Simon Raven was born [...]
Charterhouse and Kin[...]
Classics. After universit[...]
in the King's Shropshir[...]
many and Kenya wher[...]
1957 he resigned his com[...]
first novel, *The Feather[...]*
then he has written many reviews, general essays, plays (which
have been performed on both radio and television), plus a host of
successful novels including the highly acclaimed ALMS FOR
OBLIVION sequence, published for the first time in this Panther
edition in chronological order. The sequence takes its title from
a passage in Shakespeare's *Troilus and Cressida*, has been referred
to as 'a latter-day Waugh report on another generation of
Bright Young Things', and has been compared favourably with
the *romans fleuves* of Anthony Powell and C. P. Snow. Simon
Raven lives and works in Deal, Kent.

Also by Simon Raven

Novels

The Feathers of Death
Brother Cain
Doctors Wear Scarlet
Close of Play
The Fortunes of Fingel

The ALMS FOR OBLIVION sequence,
in chronological order:

Fielding Gray
Sound the Retreat
The Sabre Squadron
The Rich Pay Late
Friends in Low Places
The Judas Boy
Places Where They Sing
Come Like Shadows
Bring Forth the Body
The Survivors

Essays

The English Gentleman
Boys Will Be Boys

Plays

Royal Foundation and Other Plays

Simon Raven

Fielding Gray

PANTHER
GRANADA PUBLISHING
London Toronto Sydney New York

Published by Granada Publishing Limited
in Panther Books 1969
Reprinted 1969, 1972, 1979

ISBN 0 586 02768 8

First published by Anthony Blond Ltd 1967
Copyright © Simon Raven 1967

Granada Publishing Limited
Frogmore, St Albans, Herts AL2 2NF
and
3 Upper James Street, London W1R 4BP
1221 Avenue of the Americas, New York, NY 10020, USA
117 York Street, Sydney, NSW 2000, Australia
100 Skyway Avenue, Toronto, Ontario, Canada M9W 3A6
110 Northpark Centre, 2193 Johannesburg, South Africa
CML Centre, Queen & Wyndham, Auckland 1, New Zealand

Made and printed in Great Britain by
Cox & Wyman Ltd,
London, Reading and Fakenham
Set in Intertype Times

This book is sold subject to the condition that it
shall not, by way of trade or otherwise, be lent,
re-sold, hired out or otherwise circulated
without the publisher's prior consent in any
form of binding or cover other than that in
which it is published and without a similar
condition including this condition being imposed
on the subsequent purchaser.

Granada Publishing ®

PRINCIPAL CHARACTERS IN
ALMS FOR OBLIVION

The *Alms for Oblivion* sequence consists of ten novels. They are, in chronological order: *Fielding Gray* (FG), set in 1945; *Sound the Retreat* (SR), 1945–6; *The Sabre Squadron* (SS), 1952; *The Rich Pay Late* (RPL), 1955–6; *Friends in Low Places* (FLP), 1959; *The Judas Boy* (JB), 1962; *Places Where They Sing* (PWTS), 1967; *Come Like Shadows* (CLS), 1970; *Bring Forth the Body* (BFB), 1972; and *The Survivors* (TS), 1973.

What follows is an alphabetical list of the more important characters, showing in which of the novels they have each appeared and briefly suggesting their roles.

Albani, Euphemia: daughter of Fernando Albani *q.v.* (TS).
Albani, Fernando: Venetial merchant of late 18th and early 19th centuries. Author of manuscripts researched by Fielding Gray *q.v.* in 1973 (TS).
Albani, Maria: wife to Fernando (TS).
Albani, Piero: son of Fernando (TS). Not to be confused with the Piero *q.v.* of no known surname who lives with Lykiadopoulos in Venice in 1973 (TS).

Balliston, Hugh: an undergraduate of Lancaster College, Cambridge in 1967 (PWTS); retreats to a convent of Franciscan Friars near Venice, and is recognized in Venice by Daniel Mond in 1973 (TS).
Beatty, Miss: a secretary in the firm of Salinger & Holbrook (RPL).† 1956 (RPL).
Beck, Tony: a young Fellow of Lancaster College, well known as a literary critic (PWTS).
Beyfus, The Lord (life Peer): a social scientist, Fellow of Lancaster College (PWTS).
Blakeney, Balbo: a biochemist, Fellow of Lancaster College (PWTS); still a Fellow of Lancaster and present at Daniel Mond's funeral in 1973 (TS).
Blessington, Ivan: a school friend of Fielding Gray in 1945 (FG); later a regular officer in the 49th Earl Hamilton's Light Dra-

goons (Hamilton's Horse); ADC to his Divisional Commander in Germany in 1952 (SS); by 1955 an attaché at the British Embassy in Washington (RPL); by 1972 retired from the army and working at high level for a prominent merchant bank (BFB); pensioned off from the bank for indiscretion in 1973 (TS).

von Bremke, Herr Doktor Aeneas: a prominent mathematician at the University of Göttingen (SS).

Brockworthy, Lieutenant-Colonel: Commanding Officer of the 1st Battalion, the Wessex Fusiliers, at Berhampore in 1946 (SR).

Bunce, Basil: Squadron Sergeant-Major of the 10th Sabre Squadron of Earl Hamilton's Light Dragoons at Göttingen in 1952 (SS), and on Santa Kytherea in 1955 (FG); present at Daniel Mond's funeral in 1973 (TS).

Bungay, Piers: Subaltern officer of the 10th Sabre Squadron at Göttingen in 1952 (SS).

Buttock, Mrs Tessie: owner of Buttock's Hotel in the Cromwell Road (RPL, FLP, JB, CLS), a convenient establishment much favoured by Tom Llewyllyn and Fielding Gray q.v.

Canteloupe, The Marchioness (Molly): wife of The Marquis Canteloupe (FLP, SR).

CANTELOUPE, The Most Honourable the Marquis: father of The Earl of Muscateer (SR); distant cousin of Captain Detterling q.v. and political associate of Somerset Lloyd-James q.v.; successful operator of his 'Stately Home' and in 1959 Parliamentary Secretary for the Development of British Recreational Resources (FLP); Minister of Public Relations and Popular Media in 1962 (JB); Shadow Minister of Commerce in 1967 (PWTS); Minister of Commerce in the Conservative Government of 1970 (CLS); still Minister in 1972, though under heavy pressure (BFB). † 1973 (TS).

Carnarvon, Angus: leading male star in Pandarus/Clytemnestra Film Production of *The Odyssey* on Corfu in 1970 (CLS).

Carnwath, Doctor: a Cambridge don and historian; and old friend of Provost Constable, and a member of the Lauderdale Committee; † early 1950s (BFB).

Chead, 'Corpy': Corporal-Major (*i.e.* Colour Sergeant) of the 10th Sabre Squadron at Göttingen (SS); present at Daniel Mond's funeral in 1973 (TS).

Clewes, The Reverend Oliver: Chaplain to Lancaster College (PWTS).

CONSTABLE, Robert Reculver (Major): demobilized with special priority in the summer of 1945 to take up appointment as Tutor of Lancaster College, Cambridge (FG); by 1955 Vice-Chancellor of the University of Salop, and *éx officio* member of the Board of *Strix* (RPL); elected Provost of Lancaster in 1959 (FLP); still Provost in 1962 (JB) and 1967 (PWTS) and 1972 (BFB); ennobled as Lord Constable of Reculver Castle in 1973 (TS).

Corrington, Mona: an anthropologist, Fellow of Girton College, Cambridge, Chum of Lord Beyfus *q.v.* (PWTS).

Cruxtable, Sergeant-Major: Company Sergeant-Major of Peter Morrison's Company at the O.T.S., Bangalore, in 1945–6 (SR); 'P.T. expert' at Canteloupe's physical fitness camp in the west country (FLP).

DETTERLING, Captain: distant cousin of Lord Canteloupe; regular officer of The 49th Earl Hamilton's Light Dragoons (Hamilton's Horse) from 1937; in charge of recruiting for the Cavalry in 1945 (FG); instructor at the O.T.S., Bangalore, from late 1945 to summer 1946 (SR); by 1952 has retired from Hamilton's Horse and become a Member of Parliament (SS); still M.P. in 1955 and a political supporter of Peter Morrison *q.v.* (RPL); still M.P. in 1959, when he joins Gregory Stern *q.v.* as a partner in Stern's publishing house (FLP); still M.P. and publisher in 1962 (JB) and 1970 (CLS), and 1972, at which time he gives important assistance to those enquiring into the death of Somerset Lloyd-James (BFB); inherits his distant cousin Canteloupe's marquisate by special remainder in 1973 (TS), and insists that the spelling of the title now be changed to 'marquess'.

Dexterside, Ashley: friend and employee of Donald Salinger (RPL).

Dharaparam, H.H. The Maharajah of: an Indian Prince; Patron of the Cricket Club of the O.T.S., Bangalore (SR).

Dilkes, Henry: Secretary to the Institute of Political and Economical Studies and a member of the Board of *Strix* (RPL, FLP).

Dixon, Alastair: Member of Parliament for safe Conservative seat in the west country; about to retire in 1959 (FLP), thus creating a vacancy coveted both by Peter Morrison and Somerset Lloyd-James *q.v.*

Dolly: maid of all work to Somerset Lloyd-James in his chambers in Albany (BFB).

Drew, Vanessa: *v.* Salinger, Donald.

Engineer, Margaret Rose: a Eurasian harlot who entertains Peter Morrison *q.v.* in Bangalore (SR).

fitzAvon, Humbert: otherwise called Lord Rollesden-in-Silvis, the man with whom the manuscripts of Fernando Albani *q.v.* are principally concerned (TS).

de FREVILLE, Max: gambler and connoisseur of human affairs; runs big chemin-de-fer games in the London of the fifties (RPL), maintaining a private spy-ring for protection from possible welshers and also for the sheer amusement of it (FLP); later goes abroad to Venice, Hydra, Cyprus and Corfu, where he engages in various enterprises (FLP, JB, CLS), often in partnership with Lykiadopoulos *q.v.* and usually attended by Angela Tuck *q.v.* His Corfiot interests include a share in the 1970 Pandarus/Clytemnestra production of *The Odyssey* (CLS); still active in Corfu in 1972 (BFB); still in partnership with Lykiadopoulos, whom he accompanies to Venice in the autumn of 1973 (TS).

Frith, Hetta: girl friend of Hugh Balliston *q.v.* (PWTS).† 1967 (PWTS).

Galahead, Foxe J. (Foxy): Producer for Pandarus and Clytemnestra Films of *The Odyssey* on Corfu in 1970 (CLS).

Gamp, Jonathan: a not so young man about town (RPL, FLP, BFB).

Gilzai Khan, Captain: an Indian officer (Moslem) holding the King's Commission; an instructor at the O.T.S., Bangalore, 1945–6; resigns to become a political agitator (SR)† 1946 (SR).

Glastonbury, Major Giles: an old friend of Detterling *q.v.* and regular officer of Hamilton's Horse; temporary Lieutenant-Colonel on Lord Wavell's staff in India 1945–6 (SR); officer commanding the 10th Sabre Squadron of Hamilton's Horse at Göttingen in 1952 (SS).

Grange, Lady Susan: marries Lord Philby (RPL).

Gray, John Aloysius (Jack): Fielding Gray's father (FG). † 1945.

Gray, Mrs: Fielding Gray's mother (FG).† *c.* 1948.

GRAY, Major Fielding: senior schoolboy in 1945 (FG) with Peter Morrison and Somerset Lloyd-James *q.v.*; scholar elect of Lancaster College, but tangles with the authorities, is deprived of his scholarship before he can take it up (FG), and becomes a regular officer of Earl Hamilton's Light Dragoons; 2 i/c and then O.C. the 10th Sabre Squadron in Göttingen in 1952 (SS) and still commanding the Squadron on Santa Kytherea in 1955 (KG); badly mutilated in Cyprus in 1958 and leaves the Army to become critic and novelist with the help of Somerset Lloyd-James (FLP); achieves minor distinction, and in 1962 is sent out to Greece and Cyprus by Tom Llewyllyn *q.v.* to investigate Cypriot affairs, past and present, for BBC Television (JB); in Greece meets Harriet Ongley *q.v.*; by 1967 has won the Joseph Conrad Prize for Fiction (PWTS); goes to Corfu in 1970 to rewrite script for Pandarus/Clytemnestra's *The Odyssey* (CLS); in 1972 is engaged on a study of Joseph Conrad, which is to be published, as part of a new series, by Gregory Stern (BFB); derives considerable financial benefit from the Conrad book, and settles temporarily in Venice in the autumn of 1973 (TS). His researches into a by-water of Venetian history cause trouble among his friends and provide himself with the material for a new novel.

Grimes, Sasha: a talented young actress playing in Pandarus/Clytemnestra's *The Odyssey* on Corfu (CLS).

The Headmaster of Fielding' Gray's School (FG): a man of conscience.

Helmutt, Jacquiz: historian; research student at Lancaster College in 1952 (SS); later Fellow of Lancaster (PWTS); still a Fellow of Lancaster and present at Daniel Mond's funeral in 1973 (TS).

Holbrook, Jude: partner of Donald Salinger *q.v.* 1949–56 (RPL); 'freelance' in 1959 (FLP); reported by Burke Lawrence *q.v.* (CLS) as having gone to live in Hong Kong in the sixties; discovered to have retired, with his mother, to a villa in the Veneto 1973 (TS), having apparently enriched himself in Hong Kong.

Holbrook, Penelope: a model; wife of Jude Holbrook (RPL); by 1959, divorced from Jude and associated with Burke Lawrence (FLP); reported by Burke Lawrence (CLS) as still living in London and receiving alimony from Jude in Hong Kong.

Holeworthy, R.S.M.: Regimental Sergeant-Major of the Wessex Fusiliers at Göttingen in 1952 (SS).

Jacobson, Jules: old hand in the film world; Director of Pandarus/Clytemnestra's *The Odyssey* on Corfu in 1970 (CLS).

James, Cornet Julian: Cambridge friend of Daniel Mond *q.v.*; in 1952 a National Service officer of the 10th Sabre Squadron at Göttingen (SS).

Joe: groundsman at Detterling's old school (BFB).

Lamprey, Jack: a subaltern officer of the 10th Sabre Squadron (SS).

La Soeur, Doctor: a confidential practitioner, physician to Fielding Gray (FG, RPL, CLS).

Lawrence, Burke: 'film director' and advertising man (RPL); from *c.* 1956 to 1959 teams up with Penelope Holbrook *q.v.* in murky 'agency' (FLP); *c.* 1960 leaves England for Canada, and later becomes P.R.O. to Clytemnestra Films (CLS).

Lewson, Felicity: born Contessina Felicula Maria Monteverdi; educated largely in England; wife of Mark Lewson (though several years his senior) and his assistant in his profession (RPL)† 1959 (FLP).

Lewson, Mark: a con man (RPL, FLP)† 1959 (FLP).

Lichfield, Margaret: star actress playing Penelope in the Pandarus/Clytemnestra production of *The Odyssey* on Corfu in 1970 (CLS).

LLEWYLLYN, Tom: a 'scholarship boy' of low Welsh origin but superior education; author, journalist and contributor to *Strix* (RPL); same but far more successful by 1959, when he marries Patricia Turbot *q.v.* (FLP); given important contract by BBC Television in 1962 to produce *Today in History*, and later that year appointed Namier Fellow of Lancaster College (JB); renewed as Namier Fellow in 1965 and still at Lancaster in 1967 (PWTS); later made a permanent Fellow of the College (CLS); employed by Pandarus and Clytemnestra Films as 'Literary and Historical Adviser' to their production of *The Odyssey* on Corfu in 1970 (CLS); still a don at Lancaster in 1972, when he is reported to be winning esteem for the first volume of his *magnum opus* (published by the Cambridge University Press) on the subject of Power (BFB); comes to Venice in the autumn of 1973 (TS), nominally to do research but in fact to care for Daniel Mond.

Llewyllyn, Tullia: always called and known as 'Baby'; Tom and Patricia's daughter, born in 1960 (JB, PWTS, CLS, BFB); on the removal from the scene of her mother, is sent away to school in the autumn of 1973 (TS). Becomes a close friend of Captain Detterling, now Marquess Canteloupe.

Lloyd-James, Mrs Peregrina: widowed mother of Somerset Lloyd-James (BFB).

LLOYD-JAMES, Somerset: a senior schoolboy and friend of Fielding Gray in 1945 (FG); by 1955, Editor of *Strix*, an independent economic journal (RPL); still editor of *Strix* in 1959 (FLP) and now seeking a seat in Parliament; still editor of *Strix* in 1962 (JB), but now also a Member of Parliament and unofficial adviser to Lord Canteloupe *q.v.*; still M.P. and close associate of Canteloupe in 1967 (PWTS), and by 1970 Canteloupe's official understrapper in the House of Commons (CLS), still so employed in 1972 (BFB), with the title of Parliamentary Under-Secretary of State at the Ministry of Commerce; † 1972 (BFB).

Lykiadopoulos, Stratis: a Greek gentleman, or not far off it; professional gambler and a man of affairs (FLP) who has a brief liaison with Mark Lewson; friend and partner of Max de Freville *q.v.* (FLP), with whom he has business interests in Cyprus (JB) and later in Corfu (CLS); comes to Venice in the autumn of 1973 (TS) to run a Baccarat Bank and thus prop up his fortunes in Corfu, which are now rather shaky. Is accompanied by Max de Freville *q.v.* and a Sicilian boy called Piero *q.v.*

Maisie: a whore (RPL, FLP, JB) frequented with enthusiasm by Fielding Gray, Lord Canteloupe and Somerset Lloyd-James; apparently still going strong as late as 1967 (ref. PWTS) and even 1970 (ref. CLS), and 1972 (BFB).

Mayerston: a revolutionary (PWTS).

Mond, Daniel: a mathematician; research student of Lancaster College (SS) sent to Göttingen University in 1952 to follow up his line of research, which unexpectedly turns out to have a military potential; later Fellow of Lancaster and teacher of pure mathematics (PWTS). † in Venice in 1973 (TS).

Morrison, Helen: Peter Morrison's wife (RPL, FLP, BFB).

MORRISON, Peter: senior schoolboy with Fielding Gray and Somerset Lloyd-James *q.v.* in 1945 (FG); an officer cadet at the O.T.S., Bangalore, from late 1945 to summer 1946 (SR) and then commissioned as a Second Lieutenant in the Wessex Fusiliers, whom he joins at Berhampore; by 1952 has inherited substantial estates in East Anglia and by 1955 is a Member of Parliament (RPL) where he leads 'the Young England Group'; but in 1956 applies for Chiltern Hundreds (RPL); tries and fails to return to Parliament in 1959 (FLP); reported by Lord Canteloupe (CLS) as having finally got a seat again after a by-election in 1968 and as having retained it at the General Election in 1970; in 1972 appointed Parliamentary Under-Secretary of State at the Ministry of Commerce on the demise of Somerset Lloyd-James (BFB); appointed Minister of Commerce on death of Lord Canteloupe *q.v.* in 1973 (TS); soon after is in Venice to take a hand in industrial intrigues in Mestre.

Morrison, 'Squire': Peter's father (FG), owner of a fancied race-horse (Tiberius). † *c.* 1950.

Mortleman, Alister: an officer cadet at the O.T.S., Bangalore, 1945–6, later commissioned into the Wessex Fusiliers (SR).

Motley, Mick: Lieutenant of the R.A.M.C., attached to the Wessex Fusiliers at Göttingen in 1952 (SS).

Murphy, 'Wanker': an officer cadet at the O.T.S., Bangalore, 1945–6; later commissioned at Captain in the Education Corps, then promoted to be Major and Galloper to the Viceroy of India (SR). † 1946 (SR).

Muscateer, Earl of: son of Lord and Lady Canteloupe *q.v.*; an officer cadet at the O.T.S., Bangalore, 1945–6 (SR). † 1946 (SR).

Nicos: a Greek boy who picks up Fielding Gray (JB).

Ogden, The Reverend Andrew: Dean of the Chapel of Lancaster College (PWTS).

Ongley, Mrs Harriet: rich American widow; Fielding Gray's mistress and benefactress from 1962 onwards (JB, PWTS, CLS), but has left him by 1972 (BFB).

Pappenheim, Herr: German ex-officer of World War II; in 1952 about to rejoin new West German Army as a senior staff officer (SS).

Percival, Leonard: cloak-and-dagger man; in 1952 nominally a Lieutenant of the Wessex Fusiliers at Göttingen (SS), but by 1962 working strictly in plain clothes (JB); friend of Max de Freville, with whom he occasionally exchanges information to their mutual amusement (JB); transferred to a domestic department ('Jermyn Street') of the secret service and rated 'Home enquiries only', because of stomach ulcers in 1972, when he investigates, in association with Detterling, the death of Somerset Lloyd-James (BFB); joins Detterling (now Lord Canteloupe) in Venice in 1973 in order to investigate a 'threat' to Detterling (TS). Becomes Detterling's personal secretary and retires from 'Jermyn Street'.

Percival, Rupert: a small-town laywer in the west country (FLP), prominent among local Conservatives and a friend of Alistair Dixon *q.v.*; Leonard Percival's uncle (JB).

Philby, The Lord: proprietor of *Strix* (RPL, FLP) which he has inherited along with his title from his father, 'old' Philby.

Piero: A Sicilian boy who accompanies Lykiadopoulos *q.v.* to Venice in 1973 (TS). Becomes friend of Daniel Mond. Not to be confused with Piero Albani *q.v.*

Pough (pronounced Pew), The Honourable Grantchester Fitz-Margrave: Senior Fellow of Lancaster College, Professor Emeritus of Oriental Geography, at one time celebrated as a mountaineer; a dietary fadist (PWTS).

Pulcher, Detective Sergeant: assistant to Detective Superintendent Stupples, *q.v.* (BFB).

Restarick, Earle: American cloak-and-dagger man; in 1952 apparently a student at Göttingen University (SS) but in fact taking an unwholesome interest in the mathematical researches of Daniel Mond *q.v.*; later active in Cyprus (JB) and in Greece (CLS); at Mestre in autumn of 1973 in order to assist with American schemes for the industrialization of the area (TS); present at Daniel Mond's funeral.

Roland, Christopher: a special school friend of Fielding Gray (FG), † 1945 (FG).

Salinger, Donald: senior partner of Salinger & Holbrook, a printing firm (RPL); in 1956 marries Vanessa Drew (RPL); is deserted by Jude Holbrook *q.v.* in the summer of 1956 (RPL) but in 1959 is still printing (FLP), and still married to Vanessa; in 1972 is reported as having broken down mentally and retired to a private Nursing Home in consequence of Vanessa's death by drowning (BFB).

Schottgatt, Doctor Emile: of Montana University, Head of the 'Creative Authentication Committee' of the Oglander-Finckelstein Trust, which visits Corfu in 1970 (CLS) to assess the merits of the Pandarus/Clytemnestra production of *The Odyssey*.

Schroeder, Alfie: a reporter employed by the Billingsgate Press (RPL, FLP, SS); by 1967 promoted to columnist (PWTS); 'famous' as columnist by 1973, when he attends Daniel Mond's funeral (TS).

Sheath, Aloysius: a scholar on the staff of the American School of Greek Studies in Athens, but also assistant to Earle Restarick *q.v.* (JB, CLS).

Stern, Gregory: publisher (RPL), later in partnership with Captain Detterling *q.v.* (FLP); publishes Tom Llewyllyn and Fielding Gray *q.v.* (RPL, FLP, JB, PWTS, CLS); married to Isobel Turbot (FLP); still publishing in 1973 (TS), by which time Isobel has persuaded him into vulgar and profitable projects.

Strange, Barry: an officer cadet at the O.T.S., Bangalore, 1945–6, later commissioned into the Wessex Fusiliers, with whom he has strong family connections (SR).

Stupples, Detective Superintendent: policeman initially responsible for enquiries into the death of Somerset Lloyd-James in 1972 (BFB).

Tuck: a tea-planter in India; marries Angela, the daughter of a disgraced officer, and brings her back to England in 1945 (FG); later disappears, but turns up as an official of the Control Commission in Germany in 1952 (SS). † 1956 (RPL).

Tuck, Mrs Angela: daughter of a Colonel in the Indian Army Pay Corps, with whom she lives in Southern India (JB, FLP) until early 1945, when her father is dismissed the Service for malversation; being then *in extremis* marries Tuck the tea-planter, and returns with him to England in the summer of 1945 (FG); briefly mistress to the adolescent Somerset Lloyd-James *q.v.*, and to 'Jack' Gray (Fielding's father); despite this a trusted friend of Fielding's mother (FG); by 1955 is long separated from Tuck and now mistress to Jude Holbrook (RPL); in 1956 inherits small fortune from the intestate Tuck, from whom she had never been actually divorced *pace* her bibulous and misleading soliloquies on the subject in the text (RPL); in 1959 living in Menton and occasional companion of Max de Freville *q.v.* (FLP); later Max's constant companion (JB, CLS). † 1970 (CLS).

Turbot, The Right Honourable Sir Edwin, P.C., Kt: politician; in 1946 ex-Minister of wartime coalition accompanying all-party delegation of M.P.s to India (SR); by 1959 long since a Minister once more, and 'Grand Vizier' of the Conservative Party (FLP); father of Patricia, who marries Tom Llewyllyn (FLP), and of Isobel, who marries Gregory Stern (FLP); by 1962 reported as badly deteriorating and as having passed some of his fortune over to his daughters (JB). † by 1967 (PWTS), having left more money to his daughters.

Turbot, Isobel: *v.* Turbot, Sir Edwin, and Stern, Gregory.

Turbot, Patricia: *v.* Turbot, Sir Edwin, and Llewyllyn, Tom.

Also *v.* Llewyllyn, Tullia. Has brief walk-out with Hugh Balliston *q.v.* (PWTS) and is disobliging to Tom about money (JB, PWTS, CLS). In 1972 is reported by Jonathan Gamp to be indulging in curious if not criminal sexual preferences (BFB); as a result of these activities is finally overtaken by disaster and put away in an asylum in 1973 (TS), much to the benefit of her husband and daughter.

Weekes, James: bastard son of Somerset Lloyd-James, born in 1946 (BFB).

Weekes, Mrs Meriel: *quondam* and random associate of Somerset Lloyd-James, and mother of his bastard son (BFB).

Weir, Carton: Member of Parliament and political associate of Peter Morrison (RPL); later official aide to Lord Canteloupe (FLP, JB). P.P.S. to Canteloupe at Ministry of Commerce in 1972 (BFB); becomes P.P.S. to Peter Morrison *q.v.* when the latter takes over as Minister of Commerce on the death of Lord Canteloupe.

Winstanley, Ivor: a distinguished Latinist, Fellow of Lancaster College (PWTS).

'Young bastard': assistant groundsman at Detterling's old school (BFB).

Zaccharias: an officer cadet at the O.T.S., Bangalore, 1945–6; commissioned into a dowdy regiment of the line (SR).

'Right,' [*said Gregory Stern the publisher*] '*I'll take your two novels for an advance of £200 each, on the understanding that you'll loosen them up in the way I've suggested. Our editor has details.*'

He pressed a buzzer on his desk.

'*You'll be given a cheque now,*' *he said,* '*and you can fix an appointment with our editor for tomorrow. We'll do our best to publish the first of them – the Court-Martial one – in October. But*' – *his fingers flew over his coat buttons and then up to test his lower teeth* – '*what I'm really interested in is what you can do with that journal. I'm commissioning you to make a novel of it in the sum of £100 down, a further £100 on delivery and yet a further £100 on the day of publication – all this, of course, being an advance against royalties on the usual scale.*'

'*This is generous,*' *said Fielding Gray, who was resisting a strong impulse to cry.*

EXTRACT FROM FIELDING GRAY'S WORKING NOTE BOOK

23rd May, 1959.

This evening I have just taken my old journal out again. Originally it consisted only of scattered incidents and observations, but I put it all into coherent form while I was stationed on the island of Santa Kytherea in 1955. Although I took another look at it last year, while I was in hospital after that Cyprus business, and tidied it up for the sake of self-respect and the honour due to the English language, I never thought that it would have any value, other than as a private reminder of what I would really have done much better to forget. However, Gregory Stern is prepared to pay me handsomely to turn it into a novel. Though he has never seen it, he seems to have a very strong hunch about it, and all that on the strength of a chance word or two – for I very nearly didn't mention it at all. I thought of Christopher, and I was going to keep quiet; but then again it all happened a long time ago now, and Gregory Stern, on whom I must be largely dependent for years to come, was very pressing.

In any event, there it is. I've undertaken to turn this journal into a novel ... a work of 'fiction'. I suppose the first step is to read it through once more ...

The Journal of Fielding Gray ...

THE JOURNAL OF
FIELDING GRAY

On the second Sunday after the war in Europe ended, we had a service in the school chapel in memory of the dead. As many old boys as could be reached at short notice had been told about it, and the visitors' pews were crowded with uniforms. While all of us were wearing scruffy grey flannels and patched tweed jackets, the champions of England were hung about with every colour and device in the book. There were the black and gold hats of the guardsmen, the dark green side-caps of the rifles, kilts swaying from the hips of the highlanders, and ball buttons sprayed all over the horse artillerymen; there were macabre facings and curiously knotted lanyards; there were even the occasional pairs of boots and spurs, though these were frowned on in 1945 because of Fascist associations.

At first the service was in keeping with these sumptuous appointments. A spirited rendering of 'Jerusalem', the political implications of which escaped most present, set up a smug sense of triumph; and that passage from the Apocrypha which they always have at these affairs, though it paid a decent tribute to the rank and file, left us in no doubt that what really mattered was material wealth and traditional rule. I myself had a place in the Sixth Form block which commanded a good view of the visitors, and I could see, by this time, that the magnificent officers were openly preening themselves, as if the whole show had been got up solely in their applause. Indeed, when the role of the dead was called (a proceeding which took some time), there were unmistakable signs of boredom and pique; there was much fingering of canes and riding whips, much fidgeting with Sam Browne belts; the warriors were not assembled, it seemed, to listen at length to the achievements of others. At the very least, they appeared to feel, the list could have done with some discreet editing.

'Connaught la Poeur Beresford,' boomed the Senior Usher, 'Lieutenant, the Irish Guards. Died in a Field Hospital of wounds received at Anzio. Previously awarded the Military Cross for gallantry in the Libyan desert.'

Well, *that* was all right: even the supercilious cavalier in the cherry-coloured trousers could hardly find fault with that. But:

'Michael John Blood. Corporal, the Royal Corps of Signals.

Died of pneumonia in the Military Hospital at Aldershot.'

That, of course, really would not do at all. Or rather, it would do well enough provided that no one called attention to it. There was no need to drag it out in public, a sentiment evidently held by a young and marble-jawed major, who was obsessively stroking a huge hat of khaki felt. Watching the major sneer, I felt a guilty pang of sorrow for Michael John Blood, who had been scrofulous and bandy to the point of caricature but who had never sneered at anyone. R.I.P. Who was this major to spit on the pathetic grave?

But then again, who was I to be critical, even of a sneering bully like that? Shutting my ears to the grinding rehearsal of mortality, I reflected that my own state of mind, while perhaps less invidious than that of the gathered junkers, was comparable and quite as selfish. ('Norman Isaac Cohen. Captain, the Parachute Regiment' ... *Cohen?*) For the only feeling of which I was really conscious, on that beautiful summer's evening in the first Maytime of peace, was one of relief: relief that no one was going to kill me, that I could now proceed without let into a future which promised both pleasure and distinction. There was, for a start, a whole summer of cricket before me; and after that I was to stay on at school a further year, during which time I would be Head of my House (perhaps of the entire school) and would attempt to convert the Minor Scholarship, which I had won to Lancaster College the previous April, into a full-blooded Major Award. Thus a place at Cambridge was already awaiting me, and since my father was well provided with money (if not exactly generous), I could enter the contest with an easy mind as one whose motive was honour and not necessity.

'William King Fullworthy. Sergeant, the Intelligence Corps. Somewhere in the Burmese jungle.'

Somewhere in the jungle. It only went to show. Fullworthy, who was scarcely two years older than I was, had won, before he went for a soldier, the most brilliant of all the brilliant awards that Lancaster had to offer. But Fullworthy, it seemed, would not return to claim it: situation vacant. Whereas I, Fielding Gray, had only to step outside into the evening sun, and on all sides the world would lie serene about me, to bring me knowledge, sing my praises, yield me joy.

And so surely, I thought, in the face of this dispensation I must at least try to show gratitude. But to whom? To what?

'Tobias Ainsworth Jackson. Lieutenant-Colonel, the Royal

Army Ordnance Corps. Died of cardiac failure while commanding the 14th Supply Depot at Woking.'

Died of drink. Everyone knew the story, as Woking was not far away and Colonel Jackson, bored with running what was in effect a military funeral parlour, had frequently and calamitously visited his old school. No, I could not be grateful to him for the future which had been restored to me. But to whom else? To dead, bandy Blood? Distasteful. To the rose-lipped Cornet of the Blues, who was poutily languishing opposite? Ridiculous. To the sneering major? Never. To God? He shouldn't have let the whole thing start in the first place. To Fate then? Perhaps. Or to Luck? That, surely, was nearer the mark. One's gratitude was due to Lady Luck, who would resent, one might presume, too much concern for those she had deserted. Prudence dictated that Fullworthy, somewhere in the jungle, should be left to rot unwept.

'Alastair Edward Farquar Morrison. Captain, the Norfolk Yeomanry. Killed on the beaches of Crete, having first conducted himself with great courage and devotion to duty. Captain Morrison, being pinned down by machine-gun fire . . .'

It was very difficult not to weep for him. Alastair Morrison had been a man if ever there was one. Like his younger brother Peter. Very slowly I turned my head until I could see, further down the row, the large round face and sturdy trunk of Peter Morrison.

'. . . Upon which Captain Morrison waded back into the sea, dragged one man to safety and then returned for the other. He was shot dead a few yards before he reached shelter. Posthumously awarded the Victoria Cross.'

Peter's face, as I watched him, seemed to crumple slightly; he blinked once, then blinked again; after which he sniffed firmly, folded his arms over his chest, and resumed his usual aspect of calm, good-humoured authority. Over the years I had learned to love that look; but now, very soon, Peter would be gone – not across Styx, like his brother, yet assuredly into a different world. For Peter, a year older than myself and at present Head of our House, would leave at the end of the summer; and although I was heir apparent, I would have preferred my friend's company to his title.

'Hilary James Royce. Major, the Royal Fusiliers. Killed in the retreat from Tobruk.

'Percival Nicholas de Courcy Sangster. Second-Lieutenant, the Rajputana Rifles. Killed in the defence of Singapore.

'Lancelot Sassoon-Warburton. Brigadier, formerly of the Ninth Lancers. Killed during the evacuation of Dunkirk . . .'

Who would there be, I wondered, to replace Peter when the summer was over? There would be, of course, Somerset: Somerset Lloyd-James, my exact contemporary, who was now sitting just behind me, nostrils bubbling and spots glowing, as they always did when he was amused or excited. But Somerset, though a clever and entertaining friend, could never mean the same to me as Peter; for all his shrewdness he showed little understanding. And besides, he was in a different House. Even if he could and would help, he was not always available. Whereas Peter . . . Peter had always been there when wanted, for his home was not far from mine and we had known each other since we were tiny children.

'Cyprian Jordan Clement Willard Wyndham Trefusis, tenth and last Baron Trefoil of Truro . . . Trelawney, Squadron-Leader . . . Trevelyan . . .'

By this time the old boys were very restless indeed. The marble-jawed major was clawing ferociously at his felt hat. The cherry-trousered legs of the blasé cavalier were being crossed, re-crossed, positively entwined. Sufficient unto the day, I thought, the evil thereof. I would worry about Peter's departure when it was nearer – there were, after all, nine weeks to the end of the quarter. And there was, too, someone else. Not just Somerset Lloyd-James. Someone very different.

'The Honourable Andrew Usquebaugh Midshipman, the Royal Navy . . . Valence . . . Vallis . . . Vazey . . .' Would it never stop? All right, so they're all dead. What good will it do them or anybody else to carry on about it? 'Alan George Williams . . . Derek Williams . . . Geoffrey Alaric Williams . . .' Dear *God*.

Yes. There was someone else all right, and he would still be in the school next year. Christopher Roland, who was sitting on the other side of chapel, beyond the choir in the Fifth Form block: short wavy tow hair; square creamy forehead; mild eyes, wide-set, and soft nose; full lips curved slightly downwards; dented chin. My own age and my own House. Not clever, but easy to talk to. Not handsome, but good to look on. Strong build and bones, but a gentle skin. 'Godfery Trajan Yarborough . . .' X, Y, Z. Surely there was no demise to record under Z?

'Zaccharias,' bawled the Senior Usher, 'Pilot Officer, the Royal Air Force.

'And lastly, Emanuel Zyn, Private, The Pioneer Corps. Died of tuberculosis in the hospital of Colchester Military Prison, where he was a member of the maintenance staff.'

Although the fate of Private Zyn provoked the contempt of all present, the hymn which now followed put them in better accord with the proceedings. 'For all the Saints,' though nominally about the dead, was too brisk in metre and bracing in tune to have reference to any but the living. Joyfully, the heroes in the visitors' pews mouthed their own praises, while the boys, courteous to their guests and glad to be on their feet for a change, added their loyal support. I sang with ironic relish (or so I told myself), Peter Morrison, along the row, joined tunelessly but solidly in, Somerset Lloyd-James behind me lisped away with spirit; and from the Fifth Form block Christopher Roland turned towards me, caught my eye and smiled. One way and the other, 'For all the Saints' restored optimism and good humour all round, so that when the Headmaster mounted the pulpit during the last rollicking verse, he was assured of a friendly audience for his address.

The audience did not remain friendly for long.

'Already,' the Headmaster said, 'the expected voices are to be heard among you. "It is all over", the voices are saying: "Victory has been secured. Statesmen have wrought and politicians have intrigued; industrialists have been enriched, general officers have been ennobled; humble men have died and (we trust) will not be soon forgotten, and moralists have moralized assiduously on all these and other accounts. But now it is all over and we can return to the business and pleasure of the old, the real, life. We have endured six years of bereavement, danger, discomfort and official interference; and now we will have recompense in full".'

Now I came to think of it, this was exactly what everyone around me had indeed been saying; and to judge from the faces of the warriors it was a fair assessment of current opinion in the Mess. And what else, I asked myself, could the head man expect? Wars were fought either to annex or to preserve. This one, as we had all been told to the point of vomiting, had been fought to preserve freedom, and freedom, to all present in the chapel, meant a return to life as it had been before the struggle started. What they wanted, what I wanted, was a return to normal: an end of rationing, of regulations, of being bossed about by common little men in offices, and of depressing notices about duty all over the place. We all wanted, we had all earned, some fun; and who better to pay the bill than the ill conditioned louts who had made all the trouble in the first place?

'This,' said the Headmaster, 'is what the expected voices, the voices of common self-interest, are already saying. It is my duty to tell you, both you who have fought and you who have been made to sit helpless while your friends and brothers went out to die, that there can be no recompense and no return to the old life. This truth is both economic and political: England at present affords no substance for prizes, and the people of England (to say nothing of the world) will no longer tolerate what most of you here would mean by "the old life". But it is not on an economic or political level that I speak now. I must speak as a Christian. And as a Christian, I am to tell you that past inconvenience does not entitle you to present repayment, least of all at the expense of others, our so called enemies, who have suffered worse. "But," the expected voices will cry indignantly, "it was their fault." Their fault? The fault of ignorant peasants and misguided artisans, of children of your own age, who are at this minute starving among the rubble of their homes? *Their* fault? And even if it were, shall there be no forgiveness . . . no charity . . . no love?'

There was precious little love to be seen on the faces in the visitors' pews. There was anger, pride, incredulity, sullenness, boredom or greed: no love. And really, I thought, why should there be? People who started wars of aggression, particularly with the British, deserved everything they got; it was no good asking my sympathy for the Germans, leave alone my love. Clearly, life must go on its way, and if luck had destined me for the comfortable courts of Lancaster rather than the ruined backstreets of Berlin, then there was no point in making myself miserable about it.

'And as for a return to the old life,' the Headmaster was saying, 'I tell you, again as a Christian, that what has happened cannot be dismissed as though it had never been. You cannot say, "The war is over; let us forget it and do as we did before." The enormity has been too great; the residue of guilt is so vast that we must all bear our share of it. We cannot retire into our pleasant gardens to sit at leisure while the world's wound festers outside our wall. It is not merely a question of feeding the hungry, or curing the maimed and diseased, though these offices will be important: it will also be required of us to acknowledge and to understand a cosmic infection of hatred

22

and evil, which must henceforth be purified and for which the least of us here present must atone.'

As the Headmaster descended from the pulpit and began to walk back down the aisle towards his stall, I could hear a low and resentful muttering among the officers. One of them gestured obscenely, looked for a moment as if he were going to shout at the Headmaster's retreating back, was checked by a sharp but sympathetic nudge from his neighbour's one remaining elbow. The Headmaster was notorious for subjecting others to the exaggerated demands of his own conscience, but just this once, I felt, he might have been more tactful. Doctor Bunter at the organ, scenting trouble, broke prematurely into the introductory bars of the final hymn, with the result that half the congregation failed to find the place in time and 'The Day Thou gavest, Lord, has ended' started off like a bucolic round rendered by six hundred lugubrious drunks. But when, half way through the second verse, proper control was achieved, the sad, familiar song began to take effect. The officers relaxed and sang with restrained solidarity. The boys bellowed happily away in a sentimental trance. There was now a feeling, all through the building, as of souls melting and mingling into one another to form one huge and quivering spiritual colloid. It was a communion on the lowest possible level, a common agreement to wipe out an intolerable debt with the liquid of a few easy tears.

And Doctor Bunter had thought up a fitting climax, a final outrage of titillation. As the voices proceeded with lachrymose satisfaction through the last verse ('So be it, Lord; Thy Throne shall never/Like Earth's proud kingdoms pass away'), the organ was reinforced by the drums and bugles of the school J.T.C., symbolically stationed behind the 1914-18 Memorial Screen; and as the last echoes of the hymn were yet fading, a roll of kettle drums was succeeded, irresistibly, by the soaring notes of the Retreat. Cheeks moist, eyes shining, all listened to the call that announced the end of the day: the end of the day for the last Trefoil of Truro and for Private Zyn, for scrofulous Blood and knightly Morrison; the end of the day for boozer Jackson; for scholar Fullworthy, whose elegiac verses had been so delicate; for Connaught la Poeur Beresford; for Williams (A.) and Williams (G.); for Vallis, who had made the winning hit on another evening long ago, and for little Usquebaugh who had always funked his tackles; the end of the day for Sangster and Sassoon-Warburton, that promising young

23

brigadier; for Royce, who had died alone in the desert, and for Vazey, one of fifty suffocated in a submarine; for Captain Cohen, who had been circumcised by a Rabbi, and for Captain Yarborough, who had been circumcised by a bullet: for all these, the end of the day. Tell England with the drum and with the bugle: these, your sons, are dead.

Yet plenty, after all, remained alive; and these, having given thanks for their preservation, mingled in a grand passagio up and down the terrace which overlooked the 1st XI cricket ground.

'And what,' said Peter Morrison, 'did you think of the head man's sermon?'

'Typical,' I told him. '*They* all sat around while this horrible mess was cooking, and now they tell us we've got to clear it up.'

'The mess is there,' said Peter. 'Something must be done.'

'Of course. But need they be so mealy-mouthed? If they just said, "We're sorry, but it's happened, and now we need your help", then all right. But no. It seems we have to feel *guilty* as well.'

'Everyone has to feel guilty,' said Somerset Lloyd-James, who had just joined us; 'ever since Adam ate the apple.'

'And what,' said Peter, 'were you doing at a Church of England service? I thought you went to some foul little place in the town. Incense and images.'

'I had special dispensation,' lisped Lloyd-James, 'in order to hear the head man preach. I was anxious to ascertain his views.'

'The official line?' I said aggressively. 'Well, now you know it. Sackcloth and ashes.'

'You might have known for yourself,' said Lloyd-James, 'that your life would not suddenly become one long round of pleasure just because the war was at an end.'

'Of course I knew. I simply hoped that there would be some prospect of pleasure, that's all. Not people lecturing me about my guilt for a war which started when I was eleven.'

'Good evening, gentlemen,' said the Headmaster behind us. 'I should like you to meet Major Constable. You especially,' he said to me. 'Major Constable has been appointed Tutor of Lancaster. He is being prematurely released from the Army to take up his duties.'

Out from behind the Headmaster stepped the Major who had clawed his felt hat in chapel.

'You?' I said stupidly.

Major Constable did not seem surprised.

'Yes, me,' he said. His voice was mild, his face, as in chapel, ferocious.

'I'm sorry, er – er – Major Constable, I—'

'—Mister,' said Major Constable; 'or to you, as a future Lancaster man, Tutor. I shall be out of the army by this time tomorrow. The college is anticipating rather a rush.'

'I'll be getting on,' the Headmaster said: 'you'll write, Robert, as soon as you're settled in Lancaster?'

'Yes Headmaster,' said Constable, as intensely as if he were going to send a new instalment of the scriptures, 'I'll write.'

The Headmaster stalked off.

'He seems rather agitated today,' I said.

'He is a busy man,' Somerset Lloyd-James put in sternly.

'We're all going to be busy,' said Major-Mister Constable with an air of dedication. 'You heard what the Headmaster said in his sermon.'

'You didn't,' I said carefully, 'seem to be agreeing with him at the time.'

'On the contrary. Any emotion I showed sprang from a sense of the urgency of what he said. There has been far too much complacency these last few days.'

'Perhaps, sir,' said Peter softly, 'it's just a feeling of relief?'

I laughed in the cynical and disillusioned manner which I had been carefully cultivating ever since first reading *Dorian Gray* three months before.

'I don't know,' said Major Constable unctuously, 'that the subject is one for laughter.'

Clearly I was losing marks.

'Tell me, sir,' I said wildly, 'what is your subject?'

For a split second he wore a look of outraged vanity, as if it were unpardonable in me not to know.

'Economics ... You, the Headmaster tells me, are a classical man. Might one ask what you had in mind for the future?'

'I'm hoping to become a don ... a Fellow of the college.'

Constable twitched violently.

'Why?' he demanded.

But at this moment the Senior Usher appeared, ushering before him the cavalryman in the cherry trousers.

'I thought,' said the Senior Usher, 'that you'd all be interested to meet Captain Detterling. The only boy in the history of the school ever to make a double century in a school match.'

Detterling was not in the least like a schoolboy hero. Though elegantly got up, he had a stringy physique, an unhealthy colour, and a morose mouth. Although the evening was warm he shivered frequently. His hand, when I shook it, was very damp.

'I must congratulate you,' the Senior Usher was saying to Constable with open distaste, 'on your new appointment to Lancaster. Let's hope' – with heavy sarcasm – 'that you'll get things back to normal without delay.'

'One must look forward rather than back just now. ... You'll excuse me, gentlemen. I have a train. It's nice,' said Constable dubiously, 'to have met you.'

'A dreary man, that,' said the Senior Usher loudly before Constable had gone ten yards. 'I can't conceive what Lancaster is thinking of. He's not even a good economist. If he were, the authorities would have found him something more important to do during the war than running around with a lot of black men.'

'Gurkhas,' Captain Detterling said languidly. 'They're not really *quite* black, you know.'

'Perhaps,' said Peter, 'he wanted to help with the fighting. He seems to be a conscientious man.'

'Conscientious?' the Senior Usher snorted. 'He's as red as Detterling's ridiculous trousers.'

'Oh I say, sir.'

'Look forward rather than back, indeed. Before you can turn round, he'll have that college changed into an *institute*. He'll put a cafeteria in Hall, he'll sell the port to endow bursaries for the sons of dustmen, and he'll grow cabbages on the front lawn.'

'As it happens,' said Somerset Lloyd-James, 'he comes of a very good family. They were Hereditary Constables and Knights Banneret of Reculver Castle. Hence their name.'

'Much comfort that'll be to Gray here when his college has been turned into a night school.'

The Senior Usher sailed on his way and Detterling trailed off behind him. Peter, Somerset and I walked slowly down the steps on to the cricket ground and then towards the square at its centre. The crowd on the terrace grew thinner and the sun was low.

'The head man,' said Peter after a long pause, 'was right about one thing. The hungry must be fed and the homeless sheltered. Forget the guilt, as I propose to, and there is still a lot to be done.'

'What will you do, Peter?' I said.

'I shall grow food.'

'And you, Somerset?'

'I shall advise people for their own good,' said Lloyd-James coolly. 'Giving advice is going to be very much the thing to do. I shall be an expert in an age of experts.'

'What will you be expert about?'

'Whatever people think they are most concerned about.'

Somerset was always slow to commit himself.

'And what,' said Peter Morrison, 'are you going to do, Fielding? Your turn.'

'You heard me say. I want to be a don.'

'What sort of don?'

'A wining and dining don. A witty, worldly, *comfortable* don.'

'All that,' said Peter, 'is incidental. What will be at the centre of it?'

'Too soon to know.'

'I disagree. To me, fertility is the central object, fertility for my land – it will be mine now Alastair is dead – and also for myself. To Somerset, if I am not mistaken, the central object is power. What, Fielding, is yours?'

A bell jangled in the distance.

'I must go and count heads,' said Lloyd-James.

'So must we ... Am I to have an answer, Fielding?'

'I think ... that I want truth.'

'A tall order?'

'Not about everything. Only in my own small way. In some small corner I shall try to establish the truth.'

'Limited and limiting,' said Lloyd-James.

'Satisfying. If only to myself.'

Peter said nothing but nodded carefully. Then we separated, Lloyd-James to assist at *adsum* in his House, Peter and I to do the same office in ours.

This is a story of promise and betrayal. I am writing it, some ten years after it was enacted, on the island of Santa Kytherea, in a small white house between the mountains and the sea. I am doing so, first because there is very little else to do (the routine duties of the Squadron will be quite adequately supervised by Sergeant-Major Bunce), and secondly because I wish to establish, once and for all, what went wrong in that summer of 1945. 'Promise and betrayal.' I have written above, implying that I was the golden boy who received the traitor's kiss. But was it really like that? And if so, what, exactly, was promised, and who or what betrayed?

First things first. How did it all begin?

I have already described Christopher. Imagine him, then, on a winter's afternoon, running home from the Fives Courts: cheeks flushed, stockings down over ankles, gym shoes spattered with mud, shorts (because of clothes rationing) noticeably outgrown. It is nearly tea time and it is just getting dark. I am coming the other way, clumping along in gum-boots, having spent the afternoon drearily gardening (to help the War Effort). Our paths meet where we must both turn off for our House. Christopher waves, smiles, runs on ahead, and I just stand there, while God knows what desires are stirred inside me. And yet this was not lust – I swear it. I had had a vision, after three hours of grinding tedium among oafish and tetchy boys I had seen someone graceful and kind and gay, someone, moreover, who had waved me a share of his grace, smiled me a portion of his gaiety, as he passed in the evening light.

And that was how it all began, in December 1944, about five months before the day of the Memorial Service. And in the meantime? Outwardly just good friends, as the papers say, playing our games and gossiping our gossip, much as we always had since we first met as new boys some years before; but inwardly, as far as I was concerned, there was now a deep longing to protect and to cherish, to fondle (but only as a comforter) and (as a brother) to embrace. That smile had roused my soul. But how was I to tell Christopher? And what would he reply?

The problem was the more difficult as Christopher was a creature of very little brain. This is not to say that he was half-witted; on an everyday level he managed his affairs competently enough; but he was a boy of very conventional outlook and not pervious to ideas or books. To embark on an exegesis of Platonic love (for such this surely was), its history and implications, was therefore impossible. He would have thought I was mad. On the other hand, the fact that he was so conventional did hold out a slight hope; for convention at our school took in, as an abiding if scarcely a wholesome element in school life, the notion of the 'pash' which any boy might entertain for another, usually a younger one. With some such notion Christopher was undoubtedly familiar. But yet again, the concept of a 'pash' was so set around with petty guilt and assorted silliness that this was not at all the level on which I wanted to proceed. 'Christopher, I've got a pash on you.' No, definitely no. Whatever it was I felt for Christopher, love Platonic or love Romantic, agape, eros or caritas, it was altogether too serious to be demeaned by the idiom of the lower fourth.

Yet in the end everything turned out much easier than I had thought possible. For the truth is that Christopher had a sensibility (if not an intelligence) which I had underrated; and on the evening of the memorial service, after five months of mere cerebration on my part, he simply took the initiative himself.

Despite the severity of the Headmaster's sermon, he had proclaimed a modest concession in honour of victory. After seven o'clock *adsum* there would be no Sunday prep. and each House might conduct its own celebration, in such manner as seemed fit to its master. In our House, the Headmaster's own, a seemly sing-song was ordained. I shall never know quite how it happened, but at some point this innocent entertainment suddenly took on a grotesque, a Lupercalian licence. One moment we were all singing 'The Lincolnshire Poacher'; the next – memory recalls no interval – the monitors' gramophone was playing 'Jealousy', and the elder half of the House was coupled with the younger in a shambling, sweaty tango. Even Peter Morrison, enveloping his study fag, was performing elephantine steps across the dining-room floor. I myself was dancing with a pert and pretty little new boy, who was writhing from his hips as if his life depended on it – when a hand descended on his shoulder, there was a gruff 'Excuse me', and Christopher had taken his place.

'What's happened to everyone?' I said.

'I don't know, but it's all right. It's because the war's over. Just this once, it's all right.'

Although he did not come close, he gripped my hand and my shoulder very tight.

'All right for you being the girl?' I said fatuously.

This he ignored.

'Your hair's in your eyes,' he said.

He let go my hand and moved his own towards my forehead.

'Auburn,' he said oddly. 'That's the word, isn't it? Auburn.'

The music stopped and he quickly withdrew his hand. Someone put on 'The Girl in the Alice Blue Gown', to which we now began to waltz decorously. Christopher was a good dancer, light, yielding, following without effort as no doubt he would have led. But the choice of record was a bad one and dispelled the satyr spirit that had briefly descended. Peter Morrison released his study fag, stopped the music, banged on the panelling for silence.

'Tidy up for prayers,' he called, dismissing the incident for ever; 'and look sharp about it. The head man will be through in ten minutes.' So that's that, I thought. 'Just this once, it's all right ... Your hair ... auburn.' And then the music stopped.

But late that night, as Christopher and I were walking upstairs to bed, I felt the back of his hand brushing against mine and then his fingers curling round my own. Together we walked down the long row of cubicles, until we reached his. It was quite dark. Everyone else was asleep, or should have been, for these were junior cubicles, of which we had joint charge, and the occupants had been sent to bed two hours ago. In any case, provided we were quiet no one would realize if we both went into Christopher's cubicle; no one would interfere. The darkness was all ours and we knew it; and knowing it squeezed hands the tighter – and said good night.

For Christopher I cannot answer. For myself, it was fear which made me leave him when I did. I only wanted to be with him and hold him; but this might lead to other desires, on his part too, perhaps, and these, I thought, might end by provoking his disgust. That night outside his cubicle I loved him so much that the thought of incurring his anger or distaste made me sick with terror. What did he want? He gave no sign, I could not tell, I must not gamble; so I let go his hand and slunk away, cursing my timid heart, to my solitary school bed.

Early in June I made a hundred against Eton on our own ground, a triumph which was all the sweeter as Christopher had been batting opposite me much of the time, himself making a very decent 47. The occasion was marred, however, by the presence of my parents. When I was out I put on my blue 1st XI cricket blazer and went to join them; and hardly had I sat down before my father started getting at me. No congratulations about my century, just grinding and grudging ill humour from the moment he saw me. Since I might have been spending the time with Christopher, it was very hard to bear with.

'All that blue,' said my father, eyeing my blazer and costing

it to the nearest sixpence: 'anyone would think you were playing for the 'Varsity at Lord's.'

'And so he might,' my mother said, 'if he goes on like this.'
She paused and twitched slightly. '*You* never made a hundred,'
she said; 'you never even played for the first eleven.'

'The standard was higher in my time,' said my father, part
whining, part vicious. 'In those days the eleven played like
grown men. This is just boys' stuff.'

'Old Frank,' I told him, referring to the retired professional
who still attended every match, 'says this is one of the
strongest elevens he can remember. Frank was here in your
time, I think?'

'Frank's getting too senile to judge properly. I'm telling you,
in my day we had teams of men. Men who would have been
serving their country in time of war, not playing games at
school.'

'The war's over,' said mama.

'Not in the East.'

'I shall do my time in the Army,' I said, 'when and as they
call me.'

'When all the fighting's done.'

My father had served in the recent war with the Royal
Army Ordnance Corps and had been released early as his
business was of industrial importance.

'What does the Headmaster think?' said mama nervously,
'Will you have to go into the Army before or after you go up
to Lancaster?'

'No one knows yet.'

'And what's so certain,' said father, 'about him going up to
Lancaster?'

'But, Jack, he has a scholarship . . . And if he makes it into a
better scholarship next spring . . .'

'Scholarships don't pay for everything. Who finds the
difference?'

'If you're going to be like this, why did you decide that
Fielding could stay on at school another year?'

'Because that Headmaster of his gave me some drinks and
got round me. Said some very flattering things, I must say . . .
So I gave my word, that my son would be needing his place
here for another year, and I shan't go back on it.'

'Then why not make the best of it?' said mother.

'So I shall – for another year. If they don't call him up before,' said father gleefully.

'They won't,' I said. 'That much at least is certain. As a candidate for a further University award, I am deferred at my headmaster's request until August 1946.'

'Very nice too,' said father. 'Dreaming about Latin and Greek while others do the fighting. But hear this. After you leave this school, I'm not paying for any more Latin and Greek. If, *if* I send you to Cambridge, it'll be to do something useful.'

And so on. The usual bullying by my father, the usual pathetic or ill timed remonstrance from my mother, the usual pouts, sulks and flashes of open revolt from me. After a time Peter Morrison, who was a great favourite with my mother, came up to pay his respects.

'Not playing yourself?' said my father brutally.

Peter, who was a goodish player and had only just failed to get a place, was used to my father and took this very well.

'Too good a side for me,' he said.

'But I've just been telling him' – my father stabbed a bitten finger nail at me – 'this is children's stuff. If any of 'em were worth anything, they'd have been off at the war by now. Like me.'

At this point I couldn't bear it any more. I made up some lie about having to help, because of shortage of staff, with the arrangements for tea; then hurried away, ignoring Peter's reproachful look. Christopher was sitting at the back of the scoring box, and when I sat down beside him, he pressed his knee hard against mine. The white flannels he wore were soft and warm and very slightly damp with sweat. The contact, so childish and innocent, was of a sensuality poignant beyond desire. Thigh close against dewy flannelled thigh, chaste yet rapturous, we sat through ten minutes of indifferent batting and an eternity of love.

'Leaving me and your mother like that,' my father said before they left the next day: 'no bloody manners any more than you've got guts.'

But it would have taken more than my parents' visit to spoil that time of happiness. Dispassionate memory records that the June of 1945 was a damp, cloudy month; but another kind of memory can recall only blue, bright mornings and golden afternoons.

One such morning. Early morning school: Catullus.

'Vivamus, mea Lesbia, atque amemus,' boomed the Senior Usher,

'Rumoresque senum severiorum

Omnes unius aestimemus assis ... Now, those verse tranlations I asked you to make ... Gray.'

> 'Come, Lesbia, let us live and love
> And at a farthing's worth we'll prove
> The sour talk of crabbed old men.
> The suns which set can rise again:
> But we, once set is our brief light,
> Must sleep an everlasting night.
> Give me a thousand kisses, all your store,
> And then a hundred, then a thousand more—'

'—Thank you, that will do. I gather you approve the sentiment?'

'Yes, sir.'

'So, with qualifications, do I. This poem states briefly and without compromise the essentials of the Pagan position. A dignified if melancholy acceptance of the extinction which will follow death, accompanied by a whole-hearted relish of the available consolations.'

'And the qualifications you have, sir? Are any needed?'

'Yes. Catullus was dead and buried some fifty years before the birth of Christ. Christianity proposes a different ethic.'

Ah.

'It's not ... compulsory ... to accept the Christian ethic, sir. Lots of prominent men in the last two thousand years have rejected it.'

'But this school, Gray' – dryly and not unkindly – 'does accept it. Christianity has the official sanction here. Individuals may have their own ideas, but they must nevertheless conform with the official ones. It is a condition of belonging.'

'And if this condition is based on what is doubtful or untrue, sir?'

'You are only asked to conform. Not to believe.'

The Sixth Form stirred, scenting heresy in high places.

'But why conform,' I insisted, 'if one does not believe?'

'It is convenient to run this institution, any institution for that matter, on certain assumptions. One assumption here, as enjoined by our founder, is that Christ was the Son of God and that the morality which he preached is therefore binding. This is the basis of our rule. We cannot compel you to believe in it, indeed many of us would not wish to, but we can and must compel you to act by it. Otherwise our whole careful structure will fall apart. So for our purposes, Gray, you should behave, *not* as though you were heir to perpetual night, but as though you had an immortal soul which you may not jeopardize by showering your kisses upon Lesbia. Unless, that is, you care to marry her first.'

And suppose I wanted to shower my kisses upon Christopher? One thing was certain from what I had read: Catullus ('dead and buried some fifty years before the birth of Christ') would have seen no objection.

And one such afternoon. In the squash courts with Christopher. Squash was not much played in the summer, so we had the place to ourselves. After the game, a cold shower. Christopher under his shower (the drops clinging to the light fair hairs on his legs) displaying the whole length of his body. The young Bacchus ... no, the young Apollo. Christ, how beautiful.

But Christopher leaving the shower as soon as its function is done. Christopher drying himself, without undue haste, certainly, but without lingering. Christopher dressed. Sun beating through the skylight.

'This place is like an oven. Let's go.'

'Christopher ...'

'We'll be late for tea. Let's go.'

But as we walked up the hill, he put his hand in my arm, ran it down to hold my hand for a few paces, then brought it back to the inside of my elbow.

'Christopher ... When you still did Latin, did you get as far as Catullus?'

'No, Fielding.'

'Do you know what he wrote about?'

'No.'

'Passion.'

Christopher looked puzzled.

'Dirty-minded lot, those Romans,' he said at last.

No, it was no good trying to communicate what I had to say in words. This beautiful, ignorant child would never understand them, unless they were the plain, crude words he knew, words which I neither wanted nor dared to use. So I squeezed his hand in the crook of my elbow, and his hand squeezed back. Hand against arm on the way home from the squash courts – the poor, stifled language of our love.

'Love?' said Somerset Lloyd-James, as we walked by the river some days later. 'I should have known we wouldn't get through the summer without that nonsense coming up.'

'I didn't say I was in love with anyone,' I said. 'I was just asking what you thought about it in theory.'

'You must distinguish, for a start, between several commodities all of which are loosely called by the same name. Do you want to know about desire, affection, charity, passion or infatuation?'

'Somerset is having practice in being an expert,' Peter Morrison said.

'Well,' I persisted, 'do you believe, in the first place, in the state which is known as "being in love"?'

'That,' said Somerset promptly, 'comes under the heading of infatuation.'

'Expand.'

'A superficial physical attraction which deliberately conceals its own triviality under layers of romantic accretion.'

'How,' asked Peter, 'does it form these ... layers of romantic accretion?'

'It seizes upon anything to hand which may have poetic connotations. A sunset, say, or a bottle of wine. It seeks to arrogate to itself the splendour of the former, the legendary tradition behind the latter. A kiss at sunset receives the blessing of the departing Apollo; a giggle over cheap sherry is associated with the wildness and beauty of the young Bacchus.'

'Somerset seems to know a lot about it,' said Peter. 'I wonder whether he has ever been infatuated.'

'Of course not,' said Somerset coolly. 'I have far too clear a head.'

We passed old Frank, the retired cricket pro, who was fishing with a crony. He answered our salutes by pointing at his float and shrugging.

'Frank says he catches an average of two fish a year,' said Peter, who had inquired into the productivity of the river.

'A peaceful occupation,' I ventured.

'Pointless and debilitating,' said Somerset sternly. 'Which reminds me. What are you both going to do during the holidays? Not much more than a month to go: one cannot begin to plan too soon.'

'I shall be on our farm near Whereham,' said Peter, 'until my call-up papers come through. Which should be early in September.'

'And I shall be at home at Broughton Staithe,' I said gloomily, 'as usual.'

'A pleasant place to do some work?'

'Not with my parents around. Though they'll be going away for some of the time.'

'Without you?'

'If I have any say in the matter.'

'And of course,' said Somerset, 'you will have Peter close at hand at Whereham. I think, yes, I think I shall make a tour of the East coast to inspect you all. When shall your parents be away?'

'Late August to early September.'

'Perfect. I shall come to stay. Bringing my ration book, of course. We can comfort Peter during his last days of freedom.'

'I'm not scared of the Army,' Peter said. 'Will your parents let you come? Just like that?'

'They trust me and they pay me an adequate allowance. Within the limits imposed by their money and their trust, I am free to do as I please.'

At the top of the hill from the valley up to the school we came in sight of Founder's Court: on three sides the inelegant but oddly satisfying buildings reared in the 1860s, when the school had moved from the City; the fourth side open towards the valley; and in the middle of the grass a robust statue of the Elizabethan crook who had started the place.

'Sir Richard,' I said, indicating the statue, 'is rather like my father to look at. And they have other things in common. Greed and obstinacy for a start.'

'What a one you are for your obsessions. First love, then your parents. Tell me,' Somerset continued, 'if your father is so very unsympathetic, how did he come to choose such a nice name for you? He doesn't sound like a reader of *Tom Jones*.'

'My mother chose the name. An old friend of hers who'd been killed in the first war ... A keen cricketer who was nick-named "Fielding" since his surname was Legg. It always pleases her when I do well at cricket – as much as it annoys my father, who is jealous of the man.'

'Jealous of a man dead thirty years?' Peter murmured.

'I told you. He is both greedy and obstinate. He stores things up.'

'Quite a chapter of family history,' observed Somerset. 'Clearly, obsessions run in your blood. I think I shall come to Broughton Staithe a little early and evaluate this man.'

'Come whenever you like. My father enjoys having my friends to stay. He uses their faults as ammunition against me after they are gone.'

'Which I suppose explains why I've never been asked before. Are you sure you can risk it now?'

'Yes,' I said. 'I'm learning at last how to deal with him.'

'How?' said Peter.

'Whenever he's unpleasant, simply get up and go away. It's the only way to cope with bullies ... until you're big enough to hit back.'

'So long as you don't let him bully me instead,' Somerset said.

'You're not bullyable ... you've got the evil eye.'

And so it was arranged that Somerset should come to stay with me at my home in Broughton on about 20th August, and that we should both go on to Whereham to spend several days with Peter before he was claimed for the service of the King.

Early in July I was summoned by the Headmaster, who was also, as I have said, my Housemaster. It was in both capacities, he remarked at once, that he wished to talk to me. He gestured me into a chair, and coiled his own shambling frame into one which was opposite me and had its back to the evening light outside.

'It is time,' the Headmaster said, 'for certain things to be made plain.'

'Sir?'

'Next quarter you will be head of this House. By next cricket quarter you may well be head of the entire school. Nor could anyone say that you lacked the abilities needed.'

Outside the window the evening deepened. For some days it had been intensely hot, and now thunder threatened. A dark cloud was spiralling out of the valley; there was a drop of sweat in the cleft of the Headmaster's chin.

'No,' the Headmaster said; 'your worst enemy could not say you were unequal to such responsibilities. But. But.'

'But what, sir?'

'I wish I knew more precisely where you stood. Outwardly you do us every credit: your work, your games, your ostensible behaviour. But what what is your ... your *code*, Fielding? On what do you base your life?'

'It's a little early to know.'

'Well,' said the Headmaster, 'there's one particular thing we must both know now. What is your ... attitude ... with regard to Christopher Roland?'

So that was it. Steady now.

'The same as it always has been. I've known him for nearly four years and I'm very attached to him.'

'Yes. But now there is something about the two of you ... when you are together ... which makes me uneasy.'

'There's no reason why you should be, sir.'

'Can I accept that assurance? Can I be really certain that you are a suitable person to be my Head Monitor?'

Outside the dark cloud was swiftly growing, like a huge genie called out of its lamp. The Headmaster leaned forward in his chair and shook himself like a large, worried dog.

'You haven't been confirmed,' he said. 'Where do you stand – the question must be asked – in respect to Christianity?'

'Not an easy question, sir ... I find it hard to understand its prohibitions, its obsession with what is sinful or wrong. The Greeks put their emphasis on what is pleasant and seemly and therefore right.'

'Christ, as a Jew, had a more fastidious morality. And as the Son of God He had authority to reveal new truths and check old errors.'

'Did he?' I said.

There was a long silence between us.

'The Greeks stood for reason and decency,' I said. 'Isn't that enough?'

'Reason and decency,' the Headmaster murmured, 'but without the sanction of revealed religion ...? No, Fielding. It isn't enough. What you ignore or tolerate, I must know about and punish in order to *forgive*. Please bear the difference in mind.'

'It is a radical difference, sir.'

'Let us hope it will not divide us too far ... Will you come,' he went on abruptly, 'and stay with us in Wiltshire? Some time in September? You and I both, we shall be too busy to talk much more this quarter. But there is more to be said on the subject we have just been discussing. Not to mention practical arrangements for the autumn.'

'I should be glad to come, sir. Any time after September the seventh.'

I explained about Somerset and Peter.

'Good, good,' said the Headmaster, uncoiling himself to dismiss me. 'Meanwhile, please remember. I do not say that your position is dishonourable. Merely that it is rather too fluid for my comfort. Good night, Fielding.'

'Good night, sir.'

Lightning flashed through the window.

'Ah,' said the Headmaster; 'I always enjoy a good storm.'

We both turned to the window. A second trident of lightning forked into the valley below.

'I nearly forgot,' the Headmaster said, 'what with the very general tone of our argument ... Please let me see you less ... or at any rate less conspicuously ... in the company of Christopher Roland.'

'He says we're not to be seen together so much.'

Thunder outside the window of my tiny study. Rain dashing out of the dark against the glass. Christopher sitting in the armchair to the left of the door, myself at the desk, upright, as though interviewing him for employment.

'Why not?'

'He didn't really say. He was uneasy, he said ...'

'Uneasy about what, Fielding?'

'I don't know. Yes, I do. You see, Christopher, I'm ... I'm ...'

'Yes, Fielding?'

Such a small word, and yet I hadn't the courage to say it.

'I'm ... Both of us ... We're conspicuous people here. We must be discreet, that's all.'

'But I like being with you.'

'Same here. But we must be careful. For the sake of peace, we must be careful. Good night, Christopher.'

The thunderstorm did not clear the air. For days the heat was moist and heavy, while clouds lurked angrily round the horizon as if waiting for the moment to move in and kill. One afternoon Peter Morrison and myself, accompanied by Christopher and another boy called Ivan Blessington, took our bicycles and went for a swim in the Obelisk Pond, a sand-bottomed lake in the middle of a nearby wood, kept clean and sweet by a stream from the Thames and taking its name from a grotesque monument which an uncle of Queen Victoria's had erected to his morganatic wife.

We were not the only people there. A party of soldiers, battledress blouses flung aside, collarless shirts gaping, lolled about on the sandy shore smoking cigarettes and staring at the girls from a local private school, who were decorously bathing from some huts a hundred yards down the bank. When we arrived, the soldiers looked us over briefly, as if afraid of possible rivalry, then sneered and turned back to the bathers. An edgy mistress called to two or three girls who were swimming eagerly away from the huts as if in response to the soldiers' gaze. The girls turned back; the soldiers shrugged and swore; the four of us went into the trees to change.

When we came back, the soldiers were dressing themselves and very slowly, at the command of a rat-faced corporal, forming themselves into ranks. Bored, sweating, heavy-lidded, denied the recently promised view of young female flesh, they consoled themselves with whistling ironically at Christopher and myself, who were the first of our party to pass them. The rat-faced corporal, not above currying favour and seeing a difficult afternoon ahead, joined in the whistling, then looked anxiously at his watch.

'Eyes front,' he called: 'say good-bye to the pretty ladies.'

Chuckling morosely, the men prepared to receive orders. I walked on quickly. Christopher, trembling but resolved, turned to face the corporal.

'I'll have your name and number, please,' Christopher said.

'Who might you be?' snarled the corporal.

'A member of the public who is going to complain about your behaviour.'

'So you're going to complain about my behaviah, are you? Just you piss off double quick, my lad, before I—'

'—Will you give me your name and number?'

The corporal preened himself, inviting the squad to share his coming triumph.

'No, my lord Muck, I won't give you my name and numbah, howevah much you disapprove of my bahaviah, hah, hah, and you can just run away and play with yourself – if you've got anything to play with.'

Peter, all muscle and chest, and Ivan, who had black curling hair from his neck to his navel, had now walked down and were standing behind Christopher.

'That won't help you,' Peter said coolly. 'I know your unit. Your commanding officer comes constantly to our cricket matches. It will not be difficult for him to find out which of his men were training in these woods this afternoon. And who was in charge of them.'

'Now, look here, mate,' began the corporal with an ingratiating whine, 'it was only a joke, see, only—' But Peter, Christopher and Ivan had already walked on down to the water. The corporal looked after them, twitched, spat, turned back to his men, and began mouthing instructions in a quick, uneasy sing-song, looking over his shoulder from time to time to grin and shrug in our direction.

'Shall you report him?' said Christopher.

'Yes.'

'I don't know. Perhaps I'd sooner you didn't.'

'Then you should have ignored him. Whatever you begin with men like that must be finished. Otherwise they think they can get away with things.'

'But he'll get into trouble.'

'Exactly. Why else should you have asked for his number?'

We began swimming, black Ivan in the lead, towards the girls along the bank. Rubber-capped heads turned quickly in our direction, turned away, turned back again with intent, inter-rogatory looks. Ivan, twenty yards in front of the rest of us, skimmed the water with his hand and splashed the nearest girl.

'Jolly warm, isn't it?' he called.

The edgy school-mistress, who had regarded the invasion with mistrust, smiled with relief as she heard Ivan's safe public school voice. Nevertheless,

'Only two more minutes, girls,' she shrilled.

Myself, I duck-dived and swam under water until my ears roared. Now then; surface: what would I find? Miscalculation; I had come up short. Ahead of me some girls were standing in a ring round Ivan, who was floating on his back (the black hair on his chest and belly curling and glistening) and explaining how you could float for ever, if you only relaxed and got your breathing right, could eat your meals, wait for rescue, even sleep. Peter was swimming in a circle round a tall, slender girl with ripe breasts, talking gravely up to her as she stood and nodded. Christopher, like me, seemed somehow to be in the margin; peevish, he swam a noisy thirty yards on his back; petulant, he aimed a splash at one of the youngest girls, laughed raucously, went deep red as the child winced and backed away, her lips quivering.

'All out,' howled the mistress.

The girls withdrew. Ivan's group waved and giggled. Peter's solitary maiden walked in backwards, her eyes fixed on his round, solemn face. Christopher and I swam away fiercely and professionally, as if to indicate that the serious business of the afternoon was only now to begin.

Later, as we all lay on the strip of sand by the shore, Peter said :

'A pleasant change.'

Proud, easy, the well oiled male, fully equipped for his role.

Ivan nodded and grunted, then turned his face to the sky and laughed.

'They didn't believe a word of what I told them,' Ivan said, 'but they looked at me as though I'd been John the Baptist come to preach in the river Jordan.'

'One of their traps,' I said snappishly. 'Their biological function is to entice the male and then smother him, so that they can breed from him without fear of revolt. A little simulated worship is a well tried bait.'

Peter and Ivan grinned tolerantly.

'Who's been listening to Somerset Lloyd-James?' Peter said.

Christopher looked across at me.

'I left my watch up with my clothes,' he said. 'Those soldiers . . . I'm going to make sure it's still there.'

'I'll come with you,' I said.

Peter and Ivan assumed carefully neutral expressions. Christopher and I walked slowly and silently towards the trees. Even in the shade the afternoon was very hot . . . hot, damp, urgent. As Christopher bent down to look for his watch I put my two hands on his bare neck and started to scratch him lightly with my finger-nails. He shivered and went on searching.

'Here it is. Quite safe.'

He turned to face me, then rested his cheek against mine.

'Come on, Fielding. We must go back.'

'Let's stay here. Just a little.'

'No.'

'Why not?'

'Peter and Ivan . . . they'll think it funny.'

I turned my head and kissed his cheek. He stood quite still for perhaps ten seconds. Then he shivered – just as he had when I massaged his neck – and slipped away from me.

'Back to the others.'

I followed, wildly elated by the kiss, scarcely resenting the evasion. This must be enough, I thought tenderly, for he prefers it so. Don't be greedy. Don't ask for any more.

Back to the lake.

'Peter . . . Ivan . . .'

'Watch all right?'

'Watch?' said Christopher. 'Oh . . . yes, thanks.'

'Good. I thought you looked rather flustered.'

'Of course I'm not flustered.'

'Of course not,' said Peter serenely, 'if your watch is all right.'

A double file of schoolgirls was now trotting home along the opposite shore of the lake. Peter raised himself on one elbow to wave, and was answered by a gust of giggles, which passed across the water and into the trees like birdsong.

That night I couldn't sleep.

Vivamus, mea Lesbia, atque amemus ... The words went round and round in my head.

Give me a thousand kisses all your store.

And then a hundred, then a thousand more.

Don't be greedy, I told myself. You've had one kiss and when the time is right you'll be allowed another. That's enough. Don't go and spoil it all.

'And so,' said the Senior Usher, 'we are to be governed by the Socialists. How pleased that dismal man Constable will be.'

The rest of the school was out on a Field Day, which both myself and the Senior Usher had managed to evade. We were celebrating our holiday with what he called a 'discreet luncheon' accompanied by that great war-time luxury, a bottle of Algerian wine.

'How will it affect us here, sir?'

'A lot depends on whether or not they get in again in five years' time. Just now they've got much bigger fish to fry than us. But by about 1950 the supply will be running out. And then . . .'

'But surely, sir, they can improve the state system of education without wrecking ours? Why don't they just leave us alone?'

'Socialists,' said the Senior Usher, 'can never leave anything alone. That's the trouble. They start with one or two things that badly need reforming, and jolly good luck to them. But then it gets to be a habit. They can't stop. And that's what'll do them in. As Macaulay has it, we can make shift to live under a debauchee or even a tyrant; but to be ruled by a busybody is more than human nature can bear.'

'So how long do you give them?'

The Senior Usher took a long swig of Algerian.

'Not much more, I hope, than four years. By which time a

lot of people will have stopped being grateful for the benefits and started to resent the preaching. Particularly if it is suggested that their socialist duty required them to share their new prosperity with their less fortunate brothers in other lands.'

'And that'll be the end of the socialists?'

'For the time being ...' The Senior Usher looked suddenly glum. 'This foul wine,' he said, 'is not improved by a thunderous atmosphere ... Yes, for the time being the end of the socialists and, I hope, of our dreary friend Constable. But just at present he's in the ascendant, and I must give you a solemn warning.'

'Warning, sir?'

'Yes. Although you made none too good an impression on him back in May, he was interested by your ambition to become a don. So he has written to me to inquire about you. He may hate my guts but he respects my judgment. In his way, he's a very *just* man.'

'What did you tell him?'

'That it was early days yet but I thought you showed great promise. I added that I should be very surprised if you didn't turn your minor scholarship into one of the top awards next April.'

'Thank you, sir. But what has this to do with a warning?'

'Ah. Because of your behaviour when he met you, Constable has got it into his head that you are frivolous. He suspects your motives. He thinks you want to be a don because it is a pleasant way of life.'

'There's a lot in that,' I said.

'Of course there is, and no one but a prig like Constable would resent it. But as it is, you're handicapped – doubly handicapped. As an economist, Constable in any case tends to regard us classical scholars as parasites. And here *you* are cheerfully admitting to the status.'

'But I don't admit to the status.'

'You admit – to me – that you're out for enjoyment?'

'Among other things.'

'Then by Constable's standards you are a self-acknowledged parasite.'

'What am I meant to do? Exterminate myself?'

'You must try to disguise the fact that you are enjoying yourself. For Constable's benefit, you must turn scholarship into a duty. You must regard a fellowship as a high vocation.'

'But surely, sir, Mr. Constable's not typical of the entire college?'

'No. But he holds an important office in it. Now I've had time to think about it more closely, it's clear that Lancaster have been very shrewd in appointing him. It's clear that they saw the way the wind was blowing and installed Robert Constable as a valuable piece of camouflage.'

'Mixed metaphor.'

'Don't be pert. Their scheme is that Constable, as Tutor of the College, should go through a conspicious routine of labour and sorrow for the benefit of the socialist authorities, while the rest of them are left in peace to pursue their own amusements.'

'Then they'll be on my side?'

'Likely enough. But they won't put themselves out to protect you from Constable. He's got too important a function to fulfil: he's both a concession to and a defence against the demands of the socialist conscience. For the time being they'll let him have his way.'

'Like you said that Sunday? Let him sell the port and grow cabbages on the front lawn?'

'I doubt,' said the Senior Usher, 'whether they'll go as far as that. But they certainly won't make an issue over *you*.'

As the days went on the clouds on the horizon continued to sulk there and hour by hour the air became heavier with their threat.

'Bad for the nerves,' Peter Morrison said. 'And now, Fielding, a word in your ear.'

We went to Peter's study. Although the window was wide open, the little room was like an oven and smelt, very faintly, of Peter's feet, for it was his custom to work with his shoes off.

'Your little thing with Christopher,' said Peter. 'I don't want to seem censorious. It's happened to us all at one time or another. But that's the point. In your case the time has now come to stop.'

'Nothing's really started.'

Peter shook his head in gentle reproof.

'Something's started all right,' he said; 'the only question is how to stop it before it's too late. It's not a question of morals, Fielding. It's just that you're now too important a person to be found out. At this stage whatever happened to you would affect everybody. Corruption in high places: drums beating, heads rolling. It's bad for the House, that kind of thing. It distracts people. Disturbs good order.'

'You're preaching to the converted,' I told him. 'I don't want trouble any more than you. And I've done nothing to cause it.'

'I know how easily the converted can relapse. Take myself ... Well, no, perhaps we'd better not do that.'

Peter smiled, rather obliquely.

'If you were going to offer any practical advice ...' I prompted him.

'Practical advice of any value is hard come by in this particular field. But there's one important thing I want you to get into your head. People make a lot of fuss about all this. They talk of boys being perverted for life by their experiences at their public schools, and they then maintain that this is why, quite apart from any question of abstract morality, it's so vital to keep the place "pure". But what they can't or won't realize,' Peter said, almost angrily for him, 'is that it's not what two boys do together in private which does the permanent damage, but the hysterical row which goes on if they get caught.'

'I'm not quite with you.'

'Well, then. Two boys disappear into the bushes. Once, twice, twenty times. They get a lot of pleasure from one another, but other things being equal it does not become a permanent taste, because they grow up and go out into a wider world which offers richer diversions. All right?'

'All right.'

'But supposing they're found out. Drama, tears, denunciation, letters to parents, threats of expulsion, endless inquisition: when, how often, with whom, where, how ... And by the time that little lot's over, what would have been just a casual experience, not much more than an accident, has become ... momentous, obsessive. It has been branded on to the very core of memory and feeling. It has become something which is always with you, like a wound which will be there and keep reopening for the rest of your life. A trauma, I think the psychologists call it. But the wound was not inflicted, in most cases, by the original incident, only by the savage insistence ... by the vengefulness ... of those who chanced to find the secret out. And indeed the reactions of authority can be so extreme that they affect not only the boys immediately accused but anyone else round the place who has ever done the same thing himself. Even, perhaps, those who are completely innocent. The whole atmosphere is charged with guilt, fear and fascination. It's like this thunder hanging over us now. Can you wonder that the public schools turn out so many ... so called ... homosexuals?'

'You seem to have gone into it with some care.'

'It was no more than my duty. When I became head of this House, I had to determine how I could meet my responsibilities, how I would cope with whatever might crop up – this included.'

'And you decided that the best way was to leave people to amuse themselves in peace?'

'Let's just say that I wished the topic to be as unobtrusive as possible. Which is why I am so anxious that you, a person of prominence, should not run the risk of stirring up a conspicuous scandal. Others, you should remember, are less tolerant that I am.'

'Others?'

'In a place like this there are always inquisitive people. You don't need me to tell you.'

'No. I don't. Because I told you a long time ago – and it's still true – that I've given up ... games in the woods. I've done nothing with Christopher. Nothing whatever.'

'Keep it that way,' said Peter briskly; 'that's all.'

Peter's warning was obviously well meant, and it set me thinking. From the age of thirteen and a half, as Peter well knew, I had amused myself with a variety of boys and without any ill effects. But I had been lucky never to be found out, and knowing this, I had turned over a new leaf, for purely practical reasons, when I had become a monitor – 'a person of prominence' as Peter put it – a few months before. At this stage one simply could not afford trouble. There was also another point: ought not one to be putting away childish things by now and graduating towards women? But what might have been a firm decision never to touch a boy again had been weakened almost from the start, by two further considerations: first, that there were not, as yet, any women towards whom to graduate; and second, that it was now quite clear to me, from my reading of Greek and Latin literature, that one could have the best of both worlds. If Horace, Catullus and countless poets of the Greek anthology could have boys as well as girls, then why shouldn't I? It was of no use for the Senior Usher to point out that these authors had been superseded by the Christian morality, for that morality, with its nagging and its whining, I merely despised.

Nevertheless, for the last few months prudence had prevailed. The only danger of relapse had been Christopher, and since he was clearly resolved to impose strict limits the danger did not seem to be very serious. I was far too fond to force him (for that matter I had never forced anybody) and I was unwilling (don't be greedy) even to try to persuade him. Peter, who was very shrewd and knew both Christopher and myself very well, presumably realized this. Then why his warning?

It could only be, I decided, just *because* he knew us so well. Perhaps my prudence was a frailer vessel than I thought, and Peter had spotted this. Even so, that still left my terror of offending Christopher. Yes; but could it be that Peter had also spotted something else, in Christopher this time, that gave him cause for worry? Was this the reason for his warning – that Peter had seen, as I had not, signs that Christopher, for all his delicacy, might give way after all? Signs that determination was softening into mere reluctance, and that this in turn ...

And so it was that Peter, by warning me against what I had in any case thought to forgo, first taught me that it might yet be achieved.

'Busy, Christopher?'

'Trying to get ready for this exam tomorrow. Geography.'

'I'll just sit here and keep quiet.'

'All right. But I *must* work.'

So I perched my bottom on the little bookcase behind his chair, put my hands on his neck, and started to massage his shoulder blades.

'Please don't.'

'Just go on with your work, Christopher. This will soothe you.'

'It doesn't. It ... I'm sorry, Fielding, but please go.'

'All right. Can I come back later?'

'Come back and talk to me ... *talk* to me, Fielding ... after adsum. If I've finished this.'

'And if you haven't?'

Christopher sighed, very gently.

'Come anyway,' he said.

Exams.

' "Cum semel occideris, et de te splendida Minos Fecerit arbitria:

Non, Torquate, genus, non te facundia, non te Restituet pietas." '

' "When once you are dead and Minos has pronounced his high judgment upon you, not your lineage, Torquatus, nor all your eloquence – nor even your very virtue will bring you back again". '

I paused, I remember, and I thought: now for it, now let 'em have it straight. Then I wrote:

The passage is crucial. Moralists of the sternest persuasion would readily agree with Horace that neither high birth nor clever words can recommend the soul in the face of final judgment. But then the poet puts in his hammer blow:

> '... non te
> Restituet pietas.'

Not virtue itself is going to be any help. *All*, in fact, is vanity: not only gold and silver, not only worldly fame and accomplishment, but duty, faith and purity too. The highest moral character can procure one no preference among the shades.

I handed in my essay paper (I remember) and walked outside. There was an end of the year's exams, from which, with luck, I would pick up a prize or two. The results would not be known until the last day of the quarter. Meanwhile, there were seven days to pass and nothing to do except enjoy them. There would be a cricket match between the Scholars and the Rest, the finals of the House Matches, the junior boxing and swimming. And other sports? Ever since Peter's warning I had been watching Christopher with new eyes. It *was* possible. I was almost certain of that now. And without offending him? Yes; my body did not offend him, I knew that, he was simply nervous because it had never happened to him before. If I chose the right moment, went about it the right way, all would be well. And without scandal (Peter's voice insisted)? But no one need ever discover. And one thing above all was certain: no amount of chastity would prolong the passing summer or bring me back from the shades.

That night, at last, the storm broke, clearing the air and the sky. The next day's sun dried out the cricket pitches for the carnival matches that would close the season's play; and the weather was now set fair (or so it seemed) for ever and a day. From being sluggish and sullen, everyone turned warm-hearted and gay – except for Somerset Lloyd-James, who had never been known to be either and was in any case brooding over some problem which for the time being he declined to reveal.

The Scholars versus the Rest of the School was to be a full

day's match. So far from being a traditional fixture, this contest had never occurred before and had been promoted this year largely by the efforts of the Senior Usher (a great cricket fancier) on the strength of the unusual number of good players in the Sixth and Under-Sixth Classical. He was said to have backed the Scholars heavily at odds of two to one laid by the Master of the Lower School; whether this was true I never found out, but if so the odds were fair, for the Scholars, while distinguished by style and promise, were opposed by a much tougher and more experienced team which included eight members of the School XI.

The morning's play was dull. Batting first in easy conditions, the Scholars fiddled and finicked around for a full hour, at the end of which they could only show 30 runs on the board for a cost of three wickets. At this stage I went in myself and managed with the steady support of a young scholar called Paget, to put on fifty odd in the same number of minutes – only to be dismissed, just as I was very well set, by a gross full toss which I mistimed and lobbed straight into Christopher's hands at mid-on. Soon afterwards the players came in for lunch in the pavilion, the Scholars' score now standing at 120 for 5 – which, since the wicket was plumb and the out-field fast, was at best an indifferent performance.

Lunch, with a barrel of beer, was put up and presided over by the two pedagogues whose money allegedly rode on the match. It was a good lunch (as lunches then went), and to add to the pleasure of the occasion several distinguished non-playing guests had been invited, among them the two external examiners of the Sixth Classical, the Headmaster, and, as the school 'personality', Somerset Lloyd-James, who was sitting next to myself. Always a greedy boy when opportunity offered, Somerset now rapidly emptied three pots of beer and inspected me with the glazed look in his eye which meant (as I knew from four years' experience) that he was after help or information of more than usual importance.

'It would appear,' he said a bit thickly, 'that the biggest prize of all lies between you and me.'

'*What* does?' I said, somewhat inattentive, as I had just seen the Senior Usher point me out to one of the examiners, a tubby and voluble Warden from Oxford, and start whispering in his ear.

'The position of Head of the School next summer. The place is taken until April. After that it will be between the two of us.'

'Will it? Who told you?'

'I have my sources.'

'Why do we have to talk about it now? April's a long way off.'

'I thought you'd like to know.'

'And I suppose you want to know something in return,'
Somerset's eyes went more glassy than ever.

'If you've any . . . views . . . on the situation?'

'Well, I shan't grudge you the crown if you get it. And I
hope you can say the same. All right?'

Apparently it was, for Somerset now started shovelling food
very fast into his face, and I became involved in an up-table conversation with the tubby Warden, who wanted to know about
the reaction of my contemporaries to the Fleming Report on
the future of the public schools. Having acquitted myself as
best I could, I started to think again about the very odd exchange which Somerset, à propos of nothing at all, had introduced, and was just about to take the matter up with him,
when commotion arose at the far end of the table. Old Frank,
one of the umpires of the day, had collapsed on to his plate.

The Senior Usher, as principal host, took immediate command. Without moving an inch from his seat and merely by
giving quiet and terser instructions to those near him (including the Headmaster and the Warden) he had, within ten minutes,
established that Frank was seriously ill, administered immediate
succour, procured an ambulance, despatched Frank, arranged
a private room for him in hospital, comforted Christopher (to
whom the old gentleman had been talking when he collapsed),
convinced everyone that there was nothing more to worry about,
and appointed Somerset, who was a pundit if not a performer,
to be umpire in lieu. Part dismayed by the event, part titillated
by guilty excitement and part overcome by admiration of the
Senior Usher's expertise, I clean forgot the peculiar turn in
Somerset's conversation (for I had never been much interested
in the topic itself, only curious as to why it had been so in-
appropriately broached) and did not give it another thought
for several weeks.

After lunch, the game went better for the Scholars than we
had dared to hope. Paget, a sturdy fifteen-year-old, received
three loose beery balls in the first over and treated himself to
two straight fours and a beautiful leg sweep for six. Before the
Rest, still dazed by the refreshments and the drama offered at
lunch time, had realized what was happening, he had put on

forty quick runs; while his partner, a skinny and intelligent child from the Scholars' Remove, stood his ground against the very few balls he was allowed to receive and simply blocked them dead.

After twenty minutes of this (score now 160 odd for 5), two quick bowlers were brought on to break up the stand – and at once had every kind of ill luck. The skinny boy ('Glinter' Parkes he was called, because of his knack of flashing his spectacles) snicked two straight balls through the slips, for four; Paget, failing to keep a square cut down properly, was criminally missed at gully; and the better of the two bowlers then tripped over his own shadow, did something to his ankle, and was hauled groaning from the ground. What with all this, and what with the malaise, compounded of drowsiness, indigestion and accidie, which always assails fieldsmen at this time of the afternoon, the morale of the Rest fell apart like a rotten mackerel. 175 for 5 ... 180 ... 190 ... 195 ... The target, on such a day, was 300 or more; but anything over 270 was very acceptable and anything over 230 would leave us with some sort of chance.

205 ... 210 ... and some more smart runs from Paget. But now, with the score at 224 for 5, Peter Morrison was put on.

Peter bowled slow off-breaks which never failed to turn at exactly the same pace off the pitch and at exactly the same angle. Paget, having sent the first off-break past mid-wicket for two off the back foot, decided to do the same with the next. And there it went, bowled with Peter's usual action, flying at Peter's usual height, pitching at Peter's almost invariable length; and there was Paget, bat up and body poised – only to find that by some grotesque failure of the natural laws the ball, instead of turning in towards him, had gone absolutely straight on to hit the top of his off stump with a melancholy clack.

226 for 6 – and very nice too, when one considered the state of play before luncheon. But not so nice when the next batsman spooned his second ball to square leg, and his successor, trying to hit a six, was brilliantly caught on the long-on boundary. 226 for 8; and neither of our last two players could so much as hold his bat properly. In five balls (Peter's of all people's) we had ceased to be dominant and come to a case in which we needed every run we could scrape.

It was now that Glinter Parkes, the skinny boy, justified himself as scholar and cricketer both. After our No. 10 had somehow survived the last ball of Peter's over, Glinter faced up to a goodish 1st XI bowler of medium pace leg cutters. Instead of blocking the first of these or leaving it alone, as he would have done at any time during the last hour, Glinter placed his right foot just wide of his wicket and daintily dropped his bat on to the ball as it passed, sending it mid-way between the two slips for four runs, as pretty a late cut as ever I saw. The bowler, considering the stroke unrepeatable, bowled the same ball twice more, and was much put out when the same stroke was twice repeated. The fourth ball of the over, a quicker one on the middle-and-leg, Glinter parried with determination; off the fifth he took a short run to an indolent mid-on; and the sixth was once again survived by No. 10.

Batting now against Peter's rubbish, Glinter, who did not have the strength to hit it, once again resorted to intelligence. He stepped right across his stumps and dribbled the expected off-break down to the deserted region of fine leg, a strategem which brought him two runs off both the first two balls. Peter then moved mid-wicket down to stop this annoyance, whereupon Glinter played the ball firmly through mid-wicket's former position and took another two. In such thoughtful fashion he pushed the score past 240 to 250 and a few runs beyond, and would probably be there yet, a little Odysseus of the crease, had not the doltish No. 10 declined an easy short run at the end of one over and been dismissed at the beginning of the next. No. 11 survived with ignominy for two balls more, and then the Scholars' innings was closed for a total, passable but far from ample, of 256.

The trouble with the Scholars' side was that we had no reliable fast bowling. Although Paget could send the ball down quite quckly for someone of his age, his pace alone amounted to very little against fully grown boys and he did nothing much with the ball either in the air or off the pitch. Other bowling consisted mainly of medium or slow medium off-breaks and in-swingers, in no case with any kind of edge. However, one thing all our bowlers could do was to keep a steady length; and although the Rest found no difficulty in playing this stuff, their rate of scoring was slow.

Stumps would be drawn at half past six. By tea time (four fifteen) the Rest had been batting for just under an hour and had made only 57 runs for two wickets, both of these having been thrown away in sheer impatience. Thus the Rest needed exactly 200 to win and would have just on two hours to make them. A hundred runs an hour was nothing out of the way on our ground if once the batsmen got going; the only question was whether our bowling, uninspired as it was, could continue to contain the opposition by the exercise of patience and accuracy. The answer, unfortunately, was almost certainly 'no': for even if the bowlers did not tire of such plodding work, the Rest had players to come who were very quick on their feet and would make our medium pace good length look like any length they pleased.

The first to do so was Christopher. He came in at No. 5 only ten minutes after tea (No. 4 having carelessly allowed himself to be yorked by a half-volley from Paget) and set about his business with classical precision. A nimble mover with a long reach, he simply came to the pitch of our careful good-length bowling and drove it away where he would. Before very long, the bowlers tried dropping the ball a little shorter, but this was a common practice on our fast wickets and Christopher knew the answer: since the bounce of the ball was absolutely regular in pace and height, he could hit it, hard and almost without risk, on the lift. During his fourth over at the crease he slashed two fours through the covers and then pulled a short and sleasy off-break right off his middle stump for six, to bring the score to 94 for 3.

Christopher was a sight to see that afternoon. Hair bleached by the sun (he never played in a cap), arms brown and smooth, fair, delicate skin showing through the cleft of his unbuttoned shirt; legs moving gracefully down the pitch, bat swinging with the easy strength which only timing can give, eyes flashing with pleasure as he struck the ball full in the meat. I thought of Keat's Ode and wished, for Christopher's sake, that he might be arrested in time for ever, just at that thrilling moment of impact when the hard leather sinks, briefly but luxuriously, into the sprung willow, and the swift current of joy quivers up the blade of the bat and on through every nerve in the body. For my own sake too I wished that time might stop: so that I might stand for ever in the sun, while the trees rustled and the young voices laughed along the terrace, and watch my darling so beautiful and happy at his play. But time slipped on, and my darling started to sweat like a cart-horse, and the Scholars were faced with shameful defeat.

For by half past five the Rest had scored 183 for 4 wickets and nothing, it seemed, could save us now.

'Rather disappointing,' said Somerset Lloyd-James, as he

moved, between overs, from the wicket out to square leg.

'I don't know,' I said. Then, seeking what consolation I could and finding it very sweet, 'At least Christopher's enjoying himself.'

Somerset looked at me with attention.

'That pleases you so much?'

At the end of the next over, he said:

'Why not give young Parkes a chance to bowl?'

'It is not the umpire's province to offer advice.'

'Since you yourself are deriving a certain pleasure from your defeat' – he glanced down the wicket at Christopher – 'you might at least let some of your own side share it. It would please Parkes to bowl, and with the mess you're in it can't do any harm.'

Well, and why not? Just about everyone else had had a go. So two overs later, when the score was 210, I threw the ball to Glinter Parkes.

With modesty and concentration, Glinter requested some changes in the field. Then he took three steps to the wicket, gave a little twitch of his narrow behind, and bowled. From somewhere about his person the ball issued out in a steep parabola, reached its apex, and started to descend; meanwhile the batsman (Christopher's partner), having disdainfully plotted the curve, waited below, licking his lips. At some late stage in the ball's descent, however, it unaccountably departed from its ordained path, landed a good twelve inches shorter than it should have done, broke very sharply from the leg, and removed the puzzled batsman's off bail. Glinter blushed, and there was some embarrassed applause from the other scholars. 210 for 5.

'Natural flight, that boy's got,' said Christopher, and went to warn Peter (No. 7) who was now approaching the wicket.

'You've made 69,' Peter told him: 'watch out for your century.'

'And you watch out for Parkes's bowling,' Christopher said: 'it comes down short of where it should. About a foot short.'

Glinter listened carefully, and glinted. His next ball started the same as the one before. There was ample time to see Peter carefully working out where the ball should land and then allowing for its being a foot short. The only trouble was that this time it came down where it should have come down, so that Peter played all round it and yelped sharply when it landed (almost vertically) on the toe of his back foot.

'How's that?' said Glinter.

Somerset Lloyd-James jabbed a finger down the wicket, and away went Peter. 210 for 6. We were back in the match. Only just, but we were back.

'This is ridiculous,' Christopher said.

'A perfectly sound decision,' said Somerset huffily: 'the ball struck his back foot, which was in a direct line between the wickets.'

'I know. I meant that it just shouldn't get wickets, this kind of thing. That's all.'

'What warning are you going to give the batsman this time?' inquired Somerset with malice.

But Christopher said nothing to No. 8 as he came in, and perhaps for this reason the rest of the over passed without incident, except for a clumsy scoop of No. 8's between mid-on and mid-wicket for two runs.

Christopher then faced one of our stock bowlers from the other end and took 16 runs off him. 228 for 6. Since No. 8, (despite his horrid scoop off Glinter), was a very fair player, as was the one who would succeed him, our chances were really negligible again ... unless Glinter could produce another of his disgraceful surprises. This he promptly did, by substituting for his usual ballooning delivery a low, quick ball which knocked down No. 8's stumps while he was still looking for it half-way to the moon.

'This nonsense has got to stop,' Christopher said.

He intercepted No. 9 and spoke to him very low and earnestly. No. 9 took guard, watched Glinter like a cashier on guard against a stumer cheque, stepped right back, patted the ball slowly towards cover, and called for an easy single. Christopher then demonstrated how harmless Glinter's bowling was, if you only hung on to your wits, by advancing down the pitch and firmly hitting three successive balls full toss for four. From the last ball of the over, which he mistimed slightly (nearly giving a catch to mid-on), he only made two, bringing his own score to 99 and that of the Rest to 243.

At this stage two things happened. First No. 9 informed us that it was now definitely known that No. 11 – the bowler who had hurt his ankle earlier – was too lame to bat, which meant that we only had two wickets instead of three still to take; and secondly, No. 9 then proceeded, off the first ball of the next over, to put up one of the easiest catches in history to short leg. Fourteen runs to be got and only one wicket to fall, and No. 10, now last man in, well known for the futility of his batting.

Nevertheless, he managed to block out the rest of the over; and now, with Christopher to face the bowling, the problem was whether or not to continue with Glinter Parkes. It was true that he had taken three priceless wickets; it was also true that he had been derisively treated by Christopher. But then so had everyone else. Anyway, I wanted Christopher to get a hundred and in my heart of hearts I wanted him to carry his side to victory. So let things take their course, I thought. I threw the ball to Glinter.

Glinter's first delivery was a very high full toss. 'This is it,' I thought; 'he must get a single off this.' But it was so high and droopy that Christopher, remembering the catch he had nearly given at the end of Glinter's last over, simply stopped the ball with his bat and let it drop dead at his feet.

'May I?' he said, and bent down towards the ball.

I nodded. Christopher picked up the ball and threw it to Glinter.

'How's that?' Glinter said to Somerset.

'Don't be a silly little boy,' I said, 'I gave him permission.'

Somerset looked at me, smiled and shook his head at such naïveté, and jabbed his finger down the wicket at Christopher.

'He's still out if there's an appeal,' Somerset said. 'No one can give a player permission to break the rules.'

'That's what I thought,' Glinter said.

'Now you look here, Somerset—'

Somerset smiled and removed the bails.

'A narrow thing,' he said.

In this way did the Scholars defeat the Rest of the School in the high summer of 1945, the first time and (I believe) the last that the match has ever been played.

'It doesn't *matter,* Fielding. It wasn't your fault.'

'But you were so close to your century.'

'I hope there'll be other chances. Next summer . . .'

'What a way to win,' I said.

'I should have known better than to handle the ball.'

'Somerset was just being bloody.'

'Somerset was going by the rules. That's what an umpire's there for . . . What shall we do now? It seems funny having the whole evening free.'

'Yes . . . How did your exams go, Christopher?'

'I think I just got by.' But at the recollection his face sagged, and suddenly a surprising amount of loose flesh was hanging under his chin. That's how you'll look in twenty years' time, I thought. *Non te restituet pietas.* Piety (yours or mine) will not preserve your beauty.

'You must be tired,' I said. 'Sit down there.'

He looked at me carefully, then sat down in the chair at his desk. I sat on the bookcase behind and placed my hands on his shoulders.

'You played wonderfully today,' I said, and started to rub the top of his spine with my thumbs. 'I could have watched you for ever.'

'Easy bowling,' he grunted; his body relaxed in the chair.

'But you must feel stiff after all that batting.'

'Yes.'

'Where?'

'Everywhere.'

Don't be greedy. Kiss him, if you like, then take him to watch the Junior House Tennis in the garden. Or take him along to Peter to talk about the match. Or go to the Monitors' room and play him a record. Don't spoil it now.

'Here?'

'Yes.'

'And here?'

'Yes . . . *yes.*'

'Better now? Better, Christopher?'

'For Christ's sake, Fielding. TAKE ME SOMEWHERE SAFE.'

There was a path which led through the woods along the lip of the valley, and about half a mile down it, standing in a clearing near the edge of the trees, a group of abandoned farm-buildings, from which, long ago, they had farmed what were now our football fields. Among these buildings was a hay-loft, which was still used to store the hay from the fields each summer. Later in the year the hay would become dry and prickly, but in July it was still sweet. A fine and private place, and thither I now took him.

We came back separately. Peter met me as I came in through the door by the boot-lockers.

'I've been looking for you,' he said. 'Frank died in hospital. Half an hour ago.'

That at least, I thought in bed that night, could not be blamed on me. Frank was an old man, and now, after a long and contented life (as far as could be known), he was dead. Unconscious to the last, they said. The best way to go.

That Christopher and I had been together in the hayloft when he died was neither here nor there. There could be no connection, no guilt ... not on Frank's account. But oh dear God, what had I done to Christopher?

As soon as we had climbed up the ladder into the hayloft, he had looked at me very redly, as if to say, 'What now?' I took my coat off and he took off his; I lay down in the hay and he lay down beside me. By now I was almost more nervous than he was – far too nervous to have any sexual feeling – and so desperately anxious not to upset or disgust him that I could hardly bear to touch him. However, I undid the buttons of his shirt, loosened the top of his trousers, then stroked his hair and kissed him lightly.

'Let's get undressed,' I said.

He turned away from me, pulled off his shirt and trousers, and kept his back to me while I too undressed. When he judged that I had finished, he turned slowly back. Rather to my surprise, I saw he was very excited indeed. Since I was still too nervous to be in the least aroused, and since I was afraid lest he might notice this and perhaps be hurt, I moved right up against him and hugged him to me, the whole length of my body against the length of his. For ten seconds we lay like this, ten seconds during which I realized that all I wanted was to hold him in this way, close and without movement, without being roused myself or further rousing him, simply feeling his warmth and knowing he felt mine. I put my mouth to his ear and kissed it.

'I love you,' I said.

Then, very slowly, I moved my knuckles down his spine not to demonstrate or stir desire but to soothe, to try to tell him to be still, just to lie against me and be still. But hardly had my hand passed down betwee his shoulder blades, when his whole body seemed to jerk and stretch as though pulled by a rack and I felt him coming against my belly.

'Oh,' he whimpered, 'oh, oh, oh.'

I did what I could. I held him very tight and stroked his hair until he finished. And then I eased him away from me.

'Lie still,' I said, 'lie quite still, and soon you'll feel all right.'

But his whimpering had passed into little sobs of distress. He turned away and started, still lying down, to put on his clothes.

'Lie still,' I said. 'It doesn't matter. It often happens like that.'

'You'd know,' he sobbed, and huddled into his shirt.

'Christopher, please . . .'

'I never wanted this,' he blubbered. 'You made me want it by fingering me, messing me about. You went on and on until I couldn't help it.'

'I only wanted to show you how much I . . . How fond of you I was.'

'Then why didn't you? Why didn't you talk to me the way I asked you to? That was what I wanted – oh, so much – for us to be real friends. There were so many things you could have told me.'

'But I did, I tried—'

'—No, you didn't. You thought I was stupid, and you told me nothing. You patronized me, Fielding. Patronized me and played about with me, until it all had to end in this.'

'But nothing's ended. If only you'll lie quiet . . .'

I reached for his hand, but he snatched it from me, scrabbled through the hay, thumped down the ladder and was gone. The next time I saw him was at lock-up adsum. He was very quiet and his face was all puffy. Thank God, I thought to myself, they'll think he's been crying for Frank.

And now, as I turned in bed this way and that, I had a sense of loss that lay in my stomach like a lump of jagged iron. But surely, I thought, I can make it up to him. I can go to him, ask to be forgiven, and talk to him in the way he wants. Then everything can start again. I had a comforting vision of Christopher and myself walking arm in arm across the cricket field. 'What a lot of things you know, Fielding,' Christopher was saying as he looked into my face and smiled 'now please tell me . . .' Start again? And where would it end this time? Suddenly I had a different vision – of Christopher as he had been that evening when his body suddenly stretched against mine 'Oh . . . oh, oh, oh.' And now I felt the desire which had deserted me in the hayloft, and my hand moved down my own flesh.

'What have you done to Christopher?' Peter Morrison said.

'Nothing.'

'Don't lie to me, Fielding. I saw him last night at adsum, and so did everyone else. He looked heart-broken.'

'That was because of Frank. He was always fond of him, and he was sitting next to him when he collapsed.'

'Let's hope that's what the rest of 'em think. I know better. I saw you going off together.'

'Well, if you're going to *spy*—'

'—I was just looking out of the window, and I didn't suspect anything – until I saw him later. Do you know the damage you may have done?'

'No one need find out . . . if you don't say anything. Even if you do, no one can prove it.'

'Let's just think of Christopher. The damage to Christopher.'

'But,' I said, 'you told me that it did no harm provided no one found out and made drama.'

'Certainly I told you that, and it's usually true. But there's a special condition here: Christopher is very fond of you, he near worships you, so he'll make his own drama. Get it? When you feel like that about someone, it's very hurtful to be *used,* Fielding. You didn't think of that, did you? You simply decided that you'd have your bit of fun.'

'That's not true,' I said. 'I did think and I did try very hard . . . not to do it. It just happened, and I couldn't help it.'

'All right,' said Peter kindly. 'I accept that. If he wanted it too, and if it wasn't deliberately planned by you, then it could have been all right. But evidently something went wrong. What, Fielding?'

I told him.

'I see,' Peter said. 'So on top of everything else there's loss of control . . . humiliation . . . in front of the one person in all the world whom he wants to impress. What are you going to do?'

'Ask to be forgiven. Tell him it was all my fault, that he's got nothing to be ashamed of, and then ask him to take me back.'

'You'd better make it good. It would be a great pity if Christopher did something . . . unexpected.'

'What do you mean?'

'Guilt, disgust, and humiliation. Quite a burden. So if he got desperate and tried to off-load some of it, it would make a very nasty mess.'

'But if I can manage him?'

'Least said, soonest mended. If Christopher's all right, who am I to complain? I only hope you've learned your lesson and that it won't happen again next year.'

'Thank you, Peter.'

'But just one more thing, Fielding. I hope that Somerset

Lloyd-James wasn't looking out of his window at the same time as I was looking out of mine.'

'Somerset?'

'Yes. You must be careful of Somerset.'

'But he's our friend.'

'Somerset is growing up fast. Somerset is getting ready to break friends and influence people. There have been all the signs, even if you've been too busy to notice them.'

'I can't believe that Somerset—'

'—Just keep your eyes open, and you'll soon know all you need to and more. And that, Fielding, is my very last piece of advice. I now resign everything into your hands. When we meet in Whereham next month, you will be head of this House, I shall be a recruit under orders to join the colours. The king is dead and rather relieved to be: long live the king.'

'... Don't grovel, Fielding. It doesn't suit you.'

'Christopher. I'm trying to say I'm sorry.'

'There's nothing to be sorry about. You were very kind.'

'But you looked so awful last night. And all those things you said, about my messing you about, never talking to you properly. All that.'

'That was last night. I'm all right now.'

He looked it too. Just perceptibly older, perhaps, and certainly a little more thoughtful, but no longer ashamed or distressed. He was as bright and beautiful as ever. And yet something was missing. I did not know what it was, I only knew that something which I'd always cherished in Christopher was no longer there for me.

'You see, Fielding, I've been thinking. Yesterday was the first time for me, ever. So naturally I made rather a mess of it.' He laughed. 'Next time it'll be better, I promise you.'

'Next time?' I said stupidly.

'I could hardly sleep for thinking of it. I nearly came to you in your cube.'

There was no hesitation in his voice. Always before there'd been diffidence or deference, even when he was trying to be firm. Now he was sure of himself. And of me. I was being taken for granted.

'You see,' he said, 'I always thought that I'd hate it. Then, when it happened like that, I did hate it. But later ... when I started to remember what you looked like, how it felt having you against me ... I longed for you so much I could hardly bear it.'

There was candour in all this, candour and honesty. But what was it that had left him?

'Fielding, let's go there. Now.'

He smiled, or rather, that's what he thought he did. But his smile had changed: although the mouth and the lips were the same, there was a new look in the eyes, a look of invitation. It was no longer a smile, it was a leer. So that's what's gone, I thought: innocence. And then this look, which would have been so welcome in many others as a herald of casual pleasure, filled me, for a moment, with loathing. In others I should have thought it saucy, sexy, enticing; in Christopher I found it an obscene parody of something which I had once – only a day before – held almost sacred.

'Look,' I said: 'Peter suspects something. We must be careful.'

'We can go different ways and meet there.'

'Christopher ... we must be sensible. Next quarter I'll be head of the House. There's too much to risk.'

'There wasn't yesterday,' he said.

But yesterday you had your innocence.

'I've already said I'm sorry about that.'

His face sagged, just as it had the previous evening when I asked him about his exams. His look was no longer obscene, only pitiable. I can't just desert him, I thought. And when it comes to it, I still want him all right ... if only as an appetizing bundle of flesh. The same as all the rest of them now, but a lot of fun to be had (if only it can be safely had), a super twenty minutes in the hay. And after all, I thought, I owe him that.

'Listen,' I said. 'On the last night of quarter the door by the boot-lockers is left open all night for those with early trains. So we can go and come back in the dark and it'll be absolutely safe. Let's wait till then.'

His face brightened.

'All right,' he said. And then, 'Will you come and stay with me in the holidays? We shall be left alone most of the time. Will you come?'

'Yes – no – I'll have to think. My parents ...'

'Of course. When can you let me know?'

'In a day or two. Before we break up.'

Don't desert him, not just like that. Play for time, and ease out gently. Don't let him be hurt.

'And on the last night of quarter,' he said, 'what time?'

'After Somerset's party.'

'I shall think about it every minute.'

Tumescence, detumescence, retumescence.

But I don't think it was that simple with Christopher. I think that he was hoping for a whole new world of physical pleasure. Despite his misfortune at the first venture, he had caught a glimpse of a strange and brilliant terrain; he had seen enough, if only just enough, to promise wonders. How far he expected me to help him in his exploration would be hard to say; but for the time at least, since I had guided him in his first foray, he would want my company.

But what had I to offer? Although the magic had gone – that much was certain – might there not still be friendliness and a little cheerful lust? But then again, prudence was quickly reasserting itself. It was one thing to take risks in a daze of love, quite another to take them for a momentary and familiar pleasure.

'Sixth Classical,' announced the Headmaster from the platform: 'First, Smithson: Brackenbury Leaving Bursary, Pilch Prize for Classical studies. Second, Higgs: Brackenbury Leaving Bursary, Liddel Prize for Greek Verse. Third, Gray: Lewis Prize for Latin Elegiac Verse and Wilkinson Award for Classical Literature. Fourth, Warmsby. Fifth Scott-Malden: Muir Prize for most improved scholar of the year . . .'

So that was it. I had beaten everyone in my own year and all but the two oldest in the year above me. The Wilkinson Award was worthy twenty guineas. The academic year had ended well.

According to a pleasing custom which the Headmaster detested but suffered, on the last night of the quarter senior boys would visit and entertain each other in their different Houses. Peter and I called on Somerset Lloyd-James, who had pompously invited us, some days before, to take a little wine with him. When we arrived, Somerset was dispensing Woodbines and Gimlets.

'I sent for some hock from home,' Somerset explained, 'but my father says that war-time Railway workers cannot be trusted. Next year, when things are back to normal . . .'

'Never mind. What shall we drink to?'

A full moon looked disdainfully through Somerset's window.

'Departing friends.'

'Departing friends,' said Somerset, and hiccuped.

Six more people crowded in, among them Ivan Blessington and Christopher.

'I ordered some rather good hock,' said Somerset to the new arrivals, 'but it's finished. Gimlets on the table.'

Christopher raised his glass to me when he thought no one was looking.

'The toast,' said Somerset thickly, 'is departing friends, not returning ones.'

'Departing friends,' everybody said.

'When the Gimlets are gone,' said Somerset carefully, 'I think there is some sherry.'

'The Gimlets *are* gone.'

'Get the sherry.'

'And now,' said Peter, when everyone had poured himself some sherry, 'I shall propose another toast.'

'Good old Peter.'

'The School,' Peter said, and emitted something between a sob and a sneeze.

'Don't cry, old chap. You'll be back, you'll come and see us.'

Somerset sat down, put his head on the table, and was sick.

'I knew that sherry was a mistake. Time to go.'

I wrote a note which said, 'See you at Broughton on 20th August,' and propped it against the sherry bottle for Somerset to see when he recovered.

'After that exhibition,' I said to Peter on the way across Founder's Court, 'I don't see that Somerset needs much watching.'

'Somerset can take time out,' said Peter, 'like anybody else. Five bob to a skivvy to clear up the mess, and tomorrow is another day.'

'Home tomorrow,' shouted Ivan, who had kind parents and several jolly siblings.

'Shush. The head man hates a row.'

Christopher touched my elbow. We fell behind.

'The hay-loft,' he whispered; 'I'll start now and wait.'

But my head was humming and the moon, I thought, was dangerously large. When we reached the House, I left the rest abruptly, lay down fully dressed on my bed, and did not wake until the first light was showing and Christopher, his face drawn and dirty, was standing over me.

'You never came.'

'I fell asleep.'

'Will you come in the holidays?'

'Come where?'

'To stay with me. You said you'd let me know.'

My head ached and there was a thick sweat all over me, under my crumpled clothes.

'I still don't know myself. I'll write.'

'When?'

'In a few days.'

'I mean, when would you be coming?'

'It's difficult.' I gagged nastily and a spurt of pain flared from the base of my skull. 'Somerset's coming to me, and he mustn't get to know . . . about us.'

'Why should he get to know?'

'He sniffs things out. Peter's been warning me about him. God, I feel awful. Please go away.'

'I wish you'd be more definite.'

'How can I be? Somerset—'

Suddenly my mouth was full of a nauseous sherry-flavoured bile. Out of sheer pride I managed to swallow it back.

'Somerset's just an excuse,' Christopher was saying. 'The truth is you've finished with me. That's why you didn't come last night.'

'All right, I've finished with you. Now for God's sake go away and leave me in peace.'

'Good-bye then, Fielding.'

'*Good-bye.*'

A few seconds later, realizing, despite my discomfort, what I had done, I raised myself on my elbow to speak some word of kindness. But by then Christopher had gone.

This afternoon, when the weekly mail reached the Squadron here on the island, there was a letter for me from the Senior Usher. He has been retired for some five years now, and his leisure, despite the demands of his reading, eating and drinking, extends to an abundant correspondence with old friends. But as it happens, this is the first letter I have had from him for some months; which intermission he excuses by explaining that he has been on a cruise.

'*. . . And unlike some of one's friends, whose first concern on leaving England is to notify their entire acquaintance of the fact, I regard such expeditions as "time out", as. periods during which one's countrymen and their affairs simply cease* to exist. I neither write nor receive letters; I do not even read a newspaper. What, in heaven's name, is a holiday for?

'Even so, my dear Fielding, at one stage I found myself being very strongly reminded of you. We were making a three day call at the Piraeus, and I decided to go to Delphi, where there was to be a performance (alas, in one of those hideous Demotic versions which are now so popular) of Sophocles' Antigone. As soon as Antigone appeared on the stage, I could not but think of you. It was not so much a matter of physical likeness, though there was that, as of – how can I put it? – an aspect bestowed on her by her destiny. From the first second that the actress, a very good one, lifted her face to the audience, it was clear that Antigone was doomed, that the gods had grown bored with her and were going to have her blood. And this ... this aura of impending disaster which hung about her reminded me of you, of you ten years ago, when you appeared, with your hangover, to say good-bye to me on the last morning of that cricket quarter in 1945. You had about you the look, almost the smell, of one who is shortly to be defeated. Unlike Antigone, you had no good reason to expect this – quite the reverse, for the quarter had ended for you in every kind of triumph and the next year, as it then seemed, must hold many more. Nevertheless, and whether or not you knew it at the time, your star had turned hostile and its new malignity was reflected in your eyes.

'I hope you will pardon this piece of hindsight ...'

Did I know, that morning after Christopher left me, that already my fortunes were turning sour? Certainly, there were several causes for disquiet – my father's attitudes, the Headmaster's fussy moralism; the Senior Usher's suspicions of Constable and Peter's suspicions of Somerset; Christopher's distress, and my own uncertainty in the whole realm of love. But if there was a warning latent in all of these, there was urgency in none. I remember feeling no more than rather sad and sick that morning, as I left the Senior Usher's Lodging and walked down the hill to my train.

When I arrived home in Broughton Staithe, late in the afternoon after my drunken awakening, my mother announced that we were to go out to dinner to celebrate the beginning of the holidays. A restaurant had been chosen which was a few miles down the coast and known for its resourceful use of cheap local sea-food. At that time one might spend only five shillings a head on a meal, exclusive of any beverages which one might be lucky enough to obtain, and eat only one main course of fish or meat. The proprietor of The Lord Nelson had overcome these difficulties by combining mussels, prawns and cockles into a variety of stews and sauces; he could thus provide a full-scale Bouillabaise under the pretence of serving 'soup' (officially a minor course) and garnish a plate of chicken with a rich crustacean compote ('white sauce') which made of the 'main' course a banquet by the standards of the day.

The dinner was mama's idea. My father, who grudged the petrol needed to get there, was in any case mistrustful of what he called 'mucked up' food; and since he was also indiscriminately greedy, he liked his plate to be set before him within a few seconds of sitting down and resented the delays consequent upon the subtle attentions which were paid to the cuisine of The Lord Nelson. Knowing this as I did, being, besides, tired after my journey and feeling, almost to tears, my painful parting from Christopher, I could hardly relish the treat in store for me, the less so as I had the additional burden of simulating pleasure for my mother's sake.

Despite all this, I flatter myself that I played my part quite well. During the drive along the coast I did my best to amuse my father, whose greeting had been civil, with a non tendentious account of the closed quarter. I played down my own successes, though urged by mama to describe them in detail, made light of the important position which I was to assume the next September, and concentrated on mildly derogatory tales, which I knew from experience to be acceptable, of personalities who survived from my father's time at the school. But my father was not one to be fobbed off with a quiet evening when he was in the mood for drama. My return made it imperative for him to assert his own talents and importance, lest mama should be in danger of forgetting them, and indeed he had probably consented to come to The Lord Nelson only because the money he must pay out there entitled him, in his view, to more attention than he would have received at home.

In any event, by the time we were at table it was clear that I had made the mistake of holding the floor too long.

'It's very pleasant,' said my father self-pityingly, 'to come home after a long day with the firm at Torbeach and listen to someone who lives in a different world.'

During the ensuing silence, while mama and I assessed the quality of this gambit, a waitress removed the soup plates.

'Bring the next course quickly,' snapped my father, 'and don't worry about the frills.'

He surveyed his wife and son, waiting for comment. Since we were too experienced to volunteer this, he reverted to his original tactic.

'As I was saying,' my father said heavily, 'it's nice to know that my boring efforts in Torbeach, which neither of you want to know about, produce the means of financing a more gracious existence for my son.'

Mama and I maintained our practised silence. The waitress returned with three plates of chicken blanketed in the famous sea-food sauce.

'What's all this?' said my father, waving his hand over the plates. 'I said no frills. Take it away and bring us plain roast chicken. Plain food for plain people.'

The text-book answer to this was, once more, to say nothing and let the waitress do as my father had ordered. But I was fond of the sea-food sauce and did not see why I should be dictated to in the matter. This, of course, was the state of mind which my father's technique was calculated to provoke. He went on and on probing from different angles, until finally his opponent, however strong his resolution to keep silent, was compelled to make some protest, if only in order to prove to himself that he was still alive. And once that protest was made, however reasonably and unemphatically, my father's art would in no time inflate it into an act of treachery or rebellion.

'If you don't mind,' I said, with a sense of throwing away game, set and match, 'I'll have it as it is. It makes a change.'

'I mind?' said my father. 'Why should I? All I've got to do is pay for it. And what about you, dear? Do you share your son's preference for messed up nonsense? Or mine for honest food?'

The waitress hovered awkwardly. Mama looked at her husband, her son, and lastly at her plate. Whatever she said now, the damage was done; she was indeed fond of sea-food sauce, but knew that what was coming would prevent her from enjoying that or anything else. Seeking for a neutral factor, she glanced at the waitress.

'It seems unkind to send it back,' she mumbled 'after all that trouble . . .'

Mama had made the fatal mistake of referring to the convenience of someone other than her husband.

'You are quite right,' said my father dangerously 'one must not be inconsiderate. It is still war-time when all is said and done. That will be quite all right,' he said, grinning fiendishly at the waitress, who took her chance and was off. 'And so,' he continued, 'I find myself eating the kind of food I detest because my family refuses to back me up against a waitress.'

'Why not give it a chance?' I said. 'You knew what kind of food they have here when you arranged to come.'

'I arranged to come because your mother was so keen. She said, and I agreed, that some sort of celebration was in order to welcome you home. I simply hoped that I might be allowed to order the kind of food I like when we got here.'

Even now, perhaps, the situation was not past mending. But the sight of my father, as he messily scraped the sauce to one side and then munched great mouthfuls of chicken and potato with eyes and cheeks bulging, was too much.

'You seemed fierce enough,' I said, 'to make us have what you thought fit. If, just for once, the tables have been turned, it bloody well serves you right.'

Not clever, I thought to myself despairingly, not witty, not even effective; just raucous and crude. Here was another element in my father's technique: he induced such anger that one lost one's head; one answered with a blind violence which, alien from logic and justice, could express only personal animus.

'Thank you for that. Thank you, Fielding my son, for letting me know how you feel about me.'

'Jack, dear, he didn't mean—'

'—I know very well what he meant. That it doesn't matter what I want, because I'm only his stupid father, who doesn't care for Latin and Greek and is only fit to grind away in his factory at Torbeach and produce the money you both spend so freely.'

My father thumped his fist on the table with deliberation and looked quickly over his shoulder to see what impression he was making on the other diners.

'Bring me beer,' he shouted at the decrepit wine-waiter; 'I never really wanted this wine in the first place.'

He snatched the half-full bottle of South African hock off the table and thrust it at the terrified old man. My mother, who loved wine of all things, followed it with miserable eyes.

'Let me tell you this,' said my father, gleefully noticing mama's discomfiture over the wine. '*I* built up that business to what it is, and *I* hold it together, and *I* keep and feed you both. What I expect in return is a little loyalty and support. Do I get it? No. I get hate. Pure, bitter hate, which I can see in your eyes. I come out to a restaurant, hope for a nice evening—'

'—Please be quiet, Jack. Nobody hates you.'

'They simply,' I said, 'despise you. You've done nothing, at Torbeach or anywhere else, except bully people about and think how marvellous you are.' I had made a great effort to collect myself and my argument, and my matter was certainly well grounded. 'You haven't built that factory up: it's exactly the same as when you inherited it. *Inherited* it. You don't hold it together: your manager does. You don't feed and keep us. Grandpa's money does that. And as for support, your ideas are so mean, so vulgar, so contemptible that you deserve none. So for God's sake shut up and let us eat our meal in peace.'

My father did not mind being answered back in anger: this was necessary if a scene was to proceed at all, and he liked scenes to proceed for some time before people actually cringed. What he did not like was being told home truths; and the set which I had just advanced, to the prejudice of the fantasy in which he figured as an able and deserving self-made man, caught him on the quick. My father, when really caught on the quick, ceased to bluster and became dangerous, cunning and cool.

'There is something in what you say,' he now calmly remarked.

The wine-waiter brought his beer.

'Please bring back that wine after all,' he said: 'I think my wife would like some ... Yes,' he went on, 'There is something in what you say, Fielding. What you must remember, however, is that the factory, inherited or not, is now mine, and that the money is also mine. I can use it how I wish. Now, I was thinking of settling a little on you. A nice little sum, the income to help you through Cambridge, the capital to become yours when you finished there and to help you start up in whatever you chose to do. Because I know you don't fancy the business and I wouldn't dream of compelling you to enter it against your will. So, I thought, I'll give him a nice little sum to start him off. But after what you have just said this evening since it seems you hold me in such contempt ... I don't suppose you will want to take my money. No. You have made your position clear. I'm very sorry that you won't allow me to help you.'

'You showed no signs of doing so last time we discussed the matter.'

'Ah. I thought again. There was something to be said, I decided, for the arguments which you and your mother put forward. But now ... now that you have decided to turn spiteful and insolent ... I see that I must change my mind once more.'

My father took a long envelope from his pocket and pulled out the contents.

'A cheque for £10,000,' he said meditatively, laying this on the table 'instructions to Japhet the solicitor to hold this in trust for you until the day you graduate as Bachelor of Arts, and in the meantime to pay you quarterly the income it will yield from careful investment. Four per cent, let us say. A pity I've had the trouble of writing this letter for nothing.'

'I'm not too proud to accept £10,000 of Grandpa's money, if that's what you mean.'

'My money,' said my father wistfully, and slowly tore up the cheque. 'Since you despise me so much, you obviously can't accept it.'

I shrugged. All three of us at the table knew that had the evening gone peacefully, had no one risen to my father's bait, then the cheque and the letter would not have appeared and would simply have been destroyed in secret or kept for another occasion. But the fact that the cheque was only a stage prop did not mean that my father could not issue such a cheque if he chose. We all knew this too. And so there was always just the outside chance that this time he had really meant it ... Ten thousand pounds, an income, a nice bit of capital later ... Despite myself, I was sweating as at the loss of a genuine offer. Abruptly I pulled myself together: to dwell on this was to play my father's game for him. Best simply to be grateful that now the process of self-assertion had been gone through there would probably be peace for several days. Mama and I would be left alone – until passing time again brought father's self-esteem to the pressure point of orgasm.

At breakfast next morning there was a letter for me. I recognized Christopher's writing on the envelope and left it unopened until I was alone in my own room.

'Dear Fielding (*Christopher wrote from his home in Tonbridge*),

'*I am so sorry for making such a silly row before I left this morning. Of course I understand why you couldn't come last night. And why you are uncertain about coming to stay. If Somerset Lloyd-James is coming to stay with you, even though you told him nothing about staying with me, I think he might sort of sniff things out, as you say. I know this sounds silly, but lately I've felt that there's come to be something rather sinister about L-J, not that I know him very well. I feel that he's the kind of person who wouldn't hesitate to use anything he knew about people, if it could help him, and at the same time would pretend to be doing it because it was his duty or something. Roman Catholics have an odd way of seeing double, I mean of bringing their religion into things when it suits them and otherwise not.*

'*But even so, if you came here, say just for a night or two, either well before or well after Somerset came to you, need he ever find out? Do think it over and try to come.*

                                        '*Love from Christopher.*

'P.S. *I thought you might like the enclosed. It was taken during the Eton match.*'

My shabby treatment of Christopher had made me feel very guilty; and twenty-four hours' absence from him had revived a raging lust. Now, sooner and more easily than I had any right to hope, both problems were settled. Immediately I sat down to reply. I could come to him any time before 14th August, I said, but must be back in Broughton not later than 16th August to allow three clear days before Somerset's arrival. For there was a strong chance that he would write or ring up just before the 20th to confirm times and days; and if I failed to answer his letter, or if my mother told him on the telephone that I had gone to Tonbridge, then he would instantly become suspicious and start probing when we met.

'... So let me know quickly, Christopher, and the sooner I can come, the better, for every possible reason. Much love and many thanks for the photo ...'

In truth, however, the photograph was rather an embarrassment. The picture itself (Christopher in cricket kit, grinning, sweaty and dishevelled) was more or less all right; but on the back he had written, 'To Fielding with all my dearest love from Christopher. Please come soon, or I shan't be able to bear it.' Not the sort of thing to leave about, I thought: best tear it up and shove it down the loo. But just then I heard my mother coming down the passage towards my room, so I stuffed it at the back of my shirt drawer for future disposal.

My father was genial over the family supper.

'I met an old friend in the club house today,' he said, 'who has just come back on leave from Southern India. He may know just the thing for Fielding.'

Mama and I remained silent.

'He's a tea-planter. He says there are splendid openings. He's coming in later to discuss it.'

'Discuss what?' said mama, biting her lip.

'The openings on tea plantations in Southern India. You don't need a degree or anything, he says.'

'Then it would be a waste of Fielding's.'

'Don't you see? He needn't bother to get one. He could just do his Army service and then go right off.'

'To Southern India?' said mama.

'To Southern India. The Nilgri mountains, to be more precise.'

'And waste his place at Cambridge?'

'When a splendid chance like this comes up ... At his age, I'd have been off like a bullet. Steady money, open air life, plenty of servants, jolly good chaps to work with. What more could anyone want?'

'I could tell you,' I said, 'but I haven't the strength.'

I was bored to death. Although four days had passed since I wrote to Christopher, there had been no answer. That afternoon, desperate to talk to someone of my own age, I had rung up Peter, who had been out when I rang. So now I had put on my Dorian Gray act, which at least (I felt) made something sophisticated, even significant, out of my frustration. ('Why am I so bored, Henry?' 'Boredom, my dear Dorian, is the privilege and burden of a sensitive spirit. Coarser natures are immune.')

'What's that?' said my father.

'I don't think the life would suit me. One must get up early because there is so much to do, go to bed early because there is so little to talk about.'

Well, it would serve.

'I suppose you think that's clever. When you know more about life, you'll realize that it's practical common sense which counts, every time. Every time.'

'I'll settle for uncommon sense. As the term implies, it is rarer commodity.'

'You don't know what you're talking about.'

'All I'm trying to say,' I said, my pose dissipated by extreme irritation, 'is that I'm damned if I'll be shunted off on the unasked advice of a complete stranger, to plant tea with a pack of whisky-swilling boobies from cheap board schools.'

'Bloody little snob. *Intellectual* snob. I suppose you'd sooner sit on your behind in Cambridge for three years, talking arty nonsense while I pay the bills. Anything rather than do a proper day's work. Sometimes I think I've got a woman for a son.'

'That's right. A woman with a first eleven batting average of 37.62.'

'They haven't asked you to play for the Rest against the Lord's Schools, I notice. Or shouldn't I mention that?'

'They never asked you to play for any team at all. Or shouldn't I mention *that*?'

Mama twisted a handkerchief in her thin hands.

'You must both help me with the washing-up,' she said, with all the firmness at her command, 'or your friend will be here, Jack.'

This was not to be denied. Father declared truce by rolling up his napkin, after which, in absolute silence, we carried the dishes to the kitchen.

Mr. Tuck, the tea-planter, got smaller as he got taller. His feet were huge, his legs ample; but his hips were ungenerous, his chest meagre, and his head like a wizened grapefruit. Mr. Tuck was very sure of his opinions, which coincided in most respects with my father's, and he laughed loudly and constantly out of a mouth like a frog's which seemed almost to meet at the back of his head.

'I've brought Angela,' said Mr. Tuck on the doorstep.

Father looked puzzled, as though he had not heard of Angela, who was a real dish. She had what Browning's bishop called huge, smooth, marbly limbs, of which a pair of shorts revealed all but an inch and a half. Her breasts were prominent but not outrageous, her skin was gold with a suggestion of silver down, her hair (blonde) fell over her shoulder like Veronica Lake's, and she had teeth sound enough to chew a raw elephant. Her nose turned up exquisitely. Her ears, when they appeared from behind the curtain of her hair, issued a pressing invitation to insert one's tongue into them, and then slyly hid behind her hair again. Her eyes were the light blue of a summer's dawn. (They were also her weakest feature, being slightly crossed and rather close together.) All in all, she could not have been much more than twenty, and the turned up nose took two years off. I gaped, my father gaped. It was left for mama to restore order.

'Oh, how nice,' she said. 'Please come in, Miss Tuck.'

'*Mrs*. Tuck,' said Mr. Tuck, and brayed like a donkey.

'Oh . . . I'm so sorry.'

'That's all right, dear lady. I don't need to be told how lucky I am. I acquired this six months ago on local leave in Oute.'

We all trooped into the drawing-room, Mrs. Tuck looking vaguely annoyed, possibly at having been 'acquired' in Oute. When she sat down her shorts rode up another inch. Has she I wondered, got anything on underneath them?

My father absent-mindedly poured quadruple whiskies all round (rather stingy singles were his usual form) and conversation of a kind began.

'So this is your young hopeful,' said Mr. Tuck. 'Your father says' – turning fiercely on me – 'that you've got brains.'

I concentrated on keeping my eyes away from Mrs. Tuck's loins.

'What are you going to do with yourself?' Mr. Tuck continued with a snarl.

'It's uncertain. The Army for a time, of course. And then Cambridge. Or Cambridge,' I stammered, 'and then the Army.'

'I told you,' my father said 'he's got Cambridge on the brain.'

'He has a scholarship to Lancaster,' said mama defensively.

'What in?' asked Mr. Tuck with contempt.

'The classics. Latin and Greek.'

'Never went in for that sort of thing myself. Keener on practical things.'

'That's what I always say,' my father said.

Mrs. Tuck, looking bored, set her empty glass firmly down.

'More whisky?' said my father.

Mrs. Tuck nodded and said nothing.

'Ice, dear?' said mama, then seemed to think she had somehow used the wrong idiom. 'Ice, Mrs. Tuck?' she emended.

'Call her Angela,' said Mr. Tuck. 'I call her Ange,' he added aggressively, as though warning everyone that the privilege was exclusive; 'don't I, Ange?'

Mrs. Tuck took a long drink of whisky.

'Your father tells me,' said Mr. Tuck turning back to myself, 'that you might like to join us. We're looking for young chaps with the right background.'

'What background is that?'

'Well, you know, decent school, decent parents ... all this,' said Mr. Tuck, gesturing round the room at two water colours by mama and some hunting prints which father had bought cheap in a sale. 'Solid,' Mr. Tuck expanded; 'nothing flashy. Reliable young chaps who can do a sound job of work. And keep the Indians in their proper place.'

'Won't they be wanting their plantations back fairly soon?'

'What gave you that idea?'

'There seem to be suggestions of that kind in the air just now,' I said.

'They can't do without us, and they know it. Why only the other day I was talking to one of *their own chaps*—'

'—Jesus Christ,' said Mrs. Tuck, speaking for the first time, 'you do bore me. I think you must be the biggest bore in the world.'

She got up, put down her empty glass, and retreated to the French window.

'Steady on, old girl,' Mr. Tuck began.

But his mem-sahib was trying the handle.

'Let me,' I said. I slipped the catch and held the door open for her. 'I'll show you the garden.'

'That's right, dear,' said mama, 'you show Angela the garden.'

'But what about the discussion?' my father complained.

'It'll keep for a minute,' said Mr. Tuck. 'Let 'em go out for a blow. Leave us old fogies to the booze.' He paused for a moment. Then,

'Old Ange often blows up like that,' he said hilariously, and started to laugh more loudly than ever, straining out guffaw after guffaw as though he was taking part in some kind of endurance test.

'I'm glad you gave me an excuse to get out of that,' I said to Mrs. Tuck as the laughter died behind us.

'What have you got to complain about? At least you're not married to any of them.'

Mrs. Tuck was plainly too full of her own woes to sympathize much with anyone else's. We walked down a well kept lawn, the pride of my father, who was an assiduous amateur gardener, and then through some prettily arranged shrubs to a little pond. Mrs. Tuck sat down on a stone seat. She put her hands on her elbows and straddled heavily.

'No need for you to hang about,' she said.

'I'd like to. If I'm not in your way.'

Mrs. Tuck shrugged, not unkindly, then patted the seat by her side.

'I dare say,' she said after a little while, 'that you're surprised at me for making a scene.'

'We have them all the time in our family.'

'At least you're not hooked. You can leave any day you want to.'

I let this pass.

'Can't you?' I said.

'Daddy,' she remarked abruptly, 'was a colonel in the Indian Army Pay Corps. One day they found his accounts were rather odd. So they took him away to arrange a Court Martial and I was left alone in the bungalow. With all those spiteful women – you know the sort – coming in all the time to ask if there was anything they could do. "You poor creature",' she mimicked badly, ' "you must think of me as a mother." I had to get out. And then Tuck turned up, on leave from his plantation. Just my luck. It was Tuck or nothing,' she said, as though it were a line of a repertory play which she was repeating for the seven hundredth time.

'And your father?'

'Dismissed the service. Some old friend found him something in Hong Kong. God knows what he'll get up to there.'

You ran out, I thought: as soon as things got tough, you ran out. And you didn't even have the sense to look where you were running.

'It was lovely up there before Daddy got into trouble,' she was saying: 'race meetings, dances, golf. They had a real grass course. New people on leave all the time. And I had to get Tuck.'

'Why?'

'What do you mean, why?'

'With all those other people passing through on leave?'

'The word had gone round about Daddy. But Tuck was so potty for a juicy young woman that he just didn't care.'

So you took advantage of him and now you're being well paid out.

'If you're keen on golf,' I said, 'perhaps we might play? The course here is very good. And very beautiful. Between the sea and the saltmarshes.'

'You're rather sweet,' she said. Was it my imagination, or was her knee pressing against mine?

'Fielding? Fielding?' It was mama from the lawn.

'When?' I said gruffly.

'When what?' said Mrs. Tuck, and withdrew her knee unhurriedly, leaving me in doubt whether or not it had been there by accident.

'Golf. Tomorrow?'

'Not before Wednesday.'

'That's nearly a week.'

'I know.' She patted my hand. 'I don't want Tuck to be jealous. If we make it too soon . . .'

Delicious thought.

'All right,' I said: 'Wednesday. Half past two?'

She nodded. 'I'll look forward very much.'

'*Fielding.*' Mother was growing urgent.

'We must go,' said Mrs. Tuck softly, and held my hand until we came in sight of my mother on the lawn.

'There you are, dear. Angela too . . . I'm afraid you must come in, Fielding, because Mr. Tuck wants to ask you some questions. About your School Certificate and things.'

'For Christ's sake, mother. Father must know I won't go out there.'

'Yes, yes, dear, but if you could – well – humour him till he gets over it. You know how he is. If you pretend to fall in with the idea, he'll forget it almost at once.'

'What's the matter with going out there?' said Mrs. Tuck, puzzled.

'Nothing, I suppose. But I've got other plans. Cambridge.'

'Well, if that's what you fancy . . .' Mrs. Tuck shook her head, as if troubled by a fly. 'India can be great fun, you know.'

'I'm sure. But it's not for me.'

Mrs. Tuck looked at me blankly, then smiled a smile that turned my inwards over.

'I'll go on home,' she said, moving away easily on her strong, lovely legs. 'Tell Tuck to stay out as late as he wants so long as he doesn't disturb me when he gets in.'

'Yes, dear,' said mama, rather shocked.

Mrs. Tuck turned to smile once more.

'Wednesday,' she cooed back at me, and was gone into the night.

'*Dear Fielding (Christopher wrote),*

'*Sorry I've been so long answering your letter, but something awkward's happened. As you know, I only just managed in my exams, and the head man's suggested to my parents that I ought to have tuition during the holidays. They've found someone from Oxford who's to come and stay and be my tutor for three or four weeks in August. It's really a good idea, I suppose, but I do wish to God it wasn't happening because it means you can't come until September. I mean, there'd be room all right, but my parents think I ought to concentrate on this tuition, and anyhow it wouldn't be the same. I'm miserable about this, but there's nothing to· be done.*

'*I remember you saying that you were going to stay with the head man in Wiltshire on 7th September or thereabouts. Why not come here for a few days before going there? It's not far out of your way, only $\frac{3}{4}$ of an hour from London, which you'll have to pass through anyway. I feel ghastly about putting you off like this, and terribly disappointed, but what can I do? Please let me know that you can come in early September.*

"*All my love,*

'*Christopher.'*

'*P.S. (Two hours later) The new tutor's just arrived. He seems quite decent, but he's very ugly, rather like Somerset L-J, though no spots. Also, I'm afraid he's rather an oik, and he seems very intense. Oxford Group or something? Keep your fingers crossed for me.*

'*Christopher.'*

This letter was a blow, but perceptibly less of a blow than it would have been had I not now met Angela Tuck. Although there had been something ambiguous about the encouragement which she offered me, encouragement it had certainly been; and she had made it very plain that her marriage was not to be regarded as an inhibiting factor. Angela, in a word, was fair game; even if nothing came of the chase, the days would pass the quicker when it started. Meanwhile, I looked forward to our golf match with a mixture of acute nervousness and un-bridled reverie.

Although I had politely answered Mr. Tuck's questions and even filled in a form, thereby seeking to deny my father that sense of being opposed which alone gave spice to his activities, we still hadn't heard the last of the tea-planting scheme.

'I want to get it all settled,' my father said. 'A definite application must be made. I want to see more keenness.'

'But Jack dear, Mr. Tuck said we couldn't do anything more until we knew about Fielding's Army service.'

'Well, what about his Army service? Is he trying to find out? There must be people he could go and see.'

'I've told you,' I said: 'I've been deferred for another year because I'm a candidate for a University award.'

'But if you're going to India,' said my father with relish, 'you won't need a University award. Therefore you needn't be deferred. Why,' he said, clapping his hands spitefully together, 'we might even be able to get you into the Army this autumn. And as soon as that's out of the way you'll be free to leave for India at once.'

'It's too late to get me undeferred,' I said, uncertain whether or not this was true. 'Anyway, the Headmaster's made all his arrangements on the understanding that I'm coming back. And apart from anything else, you haven't given notice, so they'd charge you at least one quarter's fees for nothing at all.'

This argument told.

'By God, we'll see about that,' said my father, slapping his hands together once more. 'I just wouldn't pay, that's all.'

'Then they'd sue you and you'd look a frightful fool.'

My father gave a grunt of rage.

'And anyhow,' I went on, 'you said you wouldn't go back on your word. About next year.'

'These days we have to take our chances when we see them. It's all very well for that Headmaster of yours, dreaming away about Latin and Greek all day long. What does he know about the *practical* things?'

'Enough to administer a large school, and act as a house-master, and sit on several commissions in London, and get an important book written, all in the face of a horrible war and a crippling shortage of staff and materials of every kind.'

'What's the book got to do with it?'

'Nothing. That's the point. He just managed to get it written as well as coping with all the practical things, as you call them.'

But the point was lost on my father.

'Well, one thing I can do,' he said, grinding his teeth, 'is to write to Lancaster College and tell them that you won't be wanting your place there.'

'But Jack dear, supposing this tea thing falls through?'

'That's just what you'd both like, isn't it? *I'll* see it doesn't fall through. You can rely on that.'

The next day we heard that after two bombs of a new and hideously powerful kind had been dropped on cities in Japan the Japanese had surrendered unconditionally. Good, I thought: quite a chance now that I won't have to do any Army service at all.

'... *And so* [the Headmaster wrote from Wiltshire], *you need have no worries about Lancaster. They're not interested in your father's plans, about India or anything else, only in yours. It is true they will want to know where their fees are to come from; but all sorts of systems of government subsidy are now being mooted, and I've no doubt at all that your case will be covered – though it might mean doing your Army service before you go up, which is perhaps the better choice anyhow.*

(Incidentally, I don't think the end of the war in the Far East will make much difference to your military liabilities.) However, just in case your father's letter should cause the college authorities any doubts, I've written to Robert Constable the Tutor (you met him last quarter, I think?) to reassure him and to set everything straight. I know it must be tiresome for you to put up with this kind of behaviour, but you must try to remember that your father is a busy man and is no doubt suffering from the strain of these last years.'

Lolling about boasting in R.A.O.C. messes.

This is black news [the Headmaster continued], *from Japan. It is tempting to let relief, that the war is now finally over, oust any other emotion. I hope that you will not make this mistake. An element more terrible than any I could have thought possible has now obtruded itself into our lives, and I do not see any limit to the potential horrors which may develop from it. And this is to take only a selfish view. What*

*has already been done to the people of Japan, and done in our
name, is horror enough.'*

That's all very well, I thought; but then no one was going to
send *you* out there to risk your neck in the jungle.

*'My wife and I [the letter concluded], are looking forward
to seeing you about 7th September. Perhaps you will write and
let us have an exact date? By the way, I've written to Somerset
Lloyd-James and asked him to join us if he can. I felt he would
make an interesting addition to the party.'*

The hell he will, I thought. If I go to stay in Tonbridge en
route for Wiltshire, as Christopher suggests, then Somerset
will smell out my state of sin the first moment he sees me.
Or will he? For Christ's sake be reasonable. We're all beginning
to go on as if Somerset had a crystal ball. And anyway, all that
can be forgotten for the time being, because this afternoon is
golf with Angela Tuck.

Mrs. Tuck was rather late, but she was impeccably dressed
and turned out to be a thoroughly competent player. She
declared her handicap as eight; and though at first sceptical
of this, I found myself two down after the first five holes.

'I never thought you'd be so good.'

'Why not? They say women need big bottoms for golf, and
I'm well equipped there.'

She hit her ball straight down the fairway the best part of
two hundred yards. I squared up to mine, hit too hard and
lifted my head, struck the ball with the heel of the club,
and saw it hop fiercely into a bunker twenty yards away and
forty-five degrees to my left.

'Bugger,' I said, and apologized hastily to Mrs. Tuck, who
smiled and shrugged.

Excited by this tolerant behaviour, I took my No. 8, walked
into the bunker, sent my ball flopping out in a cloud of sand,
and yelled blue murder.

'Whatever's the matter?'

'Something's got in my eye.'

'Come here then.'

As she examined my eye, she came very close; her splendid
breasts brushed against my shirt, her belly pressed up against
mine. For about ten seconds she stayed quite still; then she
made a quick dab with her handkerchief and stood back.

'All right?' she said.

'I'm not sure it's really out.'

'Aren't you now? I'll have another look . . . later.'

At the end of the hole I was three down.

'Your father's been on at Tuck about your job,' Mrs. Tuck said a few holes later on. 'He wants to know what the next step is.'

'There isn't a next step.'

'You really don't want it?'

'I've told you. I want to go to Cambridge.'

Mrs. Tuck sighed gently.

'But you filled in that form, didn't you?' she said, and put her ball dead from fifty yards.

'Only to keep my father quiet. I didn't suppose your husband cared much either way.'

'Oh but he does, Fielding. When Tuck came on leave, he was told to recruit suitable young men over here. Promised a bonus if he did well at it.'

'In a few months there'll be ex-officers at a penny a score.'

'Not just any young men. Young men from good schools, to give the place a bit of tone . . . and young men whose fathers have money to invest.'

'Just let Tuck try getting money out of my father.'

'Tuck,' she said softly, 'has more ways of persuading people than you might think.'

I took my No. 6 for my chip shot and hit the ground some inches behind the ball. It described a flaccid little arc and fell lifeless, still twenty yards short of the green. I looked at it stupidly.

'Is there any way,' I said at last, 'of calling your husband off?'

'It could mean promotion for him. Important promotion.'

'What do you care?'

'Since I'm stuck with Tuck,' she said, placidly but very firmly, 'I'd sooner it was for richer than for poorer.'

She plopped in a twelve foot putt.

'Five up,' she said, 'and nine to go. I could do with a rest.'

We sat down on a sand dune, from which we could look across an empty beach to the sea. The breeze whispered through the scattered, spiky grasses; the sand was warm.

'Lonely,' said Mrs. Tuck, and shivered slightly despite the sun. She moved closer. 'Let's have another look at your eye,' she said.

With her left hand she held the lids apart, while with the

fingers of the right she gently massaged my scalp.

'That's all right,' she said. She withdrew her left hand from my eye, than ran her finger nails down the bare flesh of my arm and on down my flannelled thigh.

'Ooooh, Angela,' I said, and reached out greedily for her.

'No,' she said, pushing me away; 'you're very sweet, but no.'

'Then you shouldn't have done like that with your nails.'

'It's not that I don't like you, Fielding. I think that you're very attractive.' A hand rubbing my knee. 'It's just that . . .'

'Just that what?'

'I can't really be at ease with you as long as we're at cross purposes.'

'What on earth do you mean by that?'

'You're quite sure you want to go to Cambridge?'

'Of course. I've wanted nothing else ever since I can remember.'

'And I suppose I can understand that. But,' she said regretfully, 'it does place a barrier between us. Me brought up in India, you see, and you despising it like this.'

'I don't despise it.'

'But you refuse to go there, Fielding. I find that . . . rather hurting. I find it makes it very difficult for me . . . to get to know you better.'

'You mean . . . *You mean* that if I fall in with this sch—'

'—Don't spell it out,' she said kindly; 'it would only spoil things.'

There was a long silence while she went on rubbing my knee.

'Come on,' she said at last, taking my hand to pull me up, 'we can't sit here all day.'

I lost the match by eight and six.

The first rocket soared and sprayed over the fair-ground in the Tuesday Market Place; there were cheers, gasps, moans; the V-J celebrations in Lympne Ducis had begun.

Lympne Ducis, which was about twenty miles up the coast from Broughton Staithe, was an ancient town with modern facilities for shipping. It had a beautiful fifteenth century Customs House and also a small but well equipped harbour which had been working to capacity during the war. Although the summer fair, which was traditionally held in the Tuesday Market Place, was limited in scope by war-time restrictions as to fuel and power, the proprietors, knowing there was a lot of good money in the town and victory to grease it, had strained the regulations to bursting. The oldfashioned round-about and the tower slide were there as usual; but for the first time since 1940 there was also a big wheel and a dive-bomber, a ghost-train and bumping cars. The stalls were crammed with food and prizes, with waffles and cockles and 'Victory' sausages, with teddy bears and goldfish, with hats which bore the legends 'Blighty', 'Britannia', 'Tipperary', 'Tobruk' and 'Hiroshima'. There were lights, after the years of darkness, wreathes and festoons of lights; and as the rockets swept arching up over the gabled houses, every bell in Lympne Ducis rang out in triumph over the evil little yellow men beyond the sea.

'How exciting,' said mama; 'I wish your father had come.'

'He might at least have let us have the car,' I said.

'You know how it is, dear. This hateful petrol rationing.'

'There's always enough when *he* wants to go somewhere ...'

And now the outlines of a huge set-piece were visible high over the market place. The myriad points of light crackled and whirled and fused, formed themselves into gradually distinguishable features. Surely ... it must be ... yes, oh God of Battles, *yes*, George King and Emperor, his Queen, his daughters, all smiling serenely out of the spurting flames. The noises of the fair died, music came from the loudspeakers hung round the square, and fifteen thousand voices took up the chant:

LAND OF HOPE AND GLORY,
MOTHER OF THE FREE ...

'I think, dear,' said mama, 'that I should like to sit down somewhere.'

With some difficulty, I made way for my mother through the rapt singers and led her into the lounge of the Duke's Head. With even more difficulty I fought for and won a glass of whisky in the bar.

'There, mother. Make you feel better.'

'Thank you, dear. Don't let me spoil it for you, though. You go out and join in, and collect me later.'

'If you're sure, mama ...'

But I turned away without waiting for an answer. Outside was a vast sea of vocal euphoria.

God, that made thee mighty,
Make thee mightier yet ...

Not only us, I thought; not only us in our privileged chapel: all these people too.

GOD, *THAT MADE THEE MIGHTY,*
MAKE THEE MIGHTIER YET.

The music died, the cheers faded, the fair-ground chorus resumed. The roundabout organ; laughter, screams. A man in front of me was sick, another slipped in the mess, staggered against two young girls who were walking arm in arm, and fell violently to the ground.

'Two bloody little 'ores,' the man said.

The girls looked distressed. Pale and vulnerable, irresistibly pretty and pathetic.

'Bloody, fuckin' little 'ores,' the man shouted from the ground.

The dense crowd seemed indifferent.

'Come with me,' I said, and taking them both by the arm I swept them through a gap in the crowd to a stall which sold waffles.

'Have a waffle?'

'No, reelly ...'

'What's your name? Mine' – 'Fielding' would sound too ridiculous in this company – 'mine's Christopher.'

'Chris ... I'm Phyllis.'

'And I'm Dixie.'

Phyllis was a well set up but commonplace blonde; Dixie, who wore a 'Hiroshima' hat, was a brunette with spotty but interesting features, a weak mouth, a tilting nose.

'Have a waffle?'

'Well, all right.'

'Three waffles, please. With syrup.'

'Ooooh ...'

It was not an evening on which to rebuff invitation. All round us, set free in the name of victory, excited by the singing, made bold by the pealing bells, people were confronting one another, breaking the rule of a lifetime for this one night. Hand reached for hand, even heart (briefly) for heart; stranger clung to stranger and called him brother. Phyllis and Dixie could be no exception. We all went on the roundabout, the dive-bomber, and the tower slide, at the bottom of which the girls' skirts flew up to reveal brown, ample thighs. We went on the bumper cars; we fired air guns and threw darts; Phyllis won a goldfish in a bowl.

'The ghost-train. The ghost-train.'

'Phyllis is feared of the dark.'

'Then you come, Dixie.'

'Yes, you go, Dixie, love. I'll stand here and mind my fish.'

Into the car and through the double gates.

'Ooh, I'm so feared, I'm as bad as Phyllis, hold me tight.'

'I'm here, Dixie. Kiss me.'

Spider webs trailing in the dark. Dixie's tongue meeting mine, keen, wet, inexpert. An enormous phosphorescent skull. Into the huge mouth went the car and into Dixie's went my probing tongue.

'Hold me tighter. More. More.'

Diabolical laughter. A sudden turn, throwing me right across her. My hand on her breast – how did it get there? – a little whimper, part of guilt and part of joy.

'Chris, Chris, Christopher. Kiss me again.'

Rattle, jerk, bang, and out into the lights.

'Round again, please. Two.'

'No, Chris. Phyllis. She's waiting.'

'Just once more. I've already paid.'

Crash through the double door. *Now.* Tongue between her lips, left hand over her shoulder and cupping her breast, and with the right hand . . .

'No, Chris. No.'

'Yes, Dixie. And when we get out, we'll give Phyllis the slip and we'll—'

'—No, Christopher. No, no, *no.*'

But her legs parted slowly to admit my hand into a warm, moist country where I had never been before.

'Oh, no . . . Oh . . . Oh . . .'

'Dixie. We'll give Phyllis the slip. And then . . .'

I moved my hand to part her legs yet wider.

'I can't, I can't, I can't. She's my *sister*.'

Using both her hands, she thrust mine away from her, away from the paradisiac country. Panting and whimpering, she strained away from me. The whimpers mounted and coalesced into hysterical weeping. Christ. Christ, Christ, Christ.

'Dixie, *please* . . .'

A heavy, rending, choking, unquenchable cacophony of sobs. Rattle, jerk, bang, and out into the lights.

Run for it.

Out of the car and down the steps, just missing the astonished Phyllis (crash went the goldfish bowl – 'Oh Chris, my poor little fish'), straight through the crowd, round the tower slide and behind the stalls. Would they follow? Would they call the police? Would they collect a mob? A whistle from the distance. Could that be . . .?

Into the Duke's Head.

'Quick, mother. We'll miss the train.'

'But Fielding dear, I thought—'

'—No, no. There's no time at all.'

'If you say so—'

'—Please be *quick*, mother. This way, out of the side door . . . Down this street. It's a short cut.'

'Really, dear, anyone would think the police were after us. You know I can't hurry too much.'

'Taxi . . . *Taxi*.' By God, what a bit of luck. There weren't more than three in the whole town. I blocked the road, waving frantically.

' 'Ere, 'ere. I don't take no more fares, master. I'm off 'ome. I've used my quota for the day.'

'But the lady's ill. Just to the station.'

'Ill, be she?'

'There'll be a whole pound for you if you take us.'

'Ill she be. In you get, missis . . .'

When we were in the train, which was not due to leave the station for another thirty minutes, mama said:

'If you ask me, dear, you ought to be a little more careful of your money. A whole pound.'

'It was for you, mama.'

'Was it, dear?' said my mother equably. 'Well, if *you* think it was worth it . . .'

'Why is it,' said my father the next morning, 'that I never get any co-operation?'

'Co-operation, dear?'

'Yes, dear, co-operation, dear. I've had a letter from the so-called Tutor of Lancaster College, in which he acknowledges mine and begs to inform me that any instructions about Mr. Fielding Gray's place at the college should be sent by Mr. Fielding Gray. Don't they know that I'm his father? And that he isn't twenty-one?'

It was unlike my father to own publicly to a snub. He must have something up his sleeve, I thought. Nevertheless the opportunity to gloat was too tempting to be missed.

'It is a popular fallacy,' I said to my father, 'that parents have a legal right to dictate to their children until they are twenty-one. Provided a person pursues a responsible course of life, he can leave home and suit himself as soon as he is sixteen.'

'Then leave home and suit yourself,' my father said. 'Go on.'

'Jack, dear—'

'—I will have co-operation. And I'll tell you how I'm going to get it. Either you do as I say,' he said, thrusting his face into mine, 'or there'll be no more money for you until you do. You can live here and have your meals, since you're still under twenty-one, but there'll be no money at all for anything else.'

There was a long silence.

'Does that set you straight?' my father said.

'While we're talking of money,' I said, trembling all over, 'let me tell *you* something to set you straight. Mr. Tuck is not offering me this job to do you a favour, but because his boss in India is after some extra capital which they think you may be persuaded to provide. His wife told me all about it. They don't love you, they don't think you're marvellous, they simply want your cash.'

After this I locked myself into the lavatory and burst into tears.

'. . . *I must say* [Peter Morrison wrote from Whereham], *you seem to be having a most unpleasant holiday. I expect it will be a relief when your parents go away. Meanwhile, I only hope your father stops being so silly over this tea-planting business. I don't see you as a sahib.*

'*Which reminds me. I'm as glad as you are that there's now no prospect of getting killed in the Far East; but I don't think we should be sanguine about this bomb they've thought up. The terrible thing about it is that it makes its possessor infallible. It does away, you see, with any margin of error or need for selection. In the old days you had to aim at your target. Now, in order to be sure of destroying what you want to, you can simply destroy everything at all. Suppose such a weapon were entrusted to a man like your father (or even Somerset) who* knows *he's right?*

'*But I expect you are depressed enough without my raising additional nightmares. I hope things improve, and I look forward to seeing you and Somerset on the 24th or 25th. Please let me know which . . .*'

So at least that was all right – though quite what was to

happen about money, since my father's threat, was still obscure. One could only hope for the best, I thought; and anyhow, mama would be sure to wangle something. So I wrote to Peter to tell him that Somerset was definitely arriving at Broughton (as I had now heard) on 20th August, and that we would be coming on to him on the 24th. After that, I wrote to Christopher:

'... *So that all being well I can be with you in Tonbridge on 4th or 5th September and stay till I leave for Wiltshire on the 7th.*

'*Oh Christopher, how I wish it could be sooner. I've been so lonely without you. I expect you've been lonely too (in a way, I hope you have), but at least you're busy with this tutor of yours. There's a line from a poem by a man called Auden which keeps running in my head—*

'"*I think of you, Christopher, and wish you beside me ..."*

'*If only it was that afternoon of the Eton match again, when we sat next to each other in the scoring box ...*'

Having posted these two letters, I settled down to read *Dorian Gray*; but the afternoon was very hot and the book a sickly bore. Every ten seconds I was interrupted by memories of Christopher in the hay-loft: 'Oh ... oh, oh, oh.' Oh Christ, those long smooth legs with their fluffy down.

And then I thought of another pair of legs. Angela Tuck's. Why not go to the Tucks' bungalow and say to Angela, 'All right. I'll sign on with your husband's plantation provided you'll come to bed with me in exchange'? That was the deal she had held out, so why not take her up? Not in so many words, of course, ('Don't spell it out,' she had said) but in the same veiled terms which she had used on the golf course, so that later on I could always wriggle out of the bargain. They meant to exploit me; why shouldn't I exploit them? All these adults ranged against me made for inequitable odds; I was entitled to any little victory I could win, however treacherously, in their despite. Superior strength in the opposition (as the Senior Usher had once observed) absolved one from obeying the Queensberry Rules.

Mr. Tuck had gone to London for a few days. My father, having apparently taken my point about Tuck's motives, had sent the wretched man to Coventry; so that Tuck had doubtless felt it expedient to try his talent for recruiting elsewhere. Angela had been distant. But if I were now to present myself and make my offer? She couldn't eat me, after all, and anything was better than hanging around in the house with Dorian Gray gone stale on me.

I went to my room, washed my hands, face and feet, slicked my hair down with water, and substituted my blue 1st XI blazer and scarf for my ordinary coat and tie. Then I walked the three quarters of a mile to the Tucks' one-storey bungalow near the quay.

The curtains of one room were drawn. Angela must be having a siesta (Indian habit). On the whole, good. I was about to knock on the front door, when I reflected that she might be cross if woken up and dragged through the hall to answer. Better surprise her, quieten her as she lay vulnerable on the bed, and then introduce my business. 'I've been thinking over what you said about India, and I see that I've been very silly. It's not a chance to be missed.' Something like that. Whatever else, she could hardly pretend to be shocked.

Very quietly, I tried the front door. The catch was evidently up, for the door opened. The excitement of what was virtually house-breaking had now replaced desire. As the door opened yet further, apprehension replaced excitement. I was about to turn and run, had indeed already turned. Too late.

'Who's there?' said Angela's voice from inside a half-open door a few feet along the hall. My lips were parting to reply, when:

'Nobody's there,' said my father's voice. 'How could they be? I fastened the front door.'

'I thought—'

'—Don't be a silly girl, Angie. Your old Jackie will see you're safe.'

'And Jackie will be a good boy about you know what?'

The voice was childish, wheedling, without irony.

'I'll see that little beast signs up with Tuck. After that . . .'

'If Tuck was in a position to say that you'd guaranteed to invest a few thousand—'

'—Why can't that wait,' said my father crossly 'until the Army's finished with the boy and he's free to join?'

'Now the war's over, they're anxious to expand as soon as possible. If Tuck brings in new money *now*, they'll be very grateful.'

'Well, I'll see. If Angie's nice to Jackie, Jackie will see what he can do.'

The bed creaked.

'No. Jackie must promise Angie.'

Sweaty and furious as I was, I nevertheless had a clear mental picture of concupiscence struggling with avarice in my father's face.

There was a great wail of randiness.

'All right. Tuck can tell his boss I'll invest five thousand. Perhaps a little more if things go well on the market.'

'There's a dear, *good* Jackie.'

If she knew him as I do, I thought grimly, she'd get him to sign something this minute. But perhaps she too was keen to start. After all, I'd heard people say my father was a handsome man.

'Jackie. Oh, Jackie.'

A different tone now, all childishness gone. A woman speaking. Either she was a good actress or she was very much in earnest.

'Christ, Christ, Jackie, Christ.'

She was in earnest.

I heard my father's breathing mount. Wait. Time it carefully. You swine, Jack Gray, you disgusting swine, with your hot, panting breath.

'Soon, Angela, *soon*.'

'Oh *yes*, Jackie.'

Now. I opened the front door to its full extent and then pulled it to with all the strength in my body.

Having slammed the door on the repulsive idyll in the Tuck bungalow, I went for a walk along the beach in order to calm myself. For a long time I thought, with a mixture of lust and apprehension, of Dixie in the ghost-train. Supposing she or her parents tried to raise a complaint? Suppose the police came making inquiries? In the end, however, I persuaded myself that the police would have neither time nor good reason to look as far afield as Broughton Staithe, and that in any case Dixie probably wanted to forget the whole episode as much as I did. Though there was one aspect of it I could never forget: my first, brief visit to the lotus country of a woman's loins.

Having, with some difficulty, dismissed Dixie, I reverted to the problem of my father. He had now given Angela a definite promise that myself plus £5,000 would be signed, sealed and delivered over to Tuck. It was always possible that my father had no intention of trying to keep his bargain; but equally, why should he not? The £5,000 would probably be quite a sound investment; the arrangement would get me off his hands for good; and more than all this, he would have had the satisfaction of destroying my most cherished plans and ambitions.

Quite why my father was so set against Cambridge, I was unsure. It was not, I suspected, just a simple matter of meanness about money or jealousy of my success; there was an intensity in his attitude, an element (however perverse) of morality, the clue to which, I thought, might possibly lie in something that I had once been told by the Senior Usher.

'If there is one thing people cannot stand,' the old man had said, 'it is that someone should achieve happiness and distinction by doing work which they despise. Their indignation is grounded in genuine moral feeling: it is like the resentment which dully married women feel at the success of a famous courtesan.'

'And why,' I had asked, 'are you telling me this?'

'My dear Fielding. You propose to spend your life doing intellectual work. You may as well learn now as later that many people – most people – regard such work as effeminate and degrading.'

Yes, I thought now, it fitted near enough. '... effeminate and degrading.' 'Sometimes,' my father had said, 'I think I've got a woman for a son.' My father clearly regarded Cambridge and all it stood for as immoral or at least unmanly; the work was not proper work at all (it was far too pleasant, for a start) and no son of his was going to make a living by it. So much, I thought, for diagnosis. But what, in heaven's name, was I going to do? If my father wanted to cut off supplies, no one could stop him. The Headmaster's talk of government grants and subsidies was all very well; but hitherto I had been accustomed to ample provision and I now shrank from the prospect of going through Cambridge on a meagre official pittance, of which, in any case, I had yet to be definitely assured. And quite apart from all that, if my father persisted in his present intention it would mean no last year at school, and on this I had set my heart.

Calmer than when I had set out but even more depressed, I arrived at our front door. Just inside the hall, on a hard chair by the telephone, sat my mother, looking very peculiar indeed.

'Mama ... Why on earth are you sitting out here?'

'Something rather funny has happened,' my mother said. Her eyes glinted weirdly, part in amusement and part in shock. 'Angela Tuck rang up. Your father's just died of a heart attack.'

Quite how much my mother knew or guessed, I never found out for sure. The official version, which mama apparently accepted, was that my father had gone to Angela to ask where he could get in touch with her husband in London, as he wanted some more information about the tea-planting scheme. Angela, while entertaining him to a cup of tea, had suggested that I myself might make difficulties about this; upon which father had flown into a rage, choked, gone into violent spasms, and then relapsed into a kind of coma. Angela had rung for a doctor, but by the time he arrived my father was dead.

This seemed to me a very convenient version of the affair; inaccurate but on the whole equitable. I was glad that I myself was mentioned as in some sort contributing to father's demise; for since I had good reason to believe that this might indeed be the case, some reference to me, however wide of the actual facts, was both ironic and just. Guilt I felt none; my father had been a pestilential bully and now, by a happy accident, had been permanently removed. Even if one assumed that my own act of slamming the door had been the mortal factor (and who was ever to say that this was so?), the act had been excusable and its consequence unforeseen.

To Angela I did not speak of the matter. If she suspected that I had been the intruder that afternoon, she had yet to give any sign of it. For my part, my feelings towards her were unaltered, save that they now included considerable admiration of her resource: she must have had a most difficult and disagreeable job rigging the scene into decency against the arrival of the doctor. No doubt about it: a slut she might be but a slut to be reckoned with.

The coroner was soon satisfied that death was due to natural causes, and arrangements for the funeral were briskly made. Mama, once she had had a few hours to get over her surprise, showed more efficiency and character than in all the years I could remember.

'Tell the undertaker,' she instructed me: 'opening time to-morrow.'

'Opening time?'

'As soon as he opens his shop or whatever he calls it. No point, Fielding dear, in hanging about.'

Or again, while kneeling in the church before the service.

'The people from the firm,' she decreed, 'must come in for drinks afterwards. But not the soaks from the golf club.'

'Some of them were friends of father's.'

'You mean they'd let him buy them drinks. Not that he was so quick to do that.'

'They'll resent it, mother.'

'I don't doubt it, dear,' said mama, as she concluded her devotions and resumed a sitting position: 'but since I never want to see any of them again, it doesn't matter, does it?'

The Rector, irritated by the flippancy with which mama had convened the ceremony, cut his address to a minimum. Even what little could be said in favour of the deceased he threw away rapidly, like a bored actor whose new mistress was waiting for him in his dressing-room. 'John Aloysius Gray,' he snorted, 'served from 1940 to 1945 as captain, later major, in the Army Ordnance Corps.' An undistinguished record, it now sounded infamous.

After John Aloysius Gray had been fed to the worms, the widow stood to receive condolences. Last in the line was Angela Tuck, to whom mama was more than gracious.

'You're not to feel it was your fault, Angela dear.' (Did she then know more than she let on?) 'You come home with me and Fielding. And when I've got rid of those nuisances from the firm we can all have a nice talk.'

From that day on my mother seemed increasingly eager for the company of Angela Tuck. Since Tuck himself was still away, presumably recruiting, Angela was free to indulge mama, and was indeed invited to be present on the most intimate occasions, such as the family discussion with little Mr. Japhet, the solicitor from Lympne Ducis, about my father's will.

With the exception of a few minor bequests to old friends and senior employees of the firm, everything was left to my mother, with the suggestion that she should 'take what steps she thought fit' as to the education and subsequent provision of myself. Although this was broadly in accordance with bourgeois custom, I was disconcerted that no more definite arrangements had been made. Knowing my father as I did, I had expected either to be provided for under some restrictive form of trust, or, quite possibly, to be spitefully disinherited: what I had not expected was that the will should be merely casual. (Here, of course, I had badly misread my father's character: I should have realized that he would have seen no point in restricting or spiting people by means of his will, as he himself would not be there to enjoy their discomfiture.) Again, quite apart from the vagueness of the immediate arrangements, my father had shown a disquieting unconcern for the future: there was no kind of entail, no stipulation that mama should regard myself as her heir, indeed nothing whatever, as far as I could see, to stop her giving away the whole lot that very afternoon. While I did not doubt her good will, I had no very high opinion of her good sense: mama was simply *not* a person who should be allowed to control a fortune.

Little Mr. Japhet clearly thought the same and was busily trying to persuade her to put her affairs entirely in the discreet hands of himself and the bank manager. But mama, true to the spirit which she had shown since father's death and strongly supported by Angela, was being difficult.

'You say,' she said, 'that after death duties there'll be about £50,000 in cash and investments?'

'That's right, dear lady.'

'And what's the firm at Torbeach worth?'

'To you, dear lady, about £5,000 in a good year.'

'I don't mean yearly profits. I mean lock, stock and barrel.'

Mr. Japhet looked shocked. My stomach stirred uneasily.

'Surely, mother—' I began.

'Don't interrupt, dear,' said mama. 'Now then, Angela. Tell Mr. Japhet what you were telling me yesterday.'

'Just at the moment,' said Angela, 'there's more money around than materials or plant. It follows that a going concern like this one, fully staffed and equipped and with half a century's good will behind it, would fetch an abnormally high price.'

Shrewd enough, I thought; but I wish you'd mind your own business instead of ours.

'But,' continued Angela, 'the seller's market won't last for ever. As soon as things settle down again and they start producing more modern kinds of machinery, your bucket shop at Torbeach will be a back number.'

'*Bucket shop?*' said Mr. Japhet.

'That's what it makes, doesn't it? Buckets?'

'General hardware, madam.'

'What the hell,' said Angela.

'Anyway,' said mama, quiet but firm, 'I've made up my mind. Sell the firm . . . for money down. Not for shares in anything else or deferred bills or whatever they call them, but for money down. I've been living in the shadow of that factory for twenty years, and I never want to hear of it again.'

'But,' said Mr. Japhet primly, 'it is a family firm. The employees of the factory are also the loyal employees of your family. They will be distressed.'

'I doubt it,' said mama. 'Loyalty to families is going to be a thing of the past, if my newspaper is anything to go by.'

Despite my uneasiness, I had to admit that my mother and Angela between them had made some telling points. Now I must put in a word for myself.

'Excuse me, mother,' I said politely, 'but while Mr. Japhet is here, do you think we might come to some firm arrangement about my allowance? Could it be paid into a bank every month or something?'

'Your *allowance,* dear?' said mama softly. 'I thought your father gave you pocket money?'

'Yes, mother. But now . . .'

'I think the same sort of arrangement will still do very well, dear. For the time being . . . And now, Mr. Japhet. In a day or two I propose going away on a little holiday. I've got a lot of things to think over, and I need a change and a rest. You can arrange, I think, to have money placed at my disposal in the bank?'

'The bank will allow you to draw as you wish,' said Mr. Japhet, 'against repayment when we obtain probate.'

'That,' said mama dismissively, 'will be exceedingly convenient.'

'Mama?'

'Yes, Fielding dear?'

'Would you like me to come with you? On this holiday, I mean?'

'Oh no, dear. I wouldn't dream of asking you to put yourself out. Not that you would, would you?'

'What can you mean?'

'Simply that there's a lot of your father in you.'

'If you want me to, I'll put off—'

'—No, dear. I'll do very well by myself for a while. What day is your friend coming? Somerset Lloyd-Thing?'

'Lloyd-James. Thursday.'

'Then I'll be off on Wednesday so as to be out of your way. How long will Somerset Lloyd-Thing be staying?'

'Lloyd-James. Only a few days. Then we go to Peter at Whereham.'

'Such *nice* manners Peter always had. How kind of him to ask you.'

'And then, later on, I'm going to stay with the Headmaster in Wiltshire. So you see, mother—'

'—The Headmaster? I should have thought he saw enough of you in term time.'

'He wants to discuss arrangements for next year.'

'Does he?' said mama blankly.

'Yes. So you see, mother, I'm going to be away a lot and I shall need some money.'

'But you'll be staying with people all the time.'

'Yes, but fares and so on . . .'

'We mustn't be extravagant, dear, must we? And if the Headmaster wants to talk to you, perhaps he might be the one to pay your fare.'

'For Christ's sake, mother.'

'It's not Christ's money, dear, but mine. So I'll write you out a little cheque. But you do understand – don't you? – that just because your father's dead you can't automatically have everything you want. As it is, there'll be the extra food for Somerset Lloyd-Thing.'

An unsatisfactory letter from Christopher at Tonbridge. He was enjoying his tuition, it seemed, as his tutor from Oxford was a very kind and interesting man. He was looking forward to telling me about some of the things they had discussed. Until when, he was 'yours ever'.

If that was all he had to say, I could see no reason why he had written at all. He hadn't even remembered to confirm the dates which I had suggested for my stay in Tonbridge. So I wrote him a quick note, repeating that I could be with him on 4th or 5th September, even a day or two earlier if he liked, and asking him to reply at once as I was anxious to have it settled.

Angela dined with mama and me on both the last two nights previous to mama's departure. Indeed, I gathered that had not Tuck's return been daily expected, Angela would probably have accompanied my mother on part at least of her holiday.

Up to this time, I had been no more than vaguely irritated by this new friendship, putting it down to the loneliness of the two women. But on the night before my mother left, I began to feel almost as if the association were turning into a league – a league against myself. The women paid me none of the deference which the senior male in a household, however young, is usually accorded. They were deaf to my small requests and combined to disregard my preferences. The off-hand manner which Angela had lately adopted towards me had now become something more like contempt; while my mother's old self-effacement now seemed nearer to indifference. All in all, I was relieved that they were about to part; their influence on one another was clearly unwholesome. Yet I saw no need of worry. My mother would return from her holiday rested and in her right senses (in so far as she had any); and Angela, no doubt, would soon be swept back to India by Tuck. Meanwhile, I was to see Somerset and Peter again: at last, the longed for company of old friends.

This afternoon, when the mail-boat arrived, I received a copy of a London weekly to which I subscribe. On the second page is the announcement that the Editor, Mr. Somerset Lloyd-James, will shortly contribute a series of five long articles about the current state of our national finances; so Somerset, it seems, has realized his ambition to become an authority. At the head of the announcement is a photograph, taken, I should surmise, while he was still up at Cambridge, not so very long after I last saw him. Yet the face on the page before me might as well belong to the devil for anything it recalls of my school-boy friend. And indeed, even when he arrived in Broughton Staithe that August of 1945, he had already changed a great deal. The change, of course, had been taking place the whole of the previous quarter, but since it had been gradual, and since I had seen him daily, I had hardly noticed it (despite the comments of Peter, who, seeing him rather less often, had been more aware). But now, after I had been nearly a month away from Somerset, the metamorphosis was plain: he had matured, I might almost say he had aged, and his knack of spreading a defensive glaze over his eyes was now more than ever pronounced. Had we not still had a number of friends and interests in common (and even these were now discussed by Somerset in a new spirit, a spirit which was grudging where before it had been merely guarded), and had it not been for certain familiar tricks of manner and idiom, I should scarcely have recognized the boy who had walked with me over the cricket ground in May.

'I was sorry,' said Somerset as soon as he was out of his train, 'to hear about your father.'

'You needn't be.'

'I should have been interested to meet him. Your mother too.'

'She thought we'd sooner be left to ourselves.'

'Considerate of her,' murmured Somerset. 'As it happens, I do have one or two rather private things to say to you.'

'Fire ahead.'

'Not yet.'

'Why not?'

'Your mood is not propitious. I must wait until you are more receptive.'

'And when is that likely to be?'

Somerset was silent for several seconds. Then he said:

'Before I can tell you what I'm going to, I must first establish the new relationship between us.'

'The new relationship?'

'Yes. Hitherto I have been the ugly but amusing boy befriended by the glamorous school hero. I have been philosopher, clown and client. This is a role I am no longer willing to sustain. I must assert my claim to equality – in some respects to dominance.'

'For heaven's sake, Somerset. I've always regarded you as an *ally.*'

'No, you haven't. Whether you knew it or not, you always condescended.'

'Well, if so I'm sorry. I never for a moment—'

'—No need to be sorry,' Somerset said. 'I bear no rancour. But from now on things must be different. When I'm sure you fully understand that, I shall be ready to speak more plainly.'

A taxi appeared at last in the station yard. We piled into it with Somerset's luggage, and sat side by side in silence until we were home. There was about Somerset, I thought, the air of a scrupulous duellist – of one determined to ensure, before shedding his opponent's blood, that everything was entirely *en règle* at the outset. It was as though he were giving me fair warning, enough to let me know that combat was about to begin, not enough to let me into the stratagems which would be used. Yet if he was after my blood, why should he trouble to give warning? Perhaps his Catholic conscience would not allow him to omit this, or perhaps he was obeying some atavistic notion of chivalry, such as might have deterred his remote ancestors from 'striking horse' in a tournament. But whatever the refinements might be, an instinct told me plainly, amid much that was in question, that Somerset meant business and meant it soon.

'The atom bomb,' said Somerset at lunch, 'is just another element in the situation.'

'Peter and the head man seem to think it's too colossal to take into account. That it's beyond our control.'

'Nothing which we ourselves have made can be beyond our control. It is simply another problem which requires thought.'

'So what would you do about it?'

'To start with,' Somerset said, 'I'd put a stop to all this so-called moral protest. The atom bomb *exists*. We may as well accept the fact without whining.'

'All right. I accept the fact without whining. So what am I to do next?'

'You should remember that as far as you know only your side can make it. No one else has the secret . . . yet.'

'And so?'

'And so you should establish dominance before it's too late. Before your enemies too can make atom bombs and so achieve parity.'

'Somerset . . . You don't mean we ought to use the thing?'

'One would hope that the mere threat, the *unambiguous* threat, would be enough.'

'And who,' I asked, 'are our enemies?'

'Those who wish us ill – about three quarters of the world's population.'

'So you would establish a series of atomic bases all over the world and then hold it to ransom?'

'For its own good,' said Somerset, 'to say nothing of ours. Unfortunately, however, we can't afford it and our American friends, who can, won't finance such an undertaking. They would regard it as wicked.'

'They might not be alone in that.'

'No doubt they will have the sentimental support of all who, like themselves, are ignorant of history. The historical lesson is quite plain: if you are lucky enough to discover a new weapon, you should make full use of it. Because if you don't somebody else will, and almost certainly at your expense. A melancholy truth,' said Somerset with satisfaction, 'which applies, *mutatis mutandis*, in all human activities.'

For three days nothing much happened. We went for walks by the sea, we prepared meals and ate them, we talked of neutral topics, and we read. Somerset said no more of 'the private things' which he had to communicate; nor did he make any signal of impending battle. But always the threat was there, and I became more and more impatient for its open declaration.

On the fourth evening of Somerset's visit, having dinner at the local hotel, we saw Angela Tuck. She waved in a friendly way, and when she had finished her meal she came over, unasked, to join us.

'Introduce me to your fascinating friend,' she said.

I introduced her.

'Tuck is back tomorrow,' she announced.

'And we are off – to a friend at Whereham.'

'Then you must come round to my place,' Angela said, 'and have a drink.'

We all went down the road to the Tuck bungalow by the quay.

'Drinkies,' said Angela. She bustled out and bustled back with a tray, three glasses, and, incredibly, two bottles of champagne.

'Don't ask me where I got it from,' she said, and opened one bottle with a few expert movements.

Somerset coyly dabbled some of the wine behind his ear.

'Twenty-one today,' sang Angela raucously, and knocked back the glass in one.

'Literally?'

'Literally. I hope Tuck brings me something nice from London. He hasn't even sent a telegram, the rotten sod.'

'Let's hope he's had good hunting,' I said. 'It might make him more generous.'

Angela gave me a sly look and seemed about to reply. But by now Somerset was on his feet proposing a toast.

'To our charming hostess,' Somerset said, 'now that she has acquired the key of the door. May she always be free with it.'

'Whoops,' went Angela, and tucked into her fizz. She sat down on Somerset's lap and started to stroke his cheek.

'Little Somerset,' she said; 'and where did he learn to say such pretty things to the ladies? Open the other bottle,' she ordered me, rather sharply, and deposited a sploshing kiss on Somerset's spotty forehead.

What in God's name is she up to now, I wondered. I opened the bottle with clumsy, unfamiliar hands, while Angela went on kissing Somerset. The cork popped and a great gout of champagne shot over her dress.

'When it rains, it rains bubble-juice from heaven,' Angela sang. 'Lucky we've got some of mother's ruin for when that's gone. Better put on something dry.'

She tottered out.

'I can't understand it,' I said: 'she's usually got a head like a rock. I mean, whatever she does, there's none of this *childishness*.'

'She's been drinking all day,' said Somerset coolly.

'How do you know?'

'She's got fresh blisters on her fingers where she's burnt them with cigarettes. Drunks always do that.'

'How clever of you to notice.'

'There've been quite a few drinkers in my family.'

Angela came back in pyjamas.

'Tell you what,' she screamed 'birthday gamies. Let's all have a birthday gamey.'

'Willingly,' said Somerset, hiccuping and helping himself to the last of the champagne.

'Get the gin first,' said Angela, throwing out her bust like Volumnia.

'Where is it?'

'Kitchen.'

Somerset clumped off.

'What do you mean . . . gamies?' I said.

'Cardies.' She swayed over to a desk and came back with a pack. 'Forfeits. You'll see.'

Somerset came back with the gin and poured out stiff measures all round. Remembering the scene on the last night of the quarter, I wondered whether Somerset would be sick again: certainly drink effected a rapid change in his demeanour, a change decidedly for the better, I thought.

'Forfeits,' announced Angela.

She dealt each of us a card, face down.

'Whoever has the highest card can claim a forfeit from the one with lowest,' she explained with surprising lucidity.

'What kind of forfeit?'

Angela shrugged.

'Turn 'em up,' she said.

Somerset had the highest card, Angela the lowest.

'I claim a kiss from Angela,' Somerset said.

'You've already had some.'

'This will be a *special* kiss.' Somerset's spectacles were crooked and his lisp pronounced.

'That's the thpirit,' Angela mimicked. She crawled along the carpet to the side of Somerset's chair, knelt there and held her face up to him. Somerset took his spectacles off, leaned down, missed her mouth, and kissed her on the end of her turned up nose.

'You need your gig-lamps.'

She picked them off the arm of the chair.

'Don't meth about with my thepectacles.'

Too late. Angela had keeled over and crunched the glasses against the hearth stone. Blood came from her hand.

'My glathes,' wailed Somerset.

'Angela's hand . . .'

'Never mind my hand *or* anybody's rotten glasses. Deal the cards.'

'Luckily I remembered to bring another pair. But they're not so comfortable.'

'*Deal the cards.*'

I dealt. This time Angela had the highest card, Somerset the lowest.

'Take your trousers off,' said Angela briskly.

Knowing that Somerset was too mean to buy himself underpants from his allowance, I started to smirk. But Somerset was equal to the occasion. Having got his trousers off swiftly and with dignity, he tucked the tail of his shirt between his legs.

'Not much meat,' said Angela, pinching one of Somerset's thin white calves and leaving a trail of blood. 'Deal the cards.'

Somerset dealt. This time I won with a ten, while both Angela and Somerset had eights.

'Forfeits for both of you,' I said hilariously. 'Let's have your shirt, Somerset. And as for you, *Angie*, the top half of your pyjamas.'

Angela complied pokerfaced: Somerset seemed reluctant.

When he had removed his shirt, he was naked save for his shoes and socks, and he did not strip prettily. He placed his hand over his groin, Angela inspecting him closely as he did so. Am I trying to humiliate him, I wondered; or do I, in some unbelievably perverse way, wish to be ... associated with him?

'Cards,' said Angela, excitable no longer but grave and purposeful. She dealt each card with ponderous care; after which she turned up an Ace, Somerset and I both Kings.

'Ace high,' said Angela; 'forfeits from both.'

She looked carefully from Somerset to me and back again.

'You,' she said to Somerset, 'are interesting. Ugly and skinny, but interesting. I claim you. You,' she said rounding on me, 'are just a sexual cliché. Peaches and a little frothy cream. From you I claim privacy.'

'The game's not over yet,' I said sullenly.

'This is my house, and I'm telling you to go away and leave us alone.'

She wiped her bloody hand casually over her breast, then bent over Somerset, who was looking myopic but composed.

'Do as the kind lady asks,' said Somerset.

This time, I thought furiously, he is not going to be sick.

'I think,' said Somerset with deadly softness, 'that I shall be able to find my own way back ... even without my glasses.'

He lay back in his chair. Angela took his hand and lifted it away from his body.

'Get out,' she hissed at me; 'and don't slam the door.'

Inland from the sea, on the way to Whereham, the fields shimmered and drowsed. The bus, almost empty, nosed along the lanes and through clumps of complacent trees, made long stops in market places or in front of tiny post offices, which displayed in their windows pre-war Christmas annuals, knitting magazines and toy magic lanterns.

At one such post office I dismounted and sent a telegram to Christopher. 'Please confirm 3rd, 4th or 5th September for visit. Anxious to hear. Fielding.' After all, I thought, Christopher must have had my last letter at least five days ago; he should have answered by now.

When I returned to the bus, Somerset, who had hardly spoken since we got out of bed, inquired with bland interest:

'What was all that about?'

'Just a wire to the charwoman. Something I forgot to tell her.'

'It could have waited, surely until we reached Peter's house?'

'I suppose so. I just felt restless.'

'So I noticed. You know, I think the time has come ... now ... for me to speak to you. After what happened last night, I fancy the conditions are favourable.'

'Then make yourself plain, Somerset. For God's sake be plain and be done.'

'Very well.' Somerset took a deep breath. 'There's one thing I want,' Somerset said, 'which I don't propose to let you take from me or to spoil for me after I have it. Eight months from now, next spring, they will need a new Head of school. I propose to be that Head and I don't propose to allow you, as a subordinate Head of your own House, to challenge my authority. Nor do I propose to allow you to discredit that authority by making a mess of things in your own little area. Mismanagement or scandal in your House would also mean mismanagement or scandal in my *school*.'

'People have been warning me about you for some time,' I said slowly, 'and I sometimes thought that it might turn out to be something like that. But then I told myself, calmly and reasonably, that it simply couldn't be, because no one as sensible as you could care about anything so trivial. I'm *disappointed* that I was wrong. *Why*, Somerset?'

'You have so much already,' said Somerset, almost humbly. 'Surely you wouldn't grudge me this?'

'You can have it and welcome. I shan't stand in your way or make rude noises when you ascend your throne. But the choice isn't ours. It will be made by the Headmaster.'

'If the position is offered to you, you must refuse.'

'The head man would think it very odd.'

'You must put him off as best you can.'

'I've told you,' I said, irritated at last. 'I don't care either way and I wouldn't dream of pushing myself forward. But if the head man *should* call on me, then I'm damned if I'll grovel about saying, "No, I am not worthy, choose Somerset instead." You can't expect it.'

'Can't I? You know, Fielding, I've been following up one or two little rumours about you. About you and Christopher Roland. I don't suppose you'd much care for them to be brought to the Headmaster's attention.'

'The head man already knows I'm fond of Christopher.'

'But does he know *how* fond? He can be very sensitive, the head man, about that kind of thing. He has to be in his position.'

'There's nothing to be sensitive about.'

'Isn't there?' Somerset paused, and then proceeded with the solemn manner of one dictating his terms. 'What's happened, Fielding, was no affair of mine. I'll let the past rest and gladly, provided you do as I say. That's the first point. By-gones can be by-gones if you'll let them be.'

'Generous of you.'

'But secondly, remember this. If I get a hint of anything in this line starting up again, *next year* . . . I won't have it, Fielding. Any more of that, with Christopher or anyone else, and *I'll get you sacked.*'

'Is it pride talking, or morality?'

'Let's just say that anything of this kind would offend my sense of good order.'

'Pride.'

'Seemliness.'

'*Obsession.*'

The bus drew to a stop. I spotted Peter, who was waiting for us in front of a brick chapel of improbable denomination.

'Have it which way you will,' said Somerset, taking his case from the rack. 'Those are my terms – quite easy terms, don't you think? – and if you still want to be there wearing your pretty blue blazer next summer, you'd better keep them.'

Peter's father, an immense brown man with a trace of Norfolk in his voice, was seldom seen save in the evenings, when he liked to discuss the prospects for county cricket now that the war was over; and Peter's mother, a grave woman with an enchanting smile, was called away to a married sister's sick bed the day after Somerset and I arrived. So the three of us were left, as I had hoped we would be, to amuse ourselves. Since Somerset was prone to hay fever, Peter did not suggest that we should help in the fields. Instead he took us on long leisurely tours of his family demesne; drove us in a farm cart to markets, or in a trap (petrol being tight even for farmers) to have picnics where there was a castle or a church, a village cricket match or a summer fête. It was a time of happiness and truce. Peter gave himself up to serene enjoyment of his last few days as a civilian in his own place; Somerset was clever, affable and modest; and I myself, while conscious of the new threat posed by Somerset, was in good part reassured by the whole-some presence of Peter and lulled by the simple pleasures of his country. So the kind days of the late summer and the new peace passed, until, one morning shortly before Somerset and I must leave, we all set out for Whereham Races, along with Peter's father, who had taken a rare holiday to watch one of his own horses run.

The main event of the day was to be a three mile steeple-chase, carrying a prize of one hundred sovereigns and open to any gentleman or yeoman who, during the war, had farmed his land in the shire or borne arms for his King. Mr. Morrison's contestant for the prize, Tiberius, was to be ridden by a young tenant who had recently returned from Germany, Mr. Morrison himself being disqualified by a weight of eighteen stone. Tiberius, an ageing black stallion much loved by Peter and known for many miles around, was second in the local betting. Favourite was Lord Blakeney's Balthazar, a young, clever and quick-tempered horse, who, it was said, would worry Tiberius by his aggressive manner and finally defeat him by sheer speed and skill.

But hope stood high with the Morrison faction, and the sun shone, and the mid-day provision of food and drink, which many of Mr. Morrison's friends and tenants had been bidden to share, was ducal by the standards of the time. Flushed faces came and went, ate and drank, whispered into Mr. Morrison's ear or boomed at him across the tankards; during which time Somerset condescended to those about him in his best country manner, I was euphoristic and inclined to show off, and Peter, anxious for his beloved Tiberius, was hospitable but pre-occupied. We watched the first race, a mediocre affair over which Somerset contrived to win a little money on the out-sider, who was ridden, as he remarked, 'by the only jockey whose knees inspire confidence'. After this there was more drinking. Then came the second race, again poorly contested, again yielding money to Somerset but not to myself. By now, what with the sun and the cider, I had already lost more than I had meant to risk on the entire meeting, but this was no time for counting losses: for next on the card was the great race of the day, and any moment now Tiberius would appear in the paddock.

Peter rejoined us after a visit to the ring.

'How do they bet?' asked Mr. Morrison.

'Even money for Balthazar, sir,' said Peter, who always

addressed his father by this style: 'two to one Tiberius. Five bar.'

'Lay this down the line,' his father said, producing a thick wad of white five pound notes. 'Slowly now. Don't go sending them into a panic. And put at least a score of it with the tote.'

'Thee be sure then, 'squire?' said a wizened old man who wore a vilely dirty cloth cap and had drunk perhaps two gallons of cider since our party arrived on the course.

'Nay,' said Mr. Morrison, 'how should I be? But it's a while since I had a good bet these last years, and the price is fair.'

'Shall I take less than two to one, sir?' asked Peter.

'Go down to six to four, my dear,' his father said; 'then take the rest to the tote. And not less than twenty on the tote, mind, howsoever they bet.'

'Best be to work, master,' said the cloth cap to Peter: 'there'll be a pile of money come in for the black 'un.'

'Come with me,' said Peter to Somerset and myself. 'We'll watch by the water-jump.'

While Peter disposed of his father's money Somerset wandered off 'to see', as he put it, 'if he could get a price'. Myself, feeling that faith was the only logic of the day, I put ten of the twelve pounds I had in my pocket on Tiberius, getting one of the last offers at two to one: if he won, then I should recoup my losses and be fourteen pounds to the good; if not ... well then Peter or Somerset would have to help. But it seemed as if I were on to a good thing: although Balthazar was still favourite, his price was stretching as that of Tiberius shortened; and likely enough the prices would meet before betting was through. Peter, looking strained, came away from the tote tent and put his hand into my arm; Somerset materialized from nowhere.

'This way,' Peter said.

'Don't you want to look at him in the paddock?'

'No. This way. He'll be all right when he's out on the course, but the crowds make him nervous. I can't bear it.'

We crossed the course from the stand and walked down over the meadows towards the water-jump, which was in a slight dip some three hundred yards after the first turn. I reflected that Peter's unwillingness to watch Tiberius in the paddock amounted almost to a dereliction of loyalty, something so unusual as to indicate that he must be very strung up indeed. I could feel the palm of his hand sweating into my arm; I must find comfort for him.

'Betting go off all right?' I said.

'Betting? I suppose so. I got twos over quite a bit, then seven to four for all but thirty. I took that to the tote.'

'Quite an investment of your father's,' Somerset said. 'Did you have anything for yourself?'

'No,' said Peter shortly: 'it would be like blackmail.'

'What about you, Somerset?'

'I found rather a nice price,' said Somerset, smug but vague: 'really rather nice.'

And now we were at the water-jump, an inoffensive natural ditch and guarded only by a foot of fence, but tricky because of the downward slope which led into it and a brief marshy patch on its far side, which might make it very hard for the horses to gain the firm footing they needed in order to make a proper onset at the sharp up-hill gradient immediately beyond it. Tiberius and the rest would have to take this jump three times. Starting in front of the stand, they would go away for two hundred yards, which included one easy plain fence, then turn, very sharply, over one hundred and thirty degrees, take another plain fence after a hundred yards, and run downhill to the water-jump; after which the course looped away, round and back, over three more fences and through two more dips, till it turned into the home run. This was about quarter of a mile from turning to winning post, included two more jumps, and completed a circuit of just on a mile. Peter had barely finished a rather jerky account of all this, when the first of the horses appeared on the course and started to parade slowly in front of the stand.

'He seems all right,' said Peter, looking through his glasses. 'I'm worried about Johnny Pitts in the saddle though. He's only been back from the Army a few days and he can't but be a bit strange to it. Blakeney's man, Georgie Owen, didn't go to the war ...'

The ten horses circled in front of the stand, then one by one tailed off to stand sedately behind the starting gate.

'Well behaved bunch,' Peter said. 'I wonder we've not had trouble from Balthazar.'

A white flag went up by the starting gate.

'Orders ...'

Then there was a great cheer from the stand and all the meadows around, for the flag was down and the field away. After the first hundred yards, it was the brown Balthazar, with the Blakeney cerise and argent up, a clear leader by four lengths; the rest were in a close bunch, nothing to reckon.

'I hope he gets clear of them,' Peter mumbled; 'he doesn't like being jostled.'

And after the first fence, the bunch behind Balthazar began to string out. Two horses stayed neck and neck, second and third, while Tiberius, a length and a half behind them, was going a placid, uncrowded fourth, a position he retained without effort round the terrible angle of the bend, to negotiate which it was necessary to slow down to an extent that made the impatient Balthazar shake his head and prick his ears in anger. Over the second fence and down the slope to the water-jump; Balthazar going very fast – 'too fast, Georgie Owen ought to know better' – but proving his cleverness by a jump which cleared the treacherous morass beyond the ditch and sent him racing up the hill the other side, to go seven lengths clear of the pair behind him, who were in turn a good three in front of Tiberius.

'There's my good boy,' called Peter softly, as Mr. Morrison's light blue and black sailed easily over the ditch and beyond the marsh. For a moment it seemed to me as if the horse turned his head very slightly to acknowledge the call; but then Tiberius was galloping serenely away up the hill, gaining, little by little and without any forcing, on the two horses between him and Balthazar.

'It's when they start jumping short, late in the race,' said Peter, pointing to the patch of marsh: 'once land in that ...'

By the end of the first circuit, Balthazar was ten lengths in front of the second and third, outside and just behind whom Tiberius was running with a confidence which implied he would pass just so soon as he judged fit. Of the rest of the field, three had fallen on the loop, two were badly tailed off, but one, a little grey animal with a short, humorous face, was going very trimly some five lengths behind Tiberius.

'That grey,' Peter said. 'Fancy Man ... There's a lot of running there.'

Once again, as he rounded the great bend, Balthazar pricked with annoyance. Once again he came down the slope at a very smart pace, cleared stream and marsh, and thundered off up the hill. Second and third ran more cautiously; but the second horse took off too soon, landed with hind legs almost in the ditch, slipped, kicked, veered, kicked again, and interlocked a leg with the third horse as it landed. In a moment there was a writhing, snorting mass on the ground which seemed to block the entire course. Tiberius having switched suddenly to the far side to avoid it, rapped his right rear leg sharply against the fence post as he jumped. Landing just inside the marsh, he had to struggle and change step to get going, by which time he had lost another two lengths to Balthazar and been substantially gained upon by Fancy Man, who, apparently unimpressed by the melée and giving it the smallest possible margin, improved his position yet further by jumping like a bird.

'Never mind, boy,' called Peter. 'There's a long way to go.'

And indeed it was now apparent that Balthazar was feeling the pace. Round the loop, back into the straight, Tiberius, unworried as it seemed by his mistake at the water, tracked him with an easy, fluid action and was visibly making up ground. The gap shortened to ten lengths and then to seven; Balthazar's jumping was beginning to lose its rhythm, while Tiberius's was still as smooth as paint; but always, three lengths behind Tiberius and giving the impression that at any moment he could an if he would, came the perky little Fancy Man. And so, when they passed the post for the second time, it was a three horse race and an open one.

'Take two to one, Tiberius,' a bookie's call floated across the meadow.

'Will you now?' muttered Peter, whose eyes had been fixed into his glasses. Now he lowered them to talk.

'I don't like it,' he said; 'he's hurt. He's hiding it, bless his heart, but he's hurt. That rap last time over here ...'

And again he lifted the glasses. Looking towards Somerset, I saw that the expression of casual condescension, which he had worn all day, had somehow deepened to one of sagacity and power.

'What are you looking so pleased about?' I said.

'I'm glad Tiberius is shortening the gap.'

Which he was still doing. This time, as he rounded the bend, Balthazar seemed glad to relax his speed; he took the plain fence clumsily and came towards the water-jump without enthusiasm. Meanwhile Tiberius kept to the same powerful and, as it were, routine stride which he had used throughout the race; and always the little Fancy Man came skipping daintily behind.

'He's hurt,' mumbled Peter again and again; 'I know it.'

At the water-jump Balthazar checked, jumped nervously, landed with rear legs in the morass, floundered, panicked, threw Georgie Owen back into the ditch. Tiberius jumped gamely; but weariness (or was it pain, as Peter said?) showed through his immaculate style; he too landed in the marsh, kept his footing only with a desperate effort ('Good boy, my sweetheart, that's my good boy'), and was off, oh, very slowly, up the hill. He had beaten Balthazar; but Fancy Man, who had jumped both ditch and marsh as sharp and clever as a flute, was now gaining rapidly. For all the wear he showed he might have been at the beginning of the day.

'He can't keep him off. Even if he wasn't hurt . . .'

But as Fancy Man drew up to Tiberius the brave stallion seemed to find new heart. A slight check in his beautiful action showed that he was indeed hurt; but he found new pace from somewhere, and even though Fancy Man was gaining it was no longer with ease. There were now five fences left. Over the first Tiberius stayed clear; then down into a dip where they could not be seen; out of the dip and over the second fence Tiberius still had his shoulders ahead; then down into another dip. Out of this and over the third fence – which was also the third from home – it was neck and neck. Into the home straight.

'Now, boy. Does it hurt? Does it hurt you, boy? Does it hurt?'

The second fence from home was an artificial and heavily guarded water-jump. Tiberius, amidst applause that rang back from the sky, took it with all the grace and skill he had shown at the very start of the race. Fancy Man pecked slightly, lost half a length, but he was over safely, his nose still level with Johnny Pitts's thigh. And now, once more, with the last fence a hundred yards ahead, he started to gain.

And this was when Johnny Pitts, forgetful after four years of driving a tank with his famous cavalry regiment, made his one mistake. For the first time in the race, he took his whip to Tiberius.

'Oh God,' moaned Peter, 'oh God, oh God . . .'

For a few yards more the horses were more or less level; then Tiberius faltered and, as Pitts thrashed more and more desperately, seemed to skid to a halt. For a moment he stood upright, shaking his head slowly, then knelt (as though to pay Pitts the final courtesy of allowing him to dismount), then subsided on to his flank and lay still. Pitts, puzzled, stood looking down on him; Fancy Man prinked over the last fence and past the post; the crowd responded with a low murmur and a turning of backs; and Peter, the tears pouring from his eyes, lowered his glasses and faced his friends.

'It's no good,' he sobbed. 'It's the whip that has broken his heart. Not the pain, the exhaustion, the defeat. But the whip . . . the whip has broken his heart.'

While Peter and his father attended to the disposal of Tiberius, Somerset left me in the drink tent on pretence of wanting a pee. Watching from the entrance to the tent, I saw him go up to a bookmaker and collect a handsome wad of notes. I stood and looked and looked straight at Somerset as he walked back.

'Yes,' said Somerset, putting a cool face on it, 'it was not for nothing I was reared in the country. I liked the look of that little grey. Seven to one . . . My family has always had an eye for horses.'

'Well,' I said, swallowing my anger in my need, 'you can lend me some of it. I'm almost out of money and I don't want to bother Peter just now.'

'Try him tomorrow,' Somerset answered, putting his money carefully away. 'He'll have got over it then.'

'It's the least you can do.'

'I don't lend money, Fielding. It makes me brood, wondering when it will come back. Peter will let you have what you want. He has stronger nerves than I have, and a more generous disposition.'

'Of course,' said Peter the following afternoon. 'How much will you need?'

Somerset had gone home. 'See you at the Headmaster's,' was all he had said to me before he left. No further reference to what had passed in the bus. Happily, Peter had asked me to stay one more night, so that there was now a chance to say a great deal which would otherwise have been impossible.

'How much will you need?' Peter said.

'Fifteen pounds, if that's all right. To see me home, then down to the head man's place and back. I'll send it on to you as soon as my mother gets home from her holiday. About September the fifteenth, she said.'

'You'd best send it to the bank for me. Barclay's, Whereham. I shan't want fifteen pounds where I'm going.'

'Even in the Army one gets time off.'

'Not recruits.' He went to a drawer and produced a bundle

116

of notes. 'So that's settled. Now what is it you've been so anxious to tell me these last days?'

'You've noticed?'

'I've noticed. Let's walk.'

As we left the house, I told Peter the substance of what had been said on the bus.

'Don't say I didn't warn you,' said Peter when I had finished. And then,

'I don't suppose for a moment you've got anything you could throw back at Somerset?'

'I have, oddly enough. But no one would believe me.'

I told him about the spree at Angela Tuck's.

'You're right,' Peter said. 'It's all too remote. It might just as well have happened in Timbuctoo. They won't believe you, and you can't prove anything, and Somerset knows it. Whereas what he's got on you ... He probably can't prove it either, but it's so close to home that he might make things very awkward.'

'I know. What shall I do, Peter?'

We were walking down the old smugglers' path, which made straight as an arrow over the ten miles to the sea. The way was between high banks which were topped by overshadowing trees. It was dusty and rutted but it was also cool and secret, a fitting place to consider threat and devise counter.

'Ignore the whole thing,' Peter said at last. 'Treat it as a bluff. Somerset may make himself a bloody nuisance, but unless he's got absolute proof he can't do any more. So ignore Somerset and ignore his threat. But from now on make doubly sure you keep your nose clean. You'll remember, I hope, what I said to you last quarter about that.'

Peter sat down against the bank and I sat down beside him. The leaves rustled listlessly over our heads. They were still green, the leaves, but they already looked tired, as though they would be glad to fall in a week or two and rot away to nothing in the earth.

'Tomorrow,' said Peter, 'you must leave here. A day or so later I go to the Army. So for the time, perhaps for a long time, we are parting; and since this is so, I want you to promise me something. I want you to promise me, Fielding, for all our sakes, that you won't hurt Christopher again.'

'What happened wasn't my fault. And I've made it up with him.'

'Yes. But what have you got in mind for him this time?'

117

'To be friends. To give him what he's always wanted.'

'You're telling me the truth, Fielding? You promise that you won't . . . take advantage of him?'

'I'm going to be to Christopher exactly what he wants me to be,' I said. 'I shan't ask for anything more.'

I shan't need to, I thought.

'Good,' said Peter. 'I was afraid you might still be greedy; it's always been your trouble, you know. But now I can go away without worrying. And if you stick to what you've promised me, you'll have nothing to fear from Somerset or anyone else.'

'I'll stick to it,' I said: 'to the last syllable.'

So I returned to Broughton Staithe, to make ready for Wiltshire and the Headmaster; and Peter, three days later, packed one small bag and went for a soldier of the King. I felt sadder, more oppressed, at this parting than at any time since the morning I had left the school at the end of July. My ally, my old counsellor, was now gone; and I felt as some early Englishman might have felt, as he watched the long line of Romans file down to the ships, bound for tottering Rome and leaving England unmanned to face whatever might come out of the misty North.

The first thing I saw, when I unlocked the front door of the empty house at Broughton, was a sprawling heap of letters. Three were for me; one of them from Christopher.

'*Dear Fielding,*

'*No, I'm afraid you can't come and stay on your way to Wiltshire. It's no longer possible. I can't explain now.*

'*Yours,*
'*Christopher.*'

Unfriendly, not to say mysterious. I read the other two letters: one from my mother, saying that she was having a nice holiday and confirming that she would be back on 15th September, just after I myself returned from Wiltshire; and one from Ivan Blessington.

'*... Was passing through Tonbridge the other day and called on Christopher for tea. He looked ill and very nervous. I know my arrival was unexpected, but it can't have been that. He seemed upset that his tutor, who'd been there for most of August, was now gone; but again, it can't have been just that. There's something very wrong there, I don't pretend to know what, but you if anybody should be able to find out and help ...*'

Blunt, imperceptive Ivan. If he had spotted something wrong, then something wrong there must certainly be. I didn't care for the dictatorial tone, but Ivan surely had a point. Not only was it within my power to help, it was my plain duty. But how could I help when I had just been so brusquely warned off the grass? After some thought, I wrote to Christopher and suggested that we should meet in London for lunch and a film on the sixth of the month; we might even have dinner together, I added, as I should be staying in a hotel overnight and the journey back to Tonbridge was a short one ... or so he himself had once said. Even if this failed to flush Christopher, I thought, it must at least elicit some account of what was doing.

Dining that night in the local hotel, I saw Mr. Tuck and Angela. They seemed morose but oddly in concert. I began to wonder, not for the first time, how and where my father had originally made Tuck's acquaintance. Tuck was indeed the dreadful sort of friend I would have expected my father to have, but I could remember no reference to him, over the years, until the evening early in the holidays when his impending visit had been announced. On the one hand, my father's knowledge of Tuck had been sketchy, for he had not known about Angela until she appeared on the doorstep: on the other hand, he had apparently had sufficient confidence in the man to accept his tea-planting proposition at face value. Driven by renewed curiosity about this odd couple and bored by the prospect of a lonely evening, I suppressed the embarrassment to which memories of my last meeting with Angela inclined me and approached the Tucks, rather warily, while they were drinking coffee in the lounge.

Tuck was affable, Angela off-hand. When I asked if I might drink my coffee with them, no one seemed to care much either way, so I braved their indifference and sat down.

'Sorry to hear about your father,' Tuck said.

'It was certainly sudden ... Tell me, when did you first know him? You'll forgive me saying so, but until a few weeks ago neither mother nor I had ever heard of you.'

'Good point,' said Tuck. He laughed loudly, as though it were also a cracking good joke. 'Let's see now. When did I first meet your old man? Early in the war, it must have been. He was with some kind of Ordnance outfit in Kalyan – big transit camp near Bombay. We just met by accident in the old Taj one night. Got talking over a peg, saw a bit more of one another ... Then he was posted away. That's how it was in those days. You were just getting to know a chap, and he'd be posted away.'

He lit a particularly foul cheroot.

'And you didn't see him again until this summer?' I said.

'That's it.'

'And yet he spoke of you as an old friend, and was prepared to pull my entire career to pieces on your suggestion.'

'Your old man,' said Tuck, 'knew a good thing when he saw it.'

'Perhaps,' I said, with a glance at Angela. 'But India wouldn't have been any good for me.'

'That,' said Tuck, 'remains to be seen.'

'What do you mean?'

'Do you suppose,' Angela said, 'that this hole can produce a drink?'

'No harm in trying,' said Tuck, and rang a bell.

'What do you mean? What remains to be seen?'

An indignant woman in a tweed skirt appeared.

'Who rang the bell?' she snarled.

'I did,' Tuck snarled back, 'because I wants some service. What is there to drink?'

'No drinks in the lounge,' she said with relish. 'There's been a war on, or hadn't you heard?'

'I'd also heard it was over.'

'No drinks in the lounge,' the tweedy woman repeated spitefully, and marched out.

'Jesus Christ,' said Tuck, 'whatever is this bloody country coming to? You may find,' he said to me, 'that India's not so bad after all. At least the servants do what they're told.'

'Would you please tell me,' I said, 'what all this is about? I neither have, nor ever have had, any intention of going to India to plant tea. And now my father's dead—'

'—But old Ange,' said Tuck complacently, 'had quite a few talks with your mother before she went away. Didn't you, Ange?'

'So you've been getting at her? I suppose you want our money for your damned plantation.'

'*Her* money,' Angela emended. 'She's very concerned, you know, about your future. So are we all.'

I rose to go.

'That's very kind of you,' I said, 'but I don't need your interest. Nor does my mother.'

'No?' said Angela. 'She's very lonely . . . and very grateful for advice.'

'She's weak, if that's what you mean. Too weak to get rid of hangers-on.'

'Now then,' said Tuck: 'you're being most impolite to my wife.'

'Your wife,' I shouted at him, 'is a common whore and you're a common crook.'

Not until I was half-way home did it occur to me that Tuck had almost certainly connived at, had probably indeed ordained, Angela's infidelity with my father. That it had failed so ludicrously of its object was mere bad luck. Now they had started on my mother instead. And Somerset? Had that been just a whim of Angela's, or had she decided that Somerset too might somehow come in useful? What had they spoken of together, I wonder, that night after I was dismissed?

'*Dear Fielding* (*Christopher wrote*),–

'*I can't come to London to meet you for lunch or anything*

else. I'm sorry, but please don't write to me again until I've first written to you.

'Christopher.'

I walked along the empty beach. It was a grey, blowy day, not at all like the afternoon, a month before, when I had sat in the warm sand hills with Angela. Autumn was coming to expel the few holiday-makers who had braved the barbed wire and the gun-sites, war-time relics which, though already rusted and crumbling, brought a lingering hint of violence to the lonely dunes. Violence; savagery; threat. Somerset; my mother; Tuck. And Christopher. Christopher too seemed to betoken the same residual sense of menace as the jagged concrete and the rotting ration packs. What did he mean – 'don't write to me again until I've first written to you'? Everything had been made up between us. If he really couldn't have me to stay (parent trouble?) what could be more pleasant and obvious than a day together in London? What the devil was going on? Nervous, Ivan had said, and also upset because the tutor had gone. But it wasn't just that. 'Something very wrong there . . . you if anyone should be able to help.' But Christopher had refused my help. Should I go there despite that, force myself on him, make him tell me about it? Oh hell, I thought, and kicked an empty tin: his letters had been plain enough; if he didn't want me, he didn't.

But for my own sake I must find someone else. I thought of Dixie quivering in the ghost-train; of Angela's finger nails on my bare flesh. Both of them had sent me away unappeased. I must be appeased, I must *know*. Now that it was over with Christopher, I must be admitted, at long last, into the Lotus Country.

Thoughtfully I counted my money. Ten pounds and odd were left of what I had borrowed from Peter. I must pay for my railway ticket, also for meals and so on during the journey; and then there would be the hotel bill for the night in London – but this, as my family was known to the hotel could always be sent to my mother. Yes, I told myself: there would be, there had to be, enough.

Piccadilly, struggling back to the gaieties of peace; coloured lights which I hadn't seen since I was a child in 1939, tawdry, pathetic, out-dated: museum pieces.

Scott's, Oddenio's, Del Monico. The little streets between Piccadilly and Shaftesbury Avenue, the broken glass awnings for the cinema queues. No lack of choice, numerically. But in point of quality, all much the same: young enough, but tired, bitter, all with the angular look of predators, or (worse) with the angles blocked out by slabs of make-up.

Now or never. Choose one. This one; of the angular variety, rather too thin in the leg, a little older than the rest, but with a discernible air of kindness.

'Please could you tell me the—'

'—Like a nice time, dearie? Only just round the corner. A pound.'

'A pound?' (Surely it was more than that, admission to the Lotus Country?)

'Can't do it for less, dear. Professional, pride, you know.'

'All right.'

Over Shaftesbury Avenue and down another little street.

'Rather young, aren't you? I'm not sure I ought to be going with you. Ah well. In here.'

Up three flights of stairs. Little room, big bed, bare dressing-table. Ashtray by the bed full of lip-sticked cigarette ends.

'Pound first, please, dearie. And five bob for the maid.'

'For the maid?'

'Someone's got to clean the place up, haven't they? Ta.'

Skirt up round middle. Rather nice thighs above gartered stockings. Dixie. Angela. Christopher . . .

'Just let me get the doings, dearie . . . No, don't take your shirt off. Just let your trousers down . . . There . . . Oh, my, my . . . *There's* a naughty boy.'

Rubber sheath. The woman sitting on the side of the bed. Reaching forward with her hands.

'Can't we get properly on the bed?'

'Don't want much for a quid, do you?'

Knees suddenly raised and thighs part wide; hands under knee joints; feet hanging limply, high heels near buttocks.

'In you go, dearie.'

'I . . . I . . .'

'Be a man and get on with it. What are you gaping at?'

'I . . . *Where*?'

'For Christ's sake put it in.' Indicative fingers. 'There.'

Easy enough too. Nice, soft.

'Not bad, darling. Now, come on.'

Nice, soft. Crutch straining forward to meet mine.

'Come on, darling. Come . . . Come . . .'

'Oh . . . Oh . . . There . .'

'Finished? That's a good boy. Not bad, was it? We'll just . . . get . . . this . . . off you.'

Into the ashtray with the lip-sticked cigarettes.

And so now I knew. It had been, as my companion put it, not bad. Which was about all one could say. Not bad; just about worth a pound (and five shillings for the maid). Now back to the hotel quickly for a thorough wash.

The Headmaster's holiday retreat was in one of those little valleys which, cosy and tree-girt, are tucked away like oases in the military wilderness round Salisbury. Somerset, I was told when I arrived, was in bed at home with a chill and would not be joining us till the morrow. After an ample supper (the Headmaster's wife, besides being a capable amateur philosopher, qualified as a *bonne femme*) the Headmaster took me to his study.

'There's something,' he said, 'which I don't wish to discuss in front of Elizabeth.'

'Oh?'

'Roland,' said the Headmaster, 'Christopher Roland.'

Oh my God, had Somerset already opened his mouth? Or someone else? Or Christopher, in an agony of repentance (hence his unfriendly letters), written to confess?

'What about Christopher, sir?'

Commendably cool, on the whole.

'It's very odd and very sad. It seems he was reported to the Tonbridge police for hanging about a nearby Army camp and ... and what they call soliciting.'

'Oh my God.' Horror. Relief. Nothing to do with me at any rate.

'I can understand that you're shocked. I wondered, though, whether you could ... cast any light on the matter. After all, the two of you were very close.'

'I don't think so, sir.' Play this one with care. 'It explains, of course, some rather curious letters I've had lately.' I told him what Ivan Blessington had written, and about the two curt notes of refusal I'd had from Christopher himself. 'I was puzzled and hurt. But if this had already happened ...'

'It happened about ten days ago. Because of his youth and the good standing of his family the police have agreed to take no action, provided his parents keep him in strict supervision and arrange for him to have psychiatric treatment. He cannot, it goes without saying, come back to us next quarter.'

'I suppose not.'

'No question of it. But my duty lies, not only in taking preventive measures for the future, but in investigating any damage that may already have been done. It occurred to me ... that you might help me there.'

'But look, sir. You say he was suspected of soliciting. It can't have been more, or else the police would have acted – family or no family. So on the strength of mere suspicion, Christopher is to be confined at home, messed about by psychiatrists, and forbidden to return to school – disgraced. Can't you see the terrible injury this must do to him?'

'I have six hundred boys to consider. I can't risk contamination.'

'Where there are six hundred boys, there's bound to be contamination already. You know that, sir.'

'I can't, knowingly, add to it.'

'But what do you know? What did Christopher *do*?'

'He hung about ... with his bicycle ... near the entrance to this camp. When the men came out, he used to smile at them, try to enter into conversation.'

'There could be a dozen explanations. He could have had friends serving there, friends from school perhaps.'

'Among the private men?'

'Everyone starts in the ranks these days.'

'In special training units. Not in a serving battalion. Besides, Roland was given every chance to provide just such an explanation. His only response was to sulk. They could think what they pleased, he said.'

'Dignified.'

'Petulant. I can understand, Fielding, that you are concerned for your friend. I am too; but I must put my public duty first. And I must therefore ask you directly, to tell me anything you may know about Roland's previous behaviour, so that any damage he has done may be undone.'

'By removing more people on mere suspicion?'

'That was not worthy,' the Headmaster said wearily.

'I know, sir, and I'm sorry. But Christopher is a very dear friend and this has been a shock. Can nothing be done?'

'The psychiatrists will do all they can.'

'The shame of it will destroy him.'

'I gather lots of people these days submit quite willingly to psychiatric treatment.'

'Not people of Christopher's kind.'

'But is there anything so special about him?' said the Headmaster gently. 'He always seemed an ordinary boy to me. Pleasant but ordinary.'

'He was very proud in his own way, very . . . fastidious. This kept him away from the others and made him lonely. He wanted love.'

Careful; don't go too far.

'For someone who was fastidious he seems to have gone a very peculiar way about getting it. So I shall ask you once again: how was this wretched boy corrupted? And has he corrupted anyone else in my charge? As we both know, Fielding, you were intimate with him.'

'Yes, I was sir. And as far as I am concerned, he was innocent. His innocence . . . that's what I prized most of all.'

'But now . . . after what's happened?'

'I can't begin to understand or explain it, sir, and there's nothing more I can say.'

And that must be enough for him, I thought. After all, what I *had* told him was true enough. I certainly couldn't understand what had happened; and from where I stood, Christopher was neither corrupter nor corrupted. The terms were meaningless.

'I think,' said the Headmaster heavily, 'that Elizabeth will have coffee ready now.'

Thinking it all over in bed that night, I suddenly realized that I was glad. Despite my protest to the Headmaster, despite my genuine indignation at what had been done, I could not really have wished it undone and Christopher restored. Where Christopher now was he was truly lovable, because he could be contemplated as the image of vanished beauty: if brought back again, he would only become what he had threatened to become in July, a common pastime, to be casually lusted for, and later a common nuisance. Christopher's downfall, then, was both convenient and poetically apt. Best get such people out of the way before they lost their charm and grew ugly, boring, irrelevant. These things are so . . .

Somerset arrived the next afternoon, looking even more pasty-faced than usual as a result of his chill. After tea, however, he felt strong enough to walk with the Headmaster and myself to inspect a nearby church, the tower of which, as the Headmaster explained, had once been used for an interesting local variant of the games of Fives.

'A custom more common further west,' Somerset commented: 'in my part of the country we once had as many kinds of Fives as there were convenient church towers.'

'When was it given up?' I asked.

'Early nineteenth century,' Somerset said. 'Ball games against church walls did not suit middle-class notions of propriety.'

'It went deeper than that,' said the Headmaster. 'Even early in the nineteenth century, it was already plain that Christianity was to be dangerously attacked. Not just by irreverant ironists, as in the previous century, but by dedicated men of science and intellect and high moral principle. The threat was so serious that the church could no longer afford to be associated with everyday pleasures: the parson must cease to hunt, the layman from playing his games in the churchyard. Frivolities like these could be tolerated only in an age of faith, when the church was so firmly entrenched that even ribaldry in its own ministers could do it no damage.' He gestured amiably. 'In an age of faith, immorality itself could be seen as joyous. But once let there be doubt, and severity, even in the most trivial things, must follow. It is the first line of defence.'

'So evangelism, like the Inquisition, was a reaction against rational inquiry?' I said smugly.

'There is something in that, though a stricter study of dates would discourage so glib a summary ... There is a box-tomb which I should like you both to see. Twelfth century.'

The Headmaster led us over a small mound, through a clump of yew trees, and down into a little hollow. The tomb was of a curious faded red; it had sunk unevenly, so that on the side nearest us, which was badly cracked, it was about a foot high while on the far side the tilting slab that topped it almost dug into the grass.

'A tomb of importance,' Somerset remarked. 'One would have expected its occupant to be buried inside the church.'

'Ah,' said the Headmaster with relish. 'This tomb belongs to a renegade. Geoffery of Underavon he was called, and he was given this manor as a reward for knight service in one of the minor crusades. But Sir Geoffery had come home through Provence where he acquired the habits and graces of the Troubadors. The arts he had learned proved only too effective in the unsophisticated part of the world, where bored wives and daughters were very grateful for a little pagan zest. His songs and addresses made him notorious and then infamous:

until finally, one summer afternoon when he was riding by the river, without armour and on his way to an assignation, he was set upon and murdered by six vizored knights, none of whom displayed either pennant, crest or coat of arms. Or so said the one attendant esquire, who had made off at the first sign of trouble. The deed was approved by the local clergy, who were keen to curry favour with injured husbands, and it was decreed that the Lord Geoffery should not be buried inside any church of the diocese. However, he could not well be denied burial in holy ground, and hence this tomb, out here in a lonely corner of the churchyard.'

'Lord Geoffery of Underavon,' I murmured, touched by the tale, 'martyr for poetry. Do any of his songs survive?'

' "Ver purpuratum exiit",' said the Headmaster in his soft, deep voice.

' "Ornatus sous induit,
Aspergit terram floribus,
Ligna silvarum frondibus".'

'Sir?' objected Somerset politely.

'I know, I know. Sir Geoffery would have sung in French or Provençal. In any case, that verse comes from the Cambridge Collection and so was probably written by a clerk. But it is my fancy to imagine Geoffery singing something out of the kind. Since,' said the Headmaster sadly, turning to me, 'the answer to your questions is "no". None of his songs has come down.'

A flowered meadow by the river. The chirrup of the grasshopper, to remind him of fiercer afternoons when he had pursued the same errand in the Midi. The long robe, the lute, the two prancing heraldic dogs, the esquire riding a few paces behind. 'Will you not sing, my lord?' 'For you, boy? Why not? A song of the season.' The tone of the lute, plangent even in celebration. 'Ver purpuratum exiit ...' The coloured spring is forth ... Then six men, six black helmets, and down goes poet and lover, vulnerable in the soft robe which he wears for his tender mission. No, his songs have not come down to us. He could not even be buried in his own church. He has lain in the shadow of the yew trees for eight hundred years.

'Martyrdom,' observed Somerset, cutting into my reverie, 'is a powerful expression. Not to be used of those who dally with the arts and their neighbours' women.'

We all three circled the tomb warily.

'Still,' said the Headmaster, 'at this distance in time Sir Geoffery makes an attractive figure.'

'A joyous sinner in an age of faith, sir?' I suggested.

'If you like. He fits so beautifully, somehow, into his background.'

'So beautifully that he was murdered.'

'Then let us say,' said Somerset, 'that his story fits beautifully into his background. He was deservedly punished for importing heresy and vice.'

The Headmaster looked vaguely troubled at this. The sentiment did not match with his notion of Sir Geoffery as a Chaucerian sinner; it implied something altogether more sinister; it was, he might have said, unworthy.

'I think we can afford to be more tolerant than that,' he remarked, bending down creakily to examine a crack in the side of the tomb.

'*We* can, sir,' said Somerset, 'because it all happened so long ago. But could they?'

'Some songs and a few love affairs,' I said; 'not very injurious.'

'Scandal,' said Somerset, 'and disorder. Injurious enough.'

'So we are to equate poetry with disorder?'

'As did Plato.'

'Who has ever since been discredited for doing so.'

Our voices rose acrimoniously. The Headmaster smiled and put a finger to his lips.

'Hush,' he said, 'you will disturb the Lord Geoffery. His sins and his songs are both forgotten now. We must let him lie in peace.'

When we got back for supper, the Headmaster's wife handed him a slip of paper. He went into his study to telephone and reappeared, very grave, fifteen minutes later. He nodded apologetically to his wife.

'Supper in twenty minutes, my dear. Please come in here, Somerset, Fielding . . . It's Roland,' he said, when he had closed the door. 'The poor boy's killed himself.'

'Oh, Christopher,' I said stupidly.

'Why should he do that?' said Somerset, looking ingenuously from me to the Headmaster.

The latter told him briefly of the police complaint and Christopher's confinement.

'It seems,' he added, 'that he found a pistol of his father's, also some ammunition. He put the pistol in his mouth—'

'—I told you,' I interrupted angrily, 'I told you it could only do harm.'

'It had to be done,' said the Headmaster sternly. 'And what I must now say to both of you is this. So far, nothing in this wretched affair directly concerns the school: the whole sequence of disaster has begun and ended in the boy's own home and during the holidays. But questions may be asked, and so I must ask you: do either of you know of anything in the boy's activities at school which might have bearing on all this? Do you?' he said, turning to Somerset.

'I didn't know him very well, sir,' said Somerset, with a hint of smugness. 'Perhaps Fielding can be more helpful.'

'I've already told you what I know, sir. As far as I'm concerned, he was lonely and innocent. Which I suppose could explain what has happened,' I said, gulping back the tears which now threatened.

Briefly and viciously, Somerset smiled at me.

'A martyr to innocence?' he said.

The Headmaster looked at Somerset with a curious cross between disapproval and admiration.

'It seems there is no more to be said,' he remarked flatly; 'we must not keep my wife waiting.'

The tears which had nearly overcome me had not been for Christopher. They had been tears of vexation that there should be such unseemliness in things, that a convenient pattern should have been so crudely torn. Christopher confined had been someone who could give no more trouble and was at the same time a source of pleasantly nostalgic memories. Christopher confined had been like a well loved book, to be taken down and replaced at will. But Christopher dead was something that had to be explained, by myself to myself and, perhaps, to others as well: in either case an abiding source of concern and nuisance.

'You see now,' said Somerset later that night in the bedroom we shared, 'why I am so averse to disorder. This is the kind of thing which results.'

'You're not blaming me?'

'No,' said Somerset equably, 'I'm not. Even if I did, what's past is past, and my concern, as I've already told you, is with the future. But perhaps all this will serve to remind you that I meant what I said the other day: I will have nothing like this happen while I'm in charge, and in charge I still intend to be.'

'You mean, you'd still make use of Christopher against me?'

'If you stand in my way.'

'Even now . . . after *this*?'

'Let's not be sentimental. What you think of as Christopher Roland will soon be a mass of maggots. What survives him has gone to account elsewhere. Neither the spirit nor what's left of the flesh will worry about any use which I might make of their past.'

'I thought perhaps *you* might worry.'

'No more than you would,' said Somerset cheerfully, and turned out the light.

The inquest, so the Headmaster was able to tell us three days later, established that Christopher had taken his life while the balance of his mind was disturbed. There would be a funeral service in Tonbridge in two days' time, after which the body would be cremated. Gently but very firmly the Headmaster insisted that I myself, as Christopher's closest friend, should attend these ceremonies with him. This would mark the end of our little house party. Somerset would return home when the Headmaster and I left (by car) for Tonbridge; the Headmaster's wife would close the house and proceed to the school, where the Headmaster would join her after the funeral; and I would return from Tonbridge *via* London to Broughton Staithe.

'It's a long way to Tonbridge, sir,' I said hopelessly. 'Are you sure you'll have enough petrol?'

'I get an extra allowance. For special duties.'

'I see, sir . . . I don't at all want to come with you. I've already been to one funeral these holidays.'

'It will please the boy's parents.'

'How? I mean nothing to them – or they to me.'

'Then let us say,' said the Headmaster, 'that I myself shall value your support.'

There could be no answer to that.

'But that's not until the day after tomorrow,' the Headmaster said, his eyes brightening. 'Tomorrow is the last day of your visit, the last of my own holiday. In the midst of death we are in life. Tomorrow, yes, tomorrow we must do something memorable. We will walk to Salisbury Cathedral, like pilgrims, over the plain.'

'Somerset?' I whispered in the dark.

'Well?'

'What was . . . it . . . like with Angela?'

'Very pleasing,' said Somerset. 'Angela,' he added conceitedly, 'thought so too. I rather hope we'll get together again before she leaves for India.'

'You've arranged to meet?'

'We correspond.'

So Angela thought Somerset was worth keeping in touch with.

'But what,' I resumed, 'was it actually like? I mean, I always thought it was something quite incredibly different. But in fact . . .'

'What do you know about it?' said Somerset crossly.

'As much as you.' Piqued by Somerset's tone, I told him of my adventure in Piccadilly. Perhaps, I thought, I was being rash, but I wanted to tell somebody, and Somerset could never use this against me any more than I could use Angela against him. We were on neutral territory, territory so remote, as Peter had put it, that nothing which happened there could count.

'But buying women,' said Somerset, 'is not at all the same thing. Besides, there's a nasty shock in store for those who consort with street-walkers.'

'Oh?'

'The Lazar of Venice,' Somerset said with relish, 'the French Worm. Otherwise known as the Raw-boned Knight of Germany, the Neapolitan Bone-Ache, the Spanish Sweat, or, *tout court,* the Pox. It covers you with sores, removes your nose, rots your brain—'

'—For God's sake. We used one of those rubber things. And I washed jolly carefully.'

'Some kinds of dirt cannot be washed off,' said Somerset sententiously.

'Come to that, Angela's not exactly chaste.'

'At least she's amateur.'

'I wouldn't be so sure,' I muttered spitefully.

'What's that?'

'Nothing. Get back to the point, Somerset. Did you find it . . . well . . . the revelation one's been led to expect?'

'Candidly,' said Somerset, 'no. But then I never expected a revelation. Did you?'

'I think I expected something rather remarkable.'

'Just like all sensualists. You expect far too much of bodily

132

amusements, and then complain when you're disappointed. Ungrateful lot.'

'I'm not ungrateful.'

'You will be,' said Somerset happily, 'if you get the Spanish Sweat.'

'I'm merely surprised that everyone makes such a thing about it.'

'There you have a point. It needs putting in its proper place. As for me,' said Somerset complacently, 'if Angela makes herself available again, I shall be well content. If not, then at least I shall be spared the trouble of making my confession.'

We walked towards Salisbury by way of the Race Course. As we passed the empty stands, I told the Headmaster about Peter and Tiberius.

'We shall miss Peter Morrison,' the Headmaster said, his eyes lowered towards the cathedral spire beneath us. 'I must write to tell him about Christopher Roland. I'm afraid it will come at a bad time, just when he's starting his Army life, but I feel he should know.'

There was a long silence as we started to descend over the downs. The cathedral spire, always visible except when we walked among trees, pointed straight up out of the close like the finger of an Archangel. I accuse. At any moment, surely, the huge finger would point or beckon. 'This was my beloved son, and because of you he is now a mass of maggots. State your defence.' Please, he was so attractive. That firm body, those golden legs with the silver down ... 'What's that got to do with it? God delighteth not in any man's legs, nor in any woman's for that matter. But we'll say no more of that for the moment. Why did you desert him when he needed your love?'

'There is something,' the Headmaster broke in on this dismal fantasy, 'which I have been meaning to say to you both. A trifle awkward. The question of which of you I shall choose as Head of the School next summer.'

Somerset went poker-faced. The grey sky started to drizzle.

'I think, sir,' I said, 'that Somerset – how shall I put it? – has more appetite for the job.'

'With due respect and without prejudice, that does not necessarily make him the better man for it.'

'I shall be very busy,' I added, 'with cricket and so on.'

None of this was said to placate Somerset or from fear of his devices. Having what I already had, I did not really want more, and I was glad to make this plain. There would be quite enough, by way of business and pleasure, to occupy me next summer.

'By the beginning of May,' said the Headmaster, 'you will have been to Cambridge and either succeeded or failed in improving on your award. I cannot see that you will be as busy as all that.'

'Then let us say that I am not particularly keen.'

'That,' said the Headmaster, 'does not unfit you for the task. It might even mean that it would be very good for you. What do you think, Somerset?'

'I think, sir, that Fielding is not much concerned with whether a thing is good for him or not.'

'And does that unfit him for the position we are discussing?'

'No. I think Fielding would be a good Head of the School, if rather off-hand. I also think that I should be a better one, because I should be more . . . more dedicated.'

'To the responsibilities? Or merely to the concept?'

'To both, sir.'

'Well,' said the Headmaster, 'we shall have to see. Meanwhile, I have only raised the point in order to receive your assurances that this will not make for bad blood between you.'

'Not for my part,' I said.

'I'm sure,' said Somerset, 'that I shall have no cause to show ill will.'

As we walked on in the silence imposed by increasingly heavy rain, the huge finger once more seemed about to point at me and the voice of the Archangel spoke again, the more resentfully, I thought, for having been interrupted.

'Why did you desert Christopher when he needed your love?' I didn't desert him: I was going to him, and then he told me not to. 'But you weren't going in love; you were going there to use him.' He wanted to be used. 'He wanted to be loved.' *Whatever* he wanted he forbade me to go to him. That wasn't my fault.

'Perhaps not; but you'd already withdrawn your love and made up your mind to exploit him; so you'd already betrayed him.' *He* didn't know. 'Didn't he? And what about the relief you felt when you heard he wasn't coming back to school – because that meant he couldn't be a nuisance later on? How's that for betrayal?' He certainly didn't know about *that*. 'Betrayal nevertheless. And another thing. When you couldn't have Christopher, you went to a whore instead. How do you answer that?' She'd starve if somebody didn't. 'No good, Fielding.' The voice had now turned into Peter Morrison's. 'I've told you before. It is foolish and dangerous (leave alone the moral side of it) to use people, to take advantage. Look where it's got you. Your mother, whom you've used all these years (don't try to deny it) as a shield against your father – your mother is getting ready to hand you over to Tuck. And what is more' – the voice was blatantly mocking now, no longer Peter's but Somerset's – 'that strumpet you picked up may well have passed on the French Worm or the Neapolitan Bone-Ache or (*tout court*) the Pox.'

Tired, wet, soiled, crumpled, bored, disgusted and afraid, I entered with my companions into the clammy and obscene chill of the cathedral. The organ piped a malignant *miserere* and the skeletal banners of vanished regiments hung in menace over my head. A gargoyle verger snickered into the ear of a raven priest. In some shadow, surely, the Furies lurked; at any moment they would proclaim my guilt, infest me with the sores of the Lazar, hurl my putrefying flesh into the pit.

Regardless of Somerset and the Headmaster. I hurried away up a side-aisle, turned right, left behind a wooden screen, walked, with a cold sweat all over me, into a deep shadow. There was something which looked like a stone altar looming in front of me (surely stone altars were forbidden?); an outcast seeking sanctuary, I lurched forward and snatched at the stone block with my hands. Looking down, I saw the figure of a knight and shivered all through my body.

'Go on,' said a low, spiteful voice just behind me: 'have a good look while you're at it.'

'There's nothing for me here,' I said without turning.

'On the contrary. You've come this far and now you must face it.'

Still shivering, I looked closer. The tips of the prayerful stone fingers pointed up to a mailed chin, above which was a full mouth, turned slightly downwards, a soft nose, and mild, beseeching eyes. Christopher. From behind me the voice laughed, amused and pitiless. I turned.

'You shouldn't have run off like that,' Somerset said. 'It was very rude.'

And now another church. Smaller than Salisbury Cathedral but having the same traditional appurtenances. The banners, the tablets in the wall. And the coffin where the transept crossed the aisle.

'When faced with untimely death,' the unctuous young clergyman declaimed, 'we do well to reflect on the role played by the unexpected in this realm below. An established way of life, worldly goods, intellectual systems and disciplines – none can stand against the blind hand of fate.'

The Headmaster sat beside me, boot-faced.

'But,' said the greasy ministrant, 'even when the careful structures of our lives are shattered, when our hopes and ambitions are laid low, there is one supreme discipline to which we may always turn for comfort and instruction. If, that is, we will only make ourselves humble enough to be received into it. I refer you to the knowledge and love of Jesus Christ.'

I winced and let out a long, hissing breath. The Headmaster turned his head slightly and looked at me with mild curiosity, as if he would be vaguely interested (no more) to see what I did next.

'I deem it no more than my duty,' said the preacher, 'to say that the boy whose death we mourn today had strayed outside the knowledge and love of Christ. His plans and pleasures had ends which were inspired by influences hostile to true religion. He was young, suggestible; so we must hope and pray that he will be forgiven where he goes. But had others, whose duty it was, encouraged him to be stronger in the Way, then perhaps he would have lived to walk down it.'

I rose. 'I'll wait for you outside,' I whispered to the Headmaster, who nodded, agreeably, companionably, as if indeed he himself were only remaining in his seat because he wanted a few minutes more of rest.

'. . .Contagion and blasphemy,' the words followed me down the aisle, 'to which this unfortunate boy must have been exposed . . .'

God, I thought as I reached the open air, that bloody parson's having a go at the head man. I sat down on a convenient tombstone. 'Contagion and blasphemy.' Contagion. What was that sentence of Huxley's I had read earlier in the summer? 'Somewhere in my veins creep the maggots of the pox.' No. *No.* Christ, that poor little coffin. Christopher inside it, the smooth thighs, the full, pretty lips. Cold now, unkissable. Cold and rotting: maggots – though kinder in their way than the maggots of the Pox.

A bell started to toll. On something which resembled an

hors d'oeuvres trolley the coffin was wheeled out of the church porch and down the path towards the waiting hearse, the driver of which, having reluctantly stubbed out a cigarette and concealed the butt somewhere in his hat, busied himself with the door at the back. Christopher, oh Christopher. No knight's effigy for you. Only the consuming fire. Christopher, forgive me, for I knew not what I did. The Headmaster stood over me.

'We must take our seats in the car.'

Confess. Tell him everything. Then there will be peace.

'Sir. There is something I must tell you. Several things.'

'In the car.'

We moved slowly down the path, among the not inconsiderable crowd that had gathered for Christopher's obsequies, and watched the coffin as it was handled into the hearse. I saw a tubby little man with a red, resentful face help a gaunt yet complacent looking woman into the first car behind the hearse. Christopher's parents; the thought of meeting them later made me feel, for a moment, physically sick. '... He often spoke of you. Tell me, Mr. Gray, as his best friend, what do *you* think could have made him do such a terrible thing?' 'Having two such horrible parents.' 'Interesting, Mr. Gray, but we happen to know a thing or two—'

'—Come along, Fielding.'

The Headmaster took my elbow and urged me gently towards his car, a black 1935 Saloon of a make now defunct and eminently suitable for a drive to a crematorium.

'Funerals,' the Headmaster was saying, 'are really rather lowering, as you may have found. Particularly if there is a disagreeable sermon. You wanted to tell me something?'

'Yes, sir. I—'

'—Please, gentlemen?' said a whining voice.

We turned to see a ratty little man who was in battle-dress, which was fastened right up to the chin, and huge, wallowing Army boots.

'Please, I don't know anyone, but you looked kind, and I wondered ...'

'You want to come with us?'

'Please.'

'Of course,' the Headmaster said.

Two heavy drops of rain landed on my neck. The Headmaster opened the back near-side door, and the soldier clambered noisily in. I made for the co-driver's door, then, drawn by some lurking sense of kinship, climbed into the back to sit by the soldier instead. The Headmaster made no comment, but heaved himself into the driving seat and settled there with the gravity of a Royal coachman. It was now raining with almost tropical violence; after some difficulty with the windscreen-wiper, the Headmaster set the car cautiously into motion and then, realizing that he was already well behind the rest of the procession and did not know the way, put his foot down harder than he meant to and rode over a yellow light.

'You knew . . . Mr. Roland?' I said to the soldier.

'I didn't know him. Only I seen him.'

During the pause which followed, I watched the struggle in the man's face between the natural reluctance of the inarticulate to embark on a tricky explanation and the guilty fear that unless he did so he might appear as an interloper.

'I'm not just snooping though,' the man said with an effort.

Touched by this delicacy of feeling, I sought about for ways of helping the explanation to birth, only to realize that this was the first time in my life (since the nursery) that a conversation between myself and a member of the lower classes had been other than merely administrative, and that I had no idea whatever how to proceed with it. The Headmaster, who appeared to share this feeling, maintained a prudent silence and kept his eyes squarely into the rain.

'It was like this,' the soldier said, gallant and tortured. 'I was in detention, see, serving a week in the guardhouse. But being a handy kind of man, they didn't put me on rough work but had me paint the place up and fit new lights and things. Get it?'

The Headmaster and I got it.

'So every day,' said the soldier with growing confidence, 'I was working round this guardhouse, inside and out, and every day there was this young fellow, this Christopher Roland, used to come on his bike and stop near the gate, like he was waiting for somebody. A lonely little chap like me, see, because although I was getting it light it's no fun spending twenty-four hours of every day round a guardhouse, with only a wooden bed waiting for you in a damp cell.'

'What makes you say he was lonely?'

'The way he kept looking to see if anyone was coming he could talk to.'

'Did he talk to you?'

'No,' said the soldier bitterly. 'He couldn't come in through the gate and I couldn't go out of it. He used to smile at me, though. Every now and then, I'd look up and see him smiling. Specially when someone had been shouting at me, bawling me out to be quick with this or that, then I'd look up and I'd find him smiling, as if to say he was sorry and he hoped I'd come through.'

We were out of Tonbridge and into the country. The rain, no longer violent, had settled into a steady vertical drench.

'Then one day just before my sentence was up,' the soldier went on, 'he didn't come. I was that upset I thought I should have cried. Afterwards I heard why, about the police and all . . . It wasn't till then I even knew his name. And now this . . .'

The soldier removed the khaki beret from his head and started wringing it in thin, dirty fingers.

'So you see, you must see,' he said urgently, 'what he meant to me and why I'm grieving for him, no matter what he done. Because whatever he came there for, he was good to me. It was him that kept me going, and I can't forget him. Oh, he used to talk to anyone that went in or out – anyone who'd stop and listen—, and there was no doubt what he was after, or so I heard later from the lads. But he never forgot me. Whenever he came or went, he always had a smile for hallo or good-bye. See what I'm trying to tell you, gentlemen?'

Scruffy, sharp yet weak in the face, twitching, undersized, perhaps thirty-five years old, the soldier, I thought, looked like just the sort of man one read about in the Sunday Press. A lonely, repellent little man, who would live unloved and die unlamented, would probably die, indeed, without its even being known, until days or weeks later an employer or chance creditor, scenting something odd, suggested to the police that they might call . . . What could Christopher have seen here? Surely to God there were more attractive people in the world who would have been grateful for his smiles?

'So you came to the funeral,' was all I could think of to say.

'Yes. I'm R.C. myself, so I don't hold with this burning but that's none of my affair. I thought . . . a prayer for him . . . I didn't get dispensation to come to the church, neither, but perhaps God . . .'

'God will hear your prayer,' said the Headmaster, speaking for the first time since the procession started.

'You think so?' said the soldier doubtfully.

The engine died and the car stopped.

'Damn,' said the Headmaster vigorously.

'Petrol-pump,' said the soldier. Before anyone could say anything, he was out of the car and had the bonnet up. He administered a brisk tap.

'Press the starter,' he called, 'and we're away.'

As indeed we were.

'But,' said the soldier knowingly, 'once it starts that trick, it goes on. More and more. Till at last you're getting out every fifty yards.'

'And so?'

'New petrol-pump. Ten minutes to fit. Any proper garage.'

The car stopped. Again the soldier went out into the pouring rain and set it going.

'You see?' he said as he got in, smelling deplorably.

After the car had stopped four more times, we came to a small but apparently reputable garage. A sneering, balding man fitted a new petrol-pump.

'That'll be six quid.'

'Robbery,' the soldier said.

'Yes, er, surely—' the Headmaster began.

'Ain't you forgetting something?' the sneering man said, thrusting his face at us. 'Ain't you forgetting that there's been a war, and parts like that are hard to come by, and if you don't want it you needn't have it, because it'll only take me two ticks to whip it out again?'

'But we must have it.'

'Then it'll cost you six quid.'

'A cheque?'

'What do you take me for?'

'But I haven't got that much in cash.'

'Then you haven't got a petrol-pump either.'

The garage man made towards the engine, flourishing a spanner. The soldier slammed the bonnet down and said,

'This gentleman will give you three nicker, which is more than a fair price for the pump and your trouble. If you try to detain us, that is illegal, and we shall be within our rights using force to get away. Get into the car, gentlemen, and start her up.'

The Headmaster and I gaped, then did as we were told. The soldier looked perky and serene. The garage-man scowled and held out his hand.

'Four quid,' he said.

'Three. You give him three, sir.'

The Headmaster gave him three, and once more we were on

the road. By this time we had ceased to be strangers, had become companions in adversity and almost confederates in crime. For a number of reasons which I was not anxious to examine, I was finding this complicity irksome.

'I'm very grateful,' the Headmaster said. 'Where did you learn that bit about illegal detention?'

'I'm quite a one for finding out things like that. It helps you get your rights.'

What an abominable little man, I thought. Aloud I said:

'I suppose we're too late. For the cremation.'

At least I should not have to talk to Christopher's parents.

'I suppose so,' the Headmaster said. 'I really can't say I'm sorry.'

With much heavy breathing he managed to turn the car round.

'I was looking forward,' the soldier said, 'to seeing how it worked. The coffin being shot into the furnace and all ... Ah, well. Perhaps you'd drop me at the camp, sir? It's not far.'

When we reached the gate of the camp the soldier said:

'That's where he used to stand with his bike. Just over there by the tree. Poor little sod.'

He waved cheerfully and strutted through the gate, his huge boots spread wide in a waddle. Two regimental policemen descended on him and ushered him into the guardroom.

'He was absent without leave,' said the Headmaster bleakly. 'He couldn't get leave to come to the funeral, I suppose, so he came without. And we didn't even ask his name.'

'Now he'll be put in detention again. And every time he comes out of that guardroom,' I said with loathing, 'he'll look at that tree and think about Christopher's smile.'

The Headmaster, who seemed saddened by this remark, drove slowly but jerkily away.

'What a foul little man,' I said at length. 'How could Christopher—'

'—What were you going to tell me? Before he asked for a lift.'

Silence.

'Well, Fielding?'

'I was going to say,' I said feebly, 'how sorry I was that that clergyman tried to get at you in his sermon.'

'No, you weren't. You were going to make a confession of some kind. You were going to ask for help. And do you know,' said the Headmaster gravely, 'I was rather pleased. So pleased, that however bad it had been I would have seen you through. But now that poor little soldier has annoyed you so much that you are determined to prove that you don't need help. That you are not like him, prepared to give and receive. For a brief moment, when you were close driven, you thought you would look for comfort. But then you realized that this meant humbling yourself, and your vanity took over.'

'I merely want to be my own man.'

'All your own man. *Never* to give or receive. So be it then. I only wish it could have been otherwise.'

'It was nothing that really matters, sir. I was hysterical. That service . . . the coffin . . .'

'You don't have to protest,' said the Headmaster. 'I'm not accusing you. I'm simply sorry you did not see fit to honour me with your confidence. That way we might have become friends instead of politely disposed strangers. Now it is too late.'

'So you've been with a trollop,' said the Senior Usher. 'Why hunt me down during my hard earned leisure to tell me that?'

We were sitting in the Senior Usher's London club, where, unable to go abroad and heedless of falling bombs, he had for five years spent most of his holidays. My visit there was the result of a snap decision. When I had arrived in London the previous evening, depressed by the day's events and so more than ever inclined to remember Somerset's disquieting exegesis on the Pox, I had made my way to the Kensington Public Library and sought out the medical section. Here I had been still further depressed and thoroughly confused: as far as I could make out, venereal disease might announce itself by exhibiting almost any kind of symptom or even none. Advice must clearly be had. Peter was not available to give it; any reputable doctor, if consulted, would want to be put in touch with school or parents; to wait my turn in one of those East End hospitals advertised in lavatories was unthinkable. I needed a tolerant and knowledgeable man of the world who would not betray me, and for such, remembering conversations past, I took the Senior Usher.

'Why,' he said, 'bring this dreary item to me?'

'I want your help, sir.'

'You've gone and got clap?'

'Not yet. But supposing I did?'

'It'll hurt like hell.'

'And the other thing . . . syphilis?'

'You'd show up all the colours of the spectrum.'

The Senior Usher emptied the glass at his side and signed to a septuagenarian steward for another.

'Let's get this settled for good and all,' he said, 'and have no more worry about it. It's very easy if you only keep your head and put the thing in its proper place. You used a French Letter? Right?'

'Right.'

'Then the odds, the overwhelming odds, are that you won't have any trouble at all. But if your old man starts hurting badly or begins to look like a Turner sunset, there's something the matter and you must go to a doctor and get yourself cured. They've discovered a new drug, I'm told, which is both painless and swift. Unlike the old days.'

He gave a perceptible shudder.

'But what doctor, sir? I don't want any trouble at home . . . or with the Headmaster.'

'Quite right. It would only upset him to no purpose. So *if* anything goes wrong, I'll fix you up with a chap I know who gets his living by not asking awkward questions.'

'Thank you very much, sir.'

'Just remember two things,' said the Senior Usher. 'First, you're not old enough to have whores until you're old enough to cope with the consequences yourself instead of pestering respectable old gentlemen in their clubs. And secondly, don't come running to me the minute you get an itch or a sweat spot. If you've really got it, you'll really know it.'

'But the books say—'

'—Yes, I know they do. So just to be on the safe side, we'll arrange a blood test for you in about six weeks' time. I'll have my chum come down to the school and invite you to meet him in my Lodging.'

'Oh, thank you, sir. It's a great relief.'

'My privilege. Now go away and leave me in peace until next quarter, which God knows will be soon enough.'

So that, I thought, as I caught the train from Liverpool Street, was one matter cleared up. The Senior Usher was quite right: all that was necessary was to keep one's head and look facts in the face, to use one's powers as a rational man. One must not panic, and one must not be tempted (as I had been at Christopher's funeral) to surrender when things got rough. Instead, one must think. Whatever the difficulties which might now ensue, difficulties made by Somerset or the Headmaster, by my mother or the Tucks, all could surely be solved by the power of rational thought.

This morning, just as I was sitting down to carry on with this memoir, I was handed a special signal from the C.O. in Malta. It seems that an all-party delegation of politicians is to tour this area and visit, among other places, this island, and that Mr. Peter Morrison, M.P. for Whereham, is to make one of the delegation. It will be interesting to see him again – and also opportune, as I have spent so much of these last weeks thinking and writing about him as a boy. This exercise has suggested certain questions, which were never asked at the time and might now be usefully answered.

When I reached home, I found a letter from Christopher which was dated the day before his death.

'*Dear Fielding,*

'*I want you to know how things are with me. Because they're not at all the same as you probably think. By now you'll have heard from the head man what's happened and how I shan't be coming back next quarter. But it isn't that which is making me unhappy, or not so much. And it's not the psychiatrist either, revolting though he is, putting his hand on my knee, asking me to tell him every last detail about "the things you did at school". (Don't worry, Fielding; he's not interested in names.) No, it's none of that, miserable as it all is.*

'*It's this, Fielding. I was afraid, at the end of last quarter, that you'd gone away from me. But then you wrote and seemed so anxious to come here and I thought, it's all right, he still loves me, those last few days at school were just a bad patch. That was until I started talking to the tutor who came. After a time we got to be friendly; and because I didn't have anyone else to tell I told him about you. He encouraged me to talk about these things, you see, I think he was fond of me and wanted to get closer, and this was the only way I'd let him get close. Anyway, I told him. And he said you weren't coming because you loved me, that was obvious from what had happened, you were coming because you were bored at home and wanted me in bed. At first I wouldn't believe him, but he kept on and on, he said he only wanted me to know the truth. And at last I thought I'd ask you straight out when you came and settle it like that.*

'*Then the tutor left, earlier than he'd been meant to, I don't think my parents liked him. It was then I started going up to that Army camp. At first I just passed it by accident, then I saw the men going in and out, and I thought ... well, you know what I thought. I was so lonely, Fielding, even the tutor was gone, and I wanted someone, anyone, to be with and hold them. In the end I didn't find anyone, they were quite kind, most of them, and just went away without understanding – though I suppose one of them must have reported me because of what the police said later.*

'*But apart from all that, something horrible happened.*

*There was a soldier under punishment, a horrid little man
with a thin face and hands like claws, who used to be doing
jobs round the gate. He used to look at me with long implor-
ing looks, and I was sorry for him, in a way, so I did my best
to smile back. And then one day I realized something. I
realized that even if my tutor was wrong and you did still
love me, very soon you wouldn't and I'd be to you what that
soldier was to me, someone loathsome but always there,
someone you had to smile at to keep him happy while all the
time you just wanted him to go away and never come back.
That's what you'd feel about me, perhaps you'd felt it already,
because sometimes I'd seen in your smiles the same strain, the
same hidden disgust which I now felt in my own.*

'*And then there was the police and all the rest which the
head man will have told you. So of course you couldn't come
here and I couldn't ask you whether you loved me or not,
though I knew the answer anyway, I'd always really known
it since after that time in the hay-loft. Ivan Blessington called
in a day or two later, which made things worse, because it
reminded me of everything I wasn't going back to. But it's not
that which has made me despair. It's because of that soldier,
it's knowing, from what I thought of him, what you really
thought of me. Oh, I'm young and nice to look at, not like
him, but in the end that's all I was to you or will be to anyone.*

'*So now I'm going out to post this letter – they'll let me go
that far if I tell them first. I'm sending it to your home, not to
the head man's house in Wiltshire, which is where you'll be,
because I don't want to embarrass you. You can't say I've ever
really been a nuisance yet, and I pray I never shall be.*

'*Love, yes, love,*

'*Christopher.*'

Those peaceful days at Whereham, I thought: it must have
been about then that Christopher was hanging round the
barrack gate, waiting. Why hadn't he sent for me if the tutor
had left? Perhaps he didn't want to disturb me at Whereham
('You can't say I've ever really been a nuisance yet'), or perhaps
it was because he already knew all he needed to – 'I'd always
really known since after that time in the hay-loft.' That time in
the hay loft: the one and only time: and now this.

I tore Christopher's letter into very small pieces and let the
wind carry them away over the September sea.

'Mama . . . It's nice to see you back.'

'Is it, dear? How have you been getting on?'

'Quite well, thank you ... Mama, I'd better tell you straight away. I'm afraid I had to ask the hotel in London to send on the bill. Two nights.'

'Two nights?'

'There and back.'

'But I thought, Fielding, that I gave you money for all that.'

'Yes, mother, but it wasn't quite enough. And I'm afraid I owe Peter Morrison some money. You see—'

'—How much?'

'Fifteen pounds. You see—'

'—I'm not much interested,' my mother said, 'in whatever story you've thought up to tell me. I shall pay the hotel bill because I don't want to feel uncomfortable when I go there. As for Peter, he should have known better than to lend you so much. He'll just have to wait until you can pay him back yourself.'

'But *mama*—'

'—It's high time,' she said, 'that we got a few things straight, you and I.'

'What things, mother?'

'Your extravagant habits. This idea that you can have what you want for the asking. But just now I'm rather tired. We'll talk about it all later on.'

> '14477929, Pte. Morrison, P.,
> 3 Platoon, "A" Coy,
> 99 P.T.C.,
> Ranby Camp,
> Near Retford, Notts.
> 'September 15th, 1945.

'*My dear Fielding,*

'*If any letters are to reach me, they should be addressed exactly as above.*

'*Ranby Camp is the end of the world, but I'm rather enjoying myself. The thing is that all anyone on the training staff here can think about is how soon he will be demobbed. With the exception of a very few regulars, everyone thinks, talks, eats and sleeps nothing but release numbers and priorities, with the result that no one has much time for training or interfering with us. As far as I can make out, the British Army is one vast Heath-Robinson contrivance which exists only to fall apart, and the days pass in an atmosphere of sloth and cynicism which would, I fancy, amuse you.*

'*But of course it's all rather futile. I fail to see why I should spend perhaps three years of my life in dodging what are in any case unexacting duties and listening to repetitive stories of Neapolitan whore-shops. Still, one must make the best of a bad job; and so I've decided to apply for the Indian Army, which could be rather exciting. Nothing's settled yet, but when and if it is I shall hope to come down to school and see you all before I go.*'

After this, the ink changed colour, and it was clear that what followed had been written some time later.

'*The head man has just written about Christopher. I haven't time to say anything about it now, and anyhow I don't yet know what I want to say. I suppose we shall have to talk about it when I see you again.*

> '*Ever,*
> '*Peter.*'

'I'm just off to have dinner with the Tucks,' my Mother said. 'I might be quite late, so don't bother to wait up.'

I sat down alone in the kitchen to a tin of cold spam. There were now, I reflected, just five days before I was due to return to school. I had made all my preparations and only one thing more was needed: that my mother should pay the fees, which had to be sent, at latest, by the day before the quarter started. She might, of course, have done so already. But somehow I thought this unlikely. She had made no mention of the matter since her return two days before; indeed, she had made no mention of anything to do with my future. Her manner was of one who had plans about to mature, of one who would have an announcement to make at any minute. Meanwhile, she watched my preparations without comment and did not commit herself. When asked, for example, to drive me and my trunk to the station, so that I might send it off by P.L.A., she had simply shrugged her shoulders and said that it could wait. And so it could, I thought; but not for long. Tomorrow or the next day I must get her to declare herself; and the best way of doing so would be to remind her about the fees.

But it was my mother who took the initiative.

'It's time,' she said, after breakfast the next morning, 'that we had a little talk.'

'Gladly.'

I lowered my paper. Mama came and stood over me as I sat in what had always been my father's armchair. She looked determined and confident; formidable. In the few weeks since my father's death her body had thickened and straightened, while the drooping lines of discontent round her mouth had become strong, sardonic curves.

'Last night,' she said, 'I had a long discussion with the Tucks.'

'What have they to do with us?'

'There's no need to take that tone. Mr. Tuck made some very sensible suggestions.'

'I think I know. They want me to carry on with this absurd tea-planting scheme, and they want you to invest money. The same old story. I wonder you troubled to listen.'

'Angela Tuck has been a very good friend to me. At a time when I needed support and advice.'

'She got at you, mother, that's all.'

'You listen to me,' my mother said, leaning forward and speaking very precisely. 'You think you're going comfortably back to school and then on to Cambridge. All on my money. Well, I'm changing all that. I've written to your Headmaster and told him you won't be coming back, this term or any term.'

'Quarter.'

'It's a pity I had to pay a term's fees in lieu of notice—'

'—A quarter's fees. In that case I may as well get the benefit until Christmas—'

'—But I mean to start as I'm going to go on. No more school. Real life now. No more school and no more Cambridge . . . unless of course you can pay for it yourself.'

'Why, mother? For God's sake, why?'

For a long time I had half-consciously expected this. I had told myself that when the time came my intelligence would show me the solution. But I had been reluctant to envisage more than a token showdown, after which my mother, as she had done for years, would comply with my reasonable requests. I had not considered tactics, I had merely assured myself of my ability to cope with a feeble-minded woman. Now that this woman had made, stated and already acted upon firm plans of her own, I suddenly found myself powerless to do more than entreat.

'Why?' I asked piteously. 'Why?'

'Because I want to see you make a real life for yourself by your own efforts. To see you behave like a man, not sit around, dependent on someone else's money, amusing yourself with Latin and Greek. Latin and Greek' – she mouthed the words grotesquely – 'what *use* could they ever be to anyone?'

'But it was all carefully planned. It was to have been my career.'

'Your *career*? A career spent mouldering away under a heap of books, talking arty nonsense to a lot of clever-clever dons, who wouldn't last a minute if they weren't protected from the real world by their cosy college walls?'

My father's voice, I thought.

'It's what I wanted, mother,' I said wearily. 'And you always seemed happy about it.'

'Don't you see?' she said. She was now speaking almost into my ear. 'I had to support you against your father, or you wouldn't have wanted me, any more than you wanted him. And I didn't know what was in his will. If it had been different, if you'd been free to do what you planned, I'd have been forced to make the best of it, or lose you altogether. But now ...'

She stood back and surveyed me, hands on hips.

'My son,' she said. 'My pretty, arty son. I want a man.'

'Mother. There is enough money for me to do what I want. I'm asking you, pleading with you, to let things go on as we'd always agreed.'

'No. Real life now.'

'Do you hate me so much?'

'I simply want what's best for you. I've listened for too long while you've laughed and been so clever about ordinary people, ordinary sensible things. Now you're going to learn what the world's like for most of us. What it's been like for me these last twenty years.'

So that was it. Part morality, part vindictiveness. She wanted to make me into a 'real man' doing a 'useful job', just like anybody else, compelled to join in with 'ordinary' people and to echo their 'sensible' notions, to be bored, to conform. No good arguing now, I thought. Listen to what she says and then think later.

'So what have you arranged?' I asked.

'I've arranged to invest all the money that would have gone on your useless education with the owner of Mr. Tuck's plantation. £5,000, and probably some more later on. You'll do your Army service as soon as possible, and then you'll go out to India to join Mr. Tuck, who will take you under his personal supervision. He hopes to be a partner by then, so you'll have every chance to get on. If you work hard and show the right spirit' – Tuck's phrase, surely? – 'you'll become an important man and make good money, like Mr. Tuck. If you don't ... well, don't think you can fall back on me.'

Money, money. But no good arguing now. Keep your head, I told myself; be patient and rational; look round for a way out. Don't let her have the scene she'd like, not until you have a weapon to silence her. And what could that be? Never mind now.

'All right, mama,' I said. 'I have no choice. What do you want me to do?'

The first thing I must do, as Mr. Tuck officiously explained, was to go to the Registration authorities in Lympne Ducis, there to notify them that I no longer wished to be deferred from call up and would like to volunteer, on grounds of personal urgency, for immediate drafting.

'Now we all know where we are at last,' Tuck said, 'let's get this show on the road.'

Although I had no intention of cancelling my deferment, I was prepared to go through motions enough to stop my mother's tongue for the time, and the next afternoon I took a train to Lympne Ducis. It was, after all, an outing of a kind.

Having gone to the registration office for just long enough to look with loathing at its exterior, I made my way towards the cinema. ('Yes, mama,' I would tell her when I got home, 'they'll do what they can, they say, but it may take some time.') Crossing the empty market place in front of The Duke's Head, I heard a scampering of high heels behind me.

'Christopher ... Chris.'

Dixie. Walk on and pretend not to notice.

But she was up beside me, panting and flushed, gripping my arm.

'Don't run away, please, Chris. I only wanted to say ... I'm sorry, so sorry, for behaving like I did that night.'

'You?' I said stupidly. 'Sorry?'

'Yes. So sorry. I don't blame you for rushing off like you did. But please talk to me now. Say you've forgiven me.'

'But after what I did to you—'

'—I led you on, Christopher. I wanted you to. I don't know why I started on like that. Phyllis ... I don't know.'

I turned towards her and put my hands on her shoulders. The afternoon, gold on the gabled houses, had a chill of dying summer; but it was not this which made me shiver.

'You wanted me to?' I repeated. 'Then why not now? We'll

take a bus out to the pinewoods ... Go to the cinema ...'

Dixie drew away.

'No, Christopher,' she said gently. 'Not any more. I'm engaged now, see?'

She held up her hand and the imitation diamonds sparkled in the autumn sun.

'I'm very happy,' she said. 'So when I saw you just now, I wanted for us to part friends like. Say it, Chris. Say we part friends and wish me luck.'

Engaged. To a 'real' man no doubt, who had a 'proper' job. Engaged to grow older and older in a deadly routine of begetting and boredom and the weekly wage-packet. Engaged to watch the children grow up and leave, to slobber through loose dentures at the grand-children on their Christmas visit, engaged to die and to rot. 'Before I go, I'd like Clarry's eldest to have my engagement ring. The jewels always looked so pretty in the sun. I remember one day, many years ago in the market place ...'

'Don't they look a treat in the sun?' Dixie said.

'And in the shadow?' (My dear Dorian.)

'Christopher? What—'

'—Never mind, Dixie. Of course I wish you luck. And if we're to part as friends, you should know my proper name. I'm called Fielding, Fielding Gray.'

'What a nice name. Funny but nice. Why did you say it was Christopher?'

'I thought you'd laugh.'

'Not that sort of funny. Thank you for telling me, though. It means ... that what you say is real.'

'Real?'

'That I'm not just anybody you picked up one evening at a fair. Give us a kiss, Fielding Gray.' She pointed to her cheek. 'There.'

I made to kiss her. At the last moment she altered the angle of her head and gave me her closed lips.

'I must run now,' she said. 'Ta-ta. Be good.'

The high heels clicked away across the square. Begetting and boredom. Reality. And warmth. Was that what made the long years endurable for Dixie and her kind, engaged only to parturate and die? Michael Redgrave and John Mills, the cinema poster said: The Way to the Stars. How Dixie would thrill to the sham title, as she thrilled to the fake diamonds in the sun. But who was I to pity or condemn? I, who had only dared to let her know my real name when I was quit of her for good?

When I came home that evening, there was a letter from the Senior Usher.

'... *The Headmaster has told me of your mother's decision, and I can well imagine how disagreeable you must find your predicament. Not that the feeling can be anything but salutary: set-backs, once in a while, are excellent therapy. Provided, that is, they are not unduly prolonged and destructive. To come to the point without more ado, I object to waste and I cannot stand by while a scholar of your promise is lost to us at the whim – forgive me – of a foolish woman. There has been enough loss these last years: scholars will be rare: our side, the humanists' side, needs all the support it can get. And so, since I am a bachelor and not a poor one, I propose, if you will permit me, to undertake the expense of your further education: the expense, that is, of another year at the school here and later of whatever provision you may need, within reasonable though not frugal limits, at Cambridge. My motive is not entirely one of high-minded patronage; if I wish to keep a scholar, I also wish to oblige a friend. The loss, you see, would be personal as well as academic.*

'*I realize that your mother's attitude will be, to say the least of it, hostile, and that she will withhold money. I enclose an encashable money order for your immediate needs, and I will make arrangements, which we can discuss later, to see you all right during future school holidays. Since I have chosen to interfere, I shall interfere amply, and place you altogether beyond the reach of – forgive me once more – your mother's palpable malice.*

'*The Headmaster, whom I have of course informed of my intentions, is dubious of the scheme but prepared to accept it. I think he is afraid your mother will make trouble, will claim that I have illicitly seduced you away from her control. Legally, however, she can do nothing. You are nearly eighteen; provided your course of life is respectable and you have visible means to support it, you are entirely free to leave her as soon as you wish.*

'*In the present circumstances, I think you would be well advised to do so immediately. If ties are to be cut, they should be sharply cut. You will be welcome at my Lodging for the last few days before the quarter begins ...*'

'And so what did they tell you at the Registration office?' my mother asked.

'Nothing. I didn't go in and now I never intend to.'

'Well, my lord. And what do you intend?'

'To leave here,' I said, 'tomorrow.'

'Very forceful all of a sudden. What will you use for money?'

'I have a friend,' I said triumphantly, 'a master at the school, who will see me through my last year there. *And* through Cambridge.'

'How kind of him. But suppose, just suppose, that I object? After all, you're under twenty-one.'

'There's nothing you can do. Provided I have proper means and occupation, I can go where I wish.'

'Yes,' my mother said quietly, 'I expect you're right. We'll talk about it in the morning.'

'There's nothing to talk about, mother.'

'We'll talk about it in the morning. What time,' she inquired, 'are you off?'

'Early.'

'But I expect we'll still have time, dear, for a little talk first.'

Trunk, I thought. That can come with me in the taxi and go in the guard's van. Stop at the post office on the way to the station, cash the money order, and wire the Senior Usher to expect me in the evening. Suitcase: socks, shirts, hanks, pants; washing things in the morning. All set. Just as I had told myself: use your brains; wait until you see the way out and then take it – fast. True, I had been lucky; but I had kept my head, bided my time, avoided excessive unpleasantness and contrived, though under heavy pressure, not to commit myself. A victory for intelligence and reason. With the thrill of impending departure in my belly I went to my fitful rest.

'So you think,' said my mother the next morning, 'that you're going to walk out of here just like that?'

'I don't want to part with bad feelings, mother. You've got one idea for my future and I've got another. You can hardly blame me for preferring mine.'

'A mother knows what's best for her son. Don't you see,' said mama, with something of her old whine, 'that I'm doing all this for your sake? The Army will make a man of you, and in India you'll have a job for which any boy should be grateful.'

154

'The Army will have its chance in any case,' I said. 'But not yet. You know what I want to do, mother – what I've always wanted to do. Let's not have any more argument.'

'I'm your mother.' Self-righteous now. 'It's for me to give you money and help you with your future. Not for some interfering master at that damned school.'

'Then give me money and help me. Stop listening to the Tucks all day long and help me do what I want.'

'I bore you, I brought you up, protected you, fought for you—'

'—Yes, yes, and I'm grateful. But now—'

'—And in return I've a right to have my wishes respected.'

'It's no good, mother. There's a taxi coming for me in ten minutes. Just as soon as you change your mind and try to see things sensibly, I'll be glad to come back to you. Until then . . . well, for heaven's sake let's be nice to each other.'

'Nice to each other. As if you'd ever been nice to me in your whole life. As if you'd ever thought of me at all, except as someone to get money for you out of your father. Well, you're going to think of me now for once. Oh yes. You're going to think of me now, Fielding Gray, because you're going to have to do what I tell you. You're not going back to that school, money or no money, because I'm going to show them this.'

She fumbled in her bag.

'*This.*' She waved a photograph in front of her. Christopher in cricket kit. ' "To Fielding with all my dearest love from Christopher",' she read from the back in an obscene, mimicking voice. ' "Please come soon, or I—" '

'—Stop it, mother.'

'—"Or I shan't be able to bear it." That ought to be quite enough, after what's happened. That wretched boy dead, after offering himself to soldiers like a common whore in the street—'

'—STOP IT—'

'—Yes, this ought to be quite enough, I think. Mind you, we knew already what you'd been up to, Angela and I. She's kept in touch with your friend who came here, Somerset Lloyd-Thing—'

'—Lloyd-James—'

'—and *he* told her all about *Christopher*. It's a funny thing, but he seems to want to stop you going back too. Nice friends you have. So when he heard that Angela and I had a plan for you, he wrote back helpfully to tell her about this Christopher

. . . only there was no real proof yet, he said. *Until I found this.*
While you were slopping around in Lympne yesterday, not
doing what you were told.'

'So you were snooping, *prying*?'

'Not at all. Simply doing my duty as your mother and going
over your clothes. This was at the bottom of your shirt drawer.
Rather careless, rather forgetful for someone so very clever.'

'Mother,' I said. 'Christopher's dead and the whole dismal
story's finished. All we want to do, all of us, is to forget it.'

'Oh? I wonder whether Somerset Lloyd-Thing wants to
forget it. Anyway, you won't be able to forget it now, because
I've got proof and I won't let you. I'm going to tell your headmaster what I know; and if he lets you back into his school
after *that*, then I'll start writing round to the parents and telling them that their esteemed Headmaster is condoning
sodomy. Sodomy,' she hissed, like a dry tap.

I lurched forward.

'You mean, spiteful bitch,' I shouted. I thrust my hand out
to seize the photograph, but she drew away from me and
brandished it above her head.

'Oh no, my lad,' she said. 'Anyhow Angela's seen it. Even if
you tear it up, we can make such a scandal between us that
that Headmaster of yours will never want to hear your name
again.'

'Bitch,' I screamed, 'Bitch, *bitch*, BITCH.'

I lowered the hand which was reaching for the photograph
and hit her with a back swing of my knuckles across her cheek.
Her lips parted and the blood welled up through her teeth.

'Mama, I'm sorry, so sorry. *Please,* mama. I didn't mean—'

'—Nasty little pansy,' she lisped through the streaming
blood; 'nasty, vicious little pig.'

The door bell rang. I offered my handkerchief.

'Don't you come near me,' she said. The blood poured over
her chin and dripped down on to her dress. 'You get into your
taxi and run away back to school. And when they turn you
out, you can just come back here. You'll have to grovel,
Christ, how you'll have to grovel, but you're under twenty-one,
so I'll let you come back here.'

Be reasonable, I told myself. It was her fault. She provoked
me beyond bearing, and so I struck her. She threatened the
vilest kind of blackmail to get her way, and so I struck her. One
minute there had been relief, the generous promise of freedom

in the Senior Usher's letter, the next there had been frustration and despair, jealousy masquerading as mother love, the hideous desire to control and possess: she was destroying everything, and so I struck her. But reason could not encompass the enormity, could not blot out the picture of the bright blood pouring from my mother's mouth.

The train slunk through the debris into London. I was following my original plan and heading, as invited, for the Senior Usher's Lodging, because I had nowhere else to go; here, if anywhere, lay help and refuge. But not for long now. One or two days at most, as long as it took my mother to convince the Headmaster of what she knew. I looked down at the jagged, carious rubble. Beaten, I told myself, beaten. How were intelligence or reason to help me now?

'When a position becomes untenable,' said the Senior Usher, spreading his buttocks before an ample and illicit fire, 'it is necessary to retreat with good grace to a tenable one. You realize that you can't stay here?'

'I suppose not.'

'You see, as long as your misdeeds were extra-mural, so to speak, I could help you. This business of your trull in Piccadilly – easily seen to. But now that you're known to have sinned within these very portals ... it's too *near,* Fielding, and it can't be disregarded. You remember what I said last quarter? We don't expect you to believe in the Christian ethic – or at least I don't – but we have to insist that on our own ground you observe it.'

'A condition of belonging, you said.'

'Exactly. We can, of course, exercise some discretion. We can even ignore what we might have suspected – so long as it's safely dead and buried. But your mother has exhumed this unhappy affair, and she has made of this wretched boy Roland a kind of accusing Lazarus. You see, it's the fact of his suicide that finally settles the question. There'd be those who'd say that you were the cause of it. So you must see that we simply can't keep you.'

'I know that. I know I must leave here before the quarter starts. But what am I to do?'

'As I say, dear boy. Retreat to a tenable position. Now then. No last year here, no further award at Lancaster. But you still have a minor scholarship to the college and a place awaiting you. It's more than most people have; so settle for it.'

'But will they still accept me? If they hear about all this?'

'Of course. They are civilized and easy-going men, who do not concern themselves with the peccadilloes of adolescence. In any case, you're now too late to propose yourself for this October, so you'll have to do your military service first; and by the time that's done, the whole thing will have been forgotten.'

'The Tutor ... Robert Constable ... he didn't strike me as easy-going. Neither forgiving, I'd have said, nor forgetting.'

'You misunderstand him. He is a bore and a prig, but also a conscientious and progressive left-winger. Vintage 'thirties. Which means that he stands not only for social reform but also for intellectual and sexual freedom. It is, to him, a duty to tolerate your kind of behaviour. Though of course,' said the Senior Usher wryly, 'the more complicated and unhappy you can be about it, the better he'll be pleased. Never let on that you were simply enjoying yourself.'

'And ... money?'

'I'll stand by what I promised. If you don't qualify for some sort of ex-service grant, I'll see to it you're all right.'

'And meanwhile? *Now*, I mean? These days one can't just take the King's shilling overnight.'

The Senior Usher scratched his rump.

'If you ask me,' he said slowly, 'As things stand you'd be wise to go home and make your peace with your mother. She is, it seems, a dangerous woman. Tell her you're sorry you were rude and you'll do what she asks. Keep her quiet, dear boy, till it's too late for her to do any more damage.'

'What more can she do?'

'On the face of it, none. As I say, Lancaster is run very differently from this place, and nobody there will give a second thought to her story. They keep their chapel going as a decorative museum piece, and that's about as far as the Christian ethic gets with *them*.'

'Well then?'

'One never knows. I still think you'd be wise to calm your mother down and keep her calm till time's done its work.'

'I don't at all want to go back.'

'A little more gratitude would become you, and a little more co-operation. You can't have everything your own way.'

'I'm sorry, sir. I didn't mean to be difficult and I *am* grateful.'

'It'll be unpleasant, I know,' said the old man, relenting. 'But when a woman has a mind to do damage she can be damned ingenious. As you've already seen. So you go off home tomorrow, soothe her down, and get yourself into khaki as soon as possible. Meanwhile, I'll brief Robert Constable and get him to set your mind at rest about your place at Lancaster. And now,' he said, 'I've ordered a nice little dinner in your honour and we will talk, if you please, of something – of anything – else.'

'Good-bye, sir,' I said to the Headmaster.

On the boundary of the cricket ground the damp leaves, whirled and fell still.

'Good-bye, Fielding,' said the Headmaster. 'I'm sorry it's turned out like this. You're not to blame your mother.'

'There's no point in blaming anyone. Would you do something for me, sir?'

'What?'

'When the boys get back and you see Somerset Lloyd-James, tell him I'm sorry not to have seen him to say good-bye.'

'I'll tell him, certainly. I expect he'll be sorry too.'

'No, he won't. You'll see that from his face. Look into his face, Headmaster; look into his eyes. You're unlikely to see anything at all in them, and if you do it won't be tears.'

When I arrived home again, my mother did not, as she had threatened, make me grovel. She was distant in her greeting and received my apologies for having struck her with an ugly shrug of the shoulders; but as soon as I had made it plain (following the Senior Usher's instructions) that I had come home to toe the line, I was treated with consideration and even with affection. Since I was prepared to yield over the big issues, it seemed that I was to be humoured in the lesser ones. Once I had been to Lympne Ducis, accompanied this time by mama, and had signified to the authorities that I wish to be called up as soon as possible, my comfort and preferences were constantly consulted. On the day that I gave Mr. Tuck a formal assurance that I would join the company in India as soon as I was free from the Army, my mother handed me a cheque for £15, made out to Peter Morrison, and another, worth twice as much, for myself, and suggested that I might indulge any reasonable fancy during the few weeks before I was posted. (Even a trip to London was sanctioned, and I was able to visit the Senior Usher's doctor friend, who tested and approved my blood.) Life at Broughton Staithe, then, was easy and tranquil that autumn; and not only on the surface: for early in October I received assurance from Robert Constable that my place at Lancaster was indeed still open, so that in the very act of complying with my mother's demands I could reflect, with deep and secret satisfaction, that the last word would be mine.

'Dear Gray [*Constable had written in his own hand*],

'I have now learned, both from the Headmaster and the Senior Usher, about the circumstances of your leaving school. They give few details, but I gather there has been some sexual indiscretion. Officially, however, you have merely been withdrawn by your mother, albeit at unexpectedly short notice. This can make no difference to your prospects here; and as Tutor of the College I am pleased to notify you that you may take up your place and your Minor Scholarship as soon as you have concluded your military service.

Yours sincerely,
Robert Constable.

So that was finally settled. When I left the Army I would go to Lancaster, and there was nothing my mother or anyone else could do to stop me. Full of glee at my victory and longing to tell someone of it, I wrote off to Peter to give him a detailed account of my afflictions and of my cleverness in achieving so happy an issue.

'Well,' said Tuck the night before I left for the Army, 'here's wishing you all the best.'

Mama was giving a little dinner party in honour of my departure.

'I expect,' said Angela, 'that you'll look very different when you come home on leave.'

'Fitter,' said Tuck.

'Tougher,' said Angela.

'More grown up,' said mama.

'Where exactly are you going?' said Tuck.

'99 Primary Training Centre. At a place called Ranby.'

'His friend Peter Morrison is there,' mama said, 'who comes from Whereham. Isn't that lucky for Fielding? Such a nice, kind, helpful boy.'

'I don't suppose he'll be there for much longer,' I said. 'Primary Training only lasts for eight weeks, they tell me. After that we go to training units belonging to our own regiments.'

'Which regiment are you going to?' asked Tuck.

'The 49th Light Dragoons. Earl Hamilton's Regiment of Horse.'

'Rather grand?'

'I don't know ... My school has quite a pull with them.'

'Hmm,' muttered Tuck suspiciously. 'You'll need a bit of extra money if they give you a commission in that lot.'

'Fielding will have an allowance,' mama said. 'And it will be nice for him to be in a regiment with people from his old school.'

Now that she had won her way, my mother apparently expected no trouble from old associations. A naïvely snobbish woman, she had even encouraged me to make use of school connections in order to enter a smart regiment. As for the money which would be needed, she had already shown herself generous and was prepared to continue so. Truth to tell, mama was not really an unamiable woman; and had she, earlier in her life, received love, she would not now have needed to exercise power.

'An allowance,' Angela said, as though such a thing were beyond the dreams of avarice; 'how very kind of you.'

'So long as Fielding is sensible,' my mother said, 'I shall help him in every way I can.'

'You've got a brick of a mother,' said Tuck when the two ladies had left us.

'You might call her that.'

'I jolly well do. It took her to make you see sense about the plantation. Not many people would have had the patience.'

'She has certainly been very persistent,' I said.

'A pretty cool way of putting it.'

'We're a pretty cool family.'

'Not your mother. She's warm, generous ...'

'Tell me, if it's not a rude question. How much is she investing in the plantation?'

'Ten thousand. More later, I think. Now the factory at Torbeach has been sold, she reckons she can afford it.'

'I don't wonder you find her generous.'

'It's all for you,' Tuck said.

'Precisely. My father, if you remember, wanted something for himself.'

'Don't play games with me, boy.'

'Never again' I said: 'I promise you that.'

And so I left for Ranby Camp and the last part of this story. I expected anything up to three years of discomfort and boredom, but if Peter could face it, I told myself, so could I. It had to be gone through sometime; and always there was Lancaster College waiting for me at the end of it. Whatever had been lost, that – and it was much – was still promised.

And now, too, I should be seeing Peter again. He would not be at Ranby much longer, but there he would be. I could seek him out, discuss what had happened, receive his sympathy and applause; then talk with him of friends and enemies in common, of days past and to come. It would be good to see Peter; as the train rumbled over the dreary flats, I cheered myself by thinking of the round face that would be waiting for me and the slow, soothing voice . . .

Today, as for weeks past, the wind has thrust at the island without ceasing. The clouds are coming across so low that the little village on the hill above me has been hidden for hours. Beneath the cloud a swirling drizzle reduces everything to two dimensions and one colour, a drab yellow. But now, just as ten years ago in that train across the Lincolnshire flats, I cheer myself with thinking of Peter, who will be here, in three days' time, with his delegation of M.P.s.

Although the spell still works, it is weaker now than it was then. Then the thought of Peter's calm eyes and kind, clumsy hands was enough to quicken the dull fens to enchantment, to make the blue war-time bulbs, which darkened rather than lit the carriage, shine out for durbar. But now, glad as I am that he is coming here, I know that such reunions do not, as a general rule, come up to expectation.

At Ranby Camp they squadded me and kitted me, took away my civilian clothes and sent them home for me, and issued me with a card which entitled me to forty cigarettes a week at special rates. Then, reluctantly and spasmodically, they began to train me. A jolly red-nosed sergeant lectured me on procedure for seeking redress of grievance or applying for leave if my wife were to prove unfaithful; an officer in furlined suede boots assured me, in a fluting voice, that the Army's skills would stand me well when I returned to my civilian trade; and a neurotic corporal, who had been broken from sergeant-major for striking a Eurasian pimp in a dance hall in Deolali, opined that a properly cleaned rifle was a better friend to me than my mother.

On my second night, I set out to discover Peter. I sloshed through the mud which lapped round the nightmare archipelago of a myriad Nissen huts and at last found a door which said 'A Coy Office'. Inside, working under a dim light with five tea-cups and five empty plates in front of him, was an immense and flabby colour-sergeant.

'Permission to speak, Colour, please?'

'Put them down on the desk, laddie,' said the colour-sergeant without looking up.

'Put what down?'

'The tea and wads down.'

'I haven't got any tea and wads, I'm afraid. I've come about a friend, Private Morrison—'

'—Not got the tea and wads?'

'I'm from "H" Company, Colour. But I've got a friend called Morrison in this, and I . . .'

The colour-sergeant held up his hand for silence and began to speak in a mildly hysterical manner.

'I took over as C.S.M. of this shower,' the colour-sergeant said, 'without, I might tell you, being given the acting rank, at 1300 hours dinner time. So I couldn't tell a single one of them from the next, not if it was Jesus Christ Almighty who came round asking. That's why I'm sitting here in the middle of the night, trying to sort out the horrible mess that's been left behind. A tap at the door. Ah, I says, my tea and wads and none too soon. But instead a young gentleman arrives as bold as the colonel on his horse, and starts asking questions. It makes me want to cry.'

He looked as if he really might.

'I'm terribly sorry. If you like, I'll go to the NAAFI and get your tea and wads for you.'

'But then,' said the colour-sergeant after some thought, 'there'd be two lots. The lot that's been ordered already, see, and the new lot that you got.'

'Better two lots than no lots.'

'Yes,' said the colour-sergeant after further thought, 'I do believe you're right. So you go to the NAAFI for me and I'll look up this mucker of yours and see where he beats his meat.'

'Beats his meat?'

'What hut his wanker's in. What did you say he was called?'

When I arrived back from the NAAFI twenty minutes later with a large tray of tea and wads, I found a stringy and yellow sergeant-major, who was sitting in the colour-sergeant's chair and lighting an eighth of an inch of Woodbine.

'Permission to speak, sir, please?'

After the sergeant-major had coughed till the tears ran down his face, he nodded his permission.

'I've brought the colour-sergeant's tea and wads.'

'Too late, son. I've just taken over from him.'

'Well, would you like these, sir? It seems a pity to waste them.'

'I've been sitting here for ten minutes,' said the sergeant-major after a heroic bout of coughing, 'and three people have come in with trays of tea and wads. Poor Colour Baines can't stop himself, you see. Three days at Anzio without a bite to eat, and now he just can't stop himself, which is why I've had to take over from him.'

'So where's he gone to now, sir?'

'They've sent him back to the stores. It doesn't matter so much there, but you can't have it in a company office. What I _would_ like,' the sergeant-major said, 'is a cigarette.'

'I'm sorry, sir. I don't smoke. But I could go to the NAAFI for you.'

'That's right, son, you do that.'

I went again to the NAAFI and with the aid of my special card brought twenty cheap cigarettes. I was half afraid lest someone else might have taken over from the sergeant-major by the time I got back, but instead there was no one in the office at all. So I looked in a file called Personnel, Distribution of, and discovered that 14477929 Recruit Lance-Corporal Morrison P., who had applied for and been granted an Indian Army Cadetship, had gone on embarkation leave the day before, having been posted w.e.f. 1st November to the Officer's Training School at Bangalore. He would be back in Ranby *en passant*, it appeared, in ten days' time. Although the sergeant-major had not paid me for the cigarettes, I obeyed an instinct which twenty-four hours of my new life had already awakened in me, and decided to leave them behind.

A week later I was summoned for interview with a visiting personnage called the Cavalry (Armoured Corps) Selection Officer. This turned out to be Captain Detterling, the only boy in the school who had ever made a double century in a school match. His cherry trousers, which had seemed the last word in elegance on the school terrace last May, were rather tactless, I thought, against a background of denim overalls and mud. He was sitting in a tiny office which was warmed by a stove twice as big as the only stove we had in my Nissen hut; despite which he was wearing his officer's great coat, slung stylishly over his shoulders to resemble a cavalry cloak.

'Permission to enter, sir, please?' I said from the door.

'Good lord,' Detterling said, 'do they still teach recruits to do that?'

'Sir.'

'Well you can knock if off with me, dear boy. After all, we have met before.' He shook hands with me, waved me into a chair and inspected a form in front of him. 'Now let's see. You want to go into the 49th Earl Hamilton's Light Dragoons, it says here.'

'That's right, sir.'

Detterling pondered awhile.

'That's my regiment,' he said, as if he had just remembered, and looked down at his trousers as though for confirmation.

'Sir.' (No other comment seemed possible.)

'Well, there'll be no trouble about that. As you probably realize, a lot of us come from the old school for a start. By the way, I was down there last week. Saw your chum Morrison. He's going to India, he says.'

'So I gather.'

'He's looking forward to seeing you here first. Told me to tell you. I don't suppose,' he continued, almost as if there were some

165

connection, 'that I can interest you in taking a *regular* commission?'

'I'm afraid not. I'm going up to Cambridge, you see.'

'The Army's rather jolly in peace time, you know. I had two years of it before the last show started. Lots of cricket and servants, that sort of thing.'

'Do you suppose it will be the same, sir?'

Captain Detterling looked glum.

'I don't suppose it will ever be *quite* the same,' he conceded. 'But you might like to think about it.'

'I'm sorry. Cambridge . . .'

'Morrison was talking about that. And the rest of them.'

'The rest of them?'

'The Senior Usher. And the head man. As I told them, you're just the sort of chap we'd jump at, if you wanted a regular commission.'

'I'm sorry.'

'So am I,' said Detterling rather oddly, 'and I'm sorry to keep nagging you like this. But I'm afraid it's my job: trying to interest people in the Army as a career. Not very easy, I assure you. And the trouble is,' he prattled on, inexplicably nervous, I thought, 'that I'm meant to explain what a healthy, exciting, useful sort of life it is for good, keen chaps. As if anyone wants to listen to that. I keep telling the Board, if only there were more talk of hunting and proper dress uniforms instead of all this boring rubbish about tanks, it would make my job easier . . . But I mustn't detain you.'

'There's nowhere I'd sooner be.'

'I suppose not. *Tanks,*' said Detterling crossly, 'how I hate them. Hideous, noisy, dirty things, spoiling everyone's pleasure.'

'I do see your point.'

'But I oughtn't,' said Detterling, 'to be talking like this. You keep your nose clean in this horrible dump, and we'll take good care of you when you get to us. We'll fix you up with an emergency commission or whatever it's called in about six months. And there's no harm,' he pleaded, 'in just thinking about making it permanent, now is there?'

Although I was so preoccupied and even diverted by my new way of life that I had contrived to forget my disappointment at Peter's absence, I was eager for his return. The 'A' Company sergeant-major, gratefully remembering the cigarettes though not offering to pay for them, agreed to pass on a message; and at eight o'clock in the evening, two days after my interview with Captain Detterling, I found Peter waiting for me outside the NAAFI.

'Not here,' said Peter at once; 'I know somewhere quieter.'

He was wearing, I now saw, the insignia of an Officer Cadet: a large white celluloid disk behind his cap-badge and a white tape on each shoulder. He would have been less than prudent to show himself in the NAAFI in a get-up like that.

'This way,' Peter said. 'Sorry about the trappings, but I'm leaving tomorrow and this is what we have to wear on the boat.'

'So soon?'

'Yes.'

He led the way across a football pitch two inches deep in yellow slush, past a coal heap, a cookhouse, two rubbish dumps and a discreetly stinking urinal labelled 'Sergeants and Above', and down a path of crazy pavement to a small stone cottage. Above the door a red light-bulb dimly illuminated a text which was surmounted by a Maltese Cross:

THE CHURCH ARMY
I bring not peace but the sword.

'Nice and quiet for all that,' Peter said.

Also warm and cheerful. For threepence each we were both given a cup of thick tea and a spicy sausage roll by a woman with a wobbling bust, who invited us to make ourselves comfortable by a huge coal fire.

'So you're off tomorrow,' I said. 'The Indian Army. How long will it last?'

'For two years perhaps. Long enough for me. I do six months at the O.T.S. at Bangalore. Then the Punjab. I've always wanted to go somewhere like that before settling down.'

He was anything but settled now. There was a long pause, during which he crumbled his sausage roll. Nervous, I thought, upset. Meeting like this only to say good-bye again. It was not a happy thing.

'Tell me,' Peter said, 'wasn't Detterling here the other day? The chap with the cherry trousers?'

'He interviewed me.'

'Did he give you my message?'

'He said you were looking forward to seeing me.'

'Only that?'

'And that you'd all been talking about me back at school.'

'I don't suppose he really gathered what it was all about. You may as well know straight off, Fielding. There's bad news.'

'Bad news?'

'It's very difficult for me.' He leant forward and started to speak very quickly, not exactly with urgency but more as if he were throwing away essential but embarrassing lines in a carefully rehearsed style. 'When I was home on leave,' he said, 'I went to see your mother. She'd be lonely, I felt, and although I hadn't seen you yet I thought she might like to hear about Ranby ... She was always very kind to me when we were younger. You remember?'

'She still speaks fondly of you. Such nice manners, she always says.'

'I was ... am ... fond of her too. She was so proud of you, Fielding.'

'Victorious, you mean.'

'No. It depends how you see it, I suppose, but to me she seemed proud. She kept talking of the 49th Light Dragoons, how she longed for the day when you'd come home with a commission ...'

As Peter talked on, the scene he described flickered in my brain like an old film. Peter and mama, one each side of a fire like the one we sat by now, were mouthing silently at one another, while what they said appeared in white sub-titles at the bottom of the screen.

'... Tell me, Peter dear. What sort of uniform do they wear? In Earl Hamilton's Light Dragoons, I mean.'

'It'll be a little while before he gets to them, Mrs. Gray. He has to finish his Primary Training first.'

'I know. But when he *does* to the Dragoons?'

'They wear cherry trousers, Mrs. Gray. Most of these cavalry regiments go in for something rather dashing.'

'Will Fielding have boots and spurs?'

'They're trying to discourage those. After all, they're not much good in tanks.'

'But they look very smart ... Ah well. How soon do you suppose you'll all be released?'

'Hard to say. Three years ... Two and a half.'

'Because Fielding's got such a good job to go to. Has he told you? He's been offered a splendid position on a tea plantation in India.'

'I heard about it.'

168

'I expect you were interested, as you're going there too. Yes, it's all been arranged. One of the partners – well, he *will* be a partner – will take special care of him, and with a little luck he should do very well.'

'Mrs. Gray. You must know as well as I do that Fielding will never go to India.'

'What did you say, Peter dear?'

'I heard from him not long ago. Fielding still means, as he always has, to go up to Lancaster College.'

The screen flickered violently, then went bright and blank.

'*Why*, Peter?' I said. 'Why in God's name did you tell her that?'

'It's very difficult . . . I suddenly felt that I must speak up on your account. Set the record straight. I couldn't allow you to deceive her any more; I couldn't let this proud, kind old lady just sit there and be made a fool of.'

'Proud, kind old lady. She's behaved wickedly, abominably—'

'—She's your mother, Fielding. You owed her the truth, however hard it was for you.'

'But she's been vicious, vindictive.'

'Because you couldn't see it right. You never tried to understand. You failed in love.'

'God is love,' said a voice behind us. A bald and snuffling old man, carrying a sheaf of tracts.

'God bless,' he snuffled, putting two tracts on the table between us, 'God bless.'

'Christ,' I said, fingering a tract, 'dear Jesus Christ. So what happened then?'

'A few days later I went down to the school to say goodbye. The head man had already heard from Lancaster. Your mother had been to see Constable.'

'What could she do there? Constable doesn't give a damn what I've done. He wrote to me and said so. It's just like the Senior Usher says,' I went on wildly 'Lancaster's not like the school, it's too powerful to be intimidated by some chattering woman.'

'No one was intimidated, Fielding.'

'Well then?'

'You never knew much about Constable. The Senior Usher did, but even he didn't understand him properly. As he now admits. You see, although Constable was a progressive, a liberal – indeed *because* he was those things – he was a man of deep moral feeling.'

'We knew that. But his brand of morality didn't trouble itself about the petty sexual offences of children.'

'No. But it troubles itself about betrayal. When your mother showed Constable that photo which Christopher sent you ... and when he thought about what it implied ... he began to suspect that you had failed Christopher in some way, that you had used him and then deserted him. But he couldn't be sure, and it might not have been your fault, so he was prepared to overlook this – or so he wrote to the head man – had it been an isolated incident. But there was more.'

'What, for God's sake?'

'Constable is a man of honour. A man of his word. You remember when the Senior Usher sneered at him for not getting a good job in the war, for "running around with a lot of black men"?'

'Yes.'

'Well Constable could have had a soft job all right, only he chose to fight because he thought his honour required it. He wouldn't take the easy way out.'

'What's that to do with me?'

'When Constable heard from your mother that you'd first struck her and then, later on, lied to her—'

'—But the old man told me to lie to her. To stop any more trouble.'

'The old man's standards aren't Constable's. When Constable heard how you'd deceived your mother, letting her think you'd fall in with her plans, drawing a handsome allowance on the strength of it, when all the time you had his own letter of acceptance in your pocket, it offended both his morality and his chivalry. Treachery ... and violence ... to a woman.'

'She was treacherous to me,' I wailed.

'In Constable's eyes that does not excuse you. Nor in mine. I think it is the blow which I cannot bear. You never told me about that when you wrote, did you? And you were quite right. The rest I might have pardoned; not the blow.'

'I never meant to hit her. I was wild with anger and disappointment. I was sorry, terribly sorry, and I told her so.'

'And then went on to express your sorrow by cold-blooded deceit. But my feelings are by the way. To Constable, as he told the head man, all this added up to a pattern of exploitation and betrayal so clear and consistent that he would have nothing more to do with you. He's finished with you, Fielding. You can't go to Lancaster. Ever.'

'He might have written,' I choked out; 'someone might have written.'

'The head man was to have done that. He asked me to tell you instead.'

'But great heavens,' I said, 'if you and the head man and the Senior Usher – if you can all put up with me, why should Constable condemn me? The head man, he's moral enough, God knows, and if he—'

'—The head man,' said Peter patiently, 'like the rest of us, has had time to grow fond of you despite your faults. He's seen the good things, fallen for the charm. Not Constable. He's seen you once and he didn't much like what he saw.'

'God curse Constable,' I snivelled into the fire.

'I did warn you.'

'Yes.'

'Can I help?'

'No. You've done enough. It's your fault. I may have been foolish, but it's your fault. If you'd only held your tongue.'

'It would have come out sooner or later. What did you think you were going to do? Deceive your mother for the rest of your life? Yes, you would if you could. You'd deceive anyone if it suited you, anyone and everyone and all the time. Just as you did Christopher.'

'I didn't deceive Christopher. I loved him.'

'Until you got what you wanted, perhaps. Then you just kept him on a string. All your talk of scholarship and truth – your whole life was a lie. You had to learn,' said Peter, rising to his feet, 'if only on a practical level, that you can't get away with it. Never mind that you've failed us, failed us all, in love: I don't expect you to understand that. But what I hope you've learned, now, is that if you cheat you get found out. Sooner or later a man like Constable comes along, a man of truth who isn't put off by charm, and he reads the signs and he finds you out. When that happens, the spell is broken.'

'So you hate me too?'

'No,' said Peter, holding out his hand in farewell, 'I can't hate you after all this. But I've no illusions any more. You've shown yourself as you are this evening. A clever, shallow, charming boy, blubbering with self-pity because he's told a lie and been found out.'

Since that evening I have not seen Peter. Our correspondence, a mere matter of form, trickled, dwindled and then, years ago, ceased. And now tomorrow he will be here on this island. Despite the meagre and long discontinued letters, despite what passed in the Church Army canteen, I am ridiculously, childishly excited. How much will he have changed in ten years? Will time have confirmed his natural gift of sympathy, or will this have yielded, now that he is prominent and even powerful, to self-righteousness and pride?

The visit is over. The Members of Parliament, having expressed themselves interested and gratified by all they have seen, have climbed into their helicopters and departed for Malta.

And Peter Morrison? He was round-faced and solemn as ever; he had always, as I remembered, looked and behaved as though he were shouldering a heavy burden, and the cares of his position have therefore done little to alter his appearance. Nor has time done much. There was still, this afternoon, a bloom in his cheek, a tenderness in his eye which took me back to that summer day when Tiberius died of a broken heart. The years have been kind to Peter Morrison.

When he first saw me, he looked away slightly and waited for our Colonel, who accompanied the delegation from Malta, to make a formal introduction. Then,

'Fielding,' he said heartily. 'You'll excuse us, for a minute or two, colonel? We're old friends.'

The colonel took the hint and pottered off to join another group.

'You've not changed . . . not all that much,' Peter said.

'I try not to let it show.'

'Don't be bitter. Do you like it here? What do you do?'

'I command a Sabre Squadron on detachment. We are responsible for good order on this island.'

'I must say,' Peter said, 'it always surprised me that you chose the Regular Army.'

'What else was there? Cambridge, as you may recall, was out. And I never intended to go to India.'

'I liked it.'

'So you said – in your one letter.'

'Don't be bitter,' said Peter again. 'Why *did* you choose the Army?'

'Because it offered something rather the same as Lancaster. A closed, comfortable and privileged society. Without the intellectual interest, of course; but that, as you know, was never really important to me. I simply wanted to shine in agreeable surroundings. I hardly do that here, but at least I am obeyed.'

'Did your mother not mind? She seemed, I remember, so determined on India for you.'

'My mother died.'

'She was always delicate. When?'

'I wrote and told you.'

'I'm sorry. It's been such a long time. When?'

'About two years too late. Two years after she'd done all the damage.'

'And . . . the money?'

'She'd invested a lot of it in that Indian plantation she wanted me to go to. First of all one of the partners – a friend of hers called Tuck – tried to embezzle a lot of the capital. They rumbled him just in time, but he gave them the slip and disappeared . . . They hushed it all up to save themselves looking damned silly.'

'But the investment was still safe?'

'At first, yes. But oddly enough Tuck had been a very good manager, the only one of them who really understood anything. Soon after he'd gone the place just ran downhill and packed up altogether at Independence in '47.'

'But there was other money?'

'It was mostly in a merchant bank recommended by Japhet, the family lawyer. That went bust too, just before my mother died. I think it was what finally killed her.'

'So there was nothing left?'

'Just a little. Enough to reassure the Colonel-in-Chief when I applied to have my commission made permanent. But that's gone as well now.'

'How?'

'We won't discuss it, if you don't mind. Tell me about yourself, Peter. Your parents? I always liked your father.'

'Both dead like yours. The land's all mine now.'

'And your land is fertile?'

He smiled. For the first time I had said something which pleased him.

'You remember?' he said.

'I remember.'

'That evening on the cricket ground with Somerset . . . I see him a lot, you know. We have political circles in common. You read his magazine?'

'With admiration. Has Somerset,' I inquired, 'got political ambitions?'

'I shouldn't wonder.'

'Then let me give you back your own advice. Watch him.'

Peter gestured amiably.

'I've no objection to furthering Somerset's ambitions,' he said,

'He'll make a very good politician.'

'A better politician than friend.'

'There you wrong him. Somerset values good order, and always did. He never harmed anyone unless his sense of order was offended first.'

'The only trouble was that his sense of order required that Somerset should do all the ordering.'

'Why are you being so tough with me?' Peter said. 'Aren't you pleased to see me?'

'I've looked forward to it for weeks.'

'Then why this hostility?'

A political trick, I thought. He wants to spare himself embarrassment by getting me to say it first. Then the truth will be out, but he can pretend to deny it for the sake of politeness. The important point will have been made without his having committed himself to a single harsh word. He wants it both ways; very well, he's the guest; let him have it so, and then we can part with the appearance of decorum, with a mutual saving of face.

'You've shown me, now you're here at last,' I said, 'that to you I've become alien, totally alien. I realized, of course, that I was no longer the person you once knew. But I had hoped that there might still be ... *something* which remained, something to which you could respond. It seems that there isn't. Or rather, there might be, but it's no longer in me, in myself as I am here and now, but only in memories of the past.'

I waited for the expected denial, for the formal protest of continued affection. But Peter nodded briskly.

'That's it,' he said. 'To me you're now alien, as you say. You have been since that night in Ranby Camp. To me, Fielding Gray is the beautiful and brilliant hero of the first summer of the new peace: an illusion, as it turned out, but a bright and memorable one. After that – nothing.'

He turned and walked away towards the Land Rovers which would carry the delegation back to their helicopters down on the beach.

This evening, for once, there is no wind on the island, so that I can hear the bell from the village up on the hill. Since it is tolling very slowly, I assume that it rings for a death. To me it rings for all the alien dead: for my parents and for Peter's; for Christopher and for the brave Tiberius; and for Fielding Gray.